NO CRYSTAL STAIR

MAIRUTH SARSFIELD

NO
CRYSTAL
STAIR

a novel

Women's Press
Toronto

No Crystal Stair
Mairuth Sarsfield

Published in 2004 by
Women's Press, an imprint of Canadian Scholars' Press Inc.
180 Bloor Street West, Suite 801
Toronto, Ontario
M5S 2V6

www.womenspress.ca

First published in trade paperback in 1997 by Moulin Publishing Limited
Published in 1998 by Stoddart Publishing Co. Limited

Canadian Scholars' Press/Women's Press gratefully acknowledges financial support for our
publishing activities from the Ontario Arts Council, the Canada Council for the Arts, the
Government of Canada through the Book Publishing Industry Development Program (BPIDP),
and the Government of Ontario through the Ontario Book Publishing Tax Credit Program.

Library and Archives Canada Cataloguing in Publication

Sarsfield, Mairuth
No crystal stair : a novel / Mairuth Sarsfield.

Originally published: Norval, Ont. : Moulin Pub., 1997.
ISBN 0-88961-451-2

I. Title.

PS8587.A38463N62 2004   C813'.54   C2004-906413-4

04 05 06 07 08   5 4 3 2 1

Printed and bound in Canada by AGMV Marquis Imprimeur, Inc.

To Jennifer and Jeremy, who provided such pleasure and love during their all-too-brief lifetimes; to my graceful mother, Anne Vaughan Packwood; to my wise granddaughter, Zinzi de Silva; and, above all, to my beloved 6'2" groom, who imagines still that he's with the Irish Guards.

Acknowledgements

So many gave encouragement, some, constructive criticism, and many more, with blind faith, waited for *No Crystal Stair* to be completed. Special thanks are due to: Ken Alexander, Austin Clarke, Lucille Cuevas, Deirdre Jones-Nishimura, Almeta Speaks, and John Wyllie.

Canada Council's Exploration Grant allowed me to develop it, while the Canadian Heritage Multicultural Program made it possible to wrap it all up.

CHAPTER I

M arion Willow had less than thirty-five minutes to get to the Westmount Y on Sherbrooke Street. Normally, it was a brisk but invigorating stroll under the tall elms that shade Westmount Boulevard, past ostentatious homes built by Scottish robber barons who'd made their fortunes building railroads. But today, Mademoiselle Laroche, Marion's morning employer, had delayed her, equating the situation of the French in Canada with the plight of Blacks in the United States. Only when an old gentleman doffed his bowler, murmuring "Good afternoon," did her resentment begin to seep away. "*Les nègres blancs*, indeed!" Marion huffed, without breaking her stride.

In faraway Europe, that spring of 1942, the Second World War was raging. France had fallen, Britain was being blitzkrieged, and North Africa was Hitler's battleground of choice. Many of Denise Laroche's contemporaries, including the former mayor of Montreal, Camillien Houde, considered Canada's involvement in the war an affront to its French population. But in English upper-crust Westmount, apart from finding rationing a bit of a nuisance, the citizens considered the war a great opportunity to fly the Union Jack, carry on for "King and Country," and listen to speeches by that wily old warhorse, Winston Churchill.

Marion picked up her pace across St. Stephen's Park. She envied the mothers whose children could roll on fresh cut lawns and build castles in clean sandboxes. Below the park and to the west, Lansdowne Avenue wound steeply downhill. Its halfway mark was the mock-Tudor duplex where she had once worked for a miserly woman. Rushing past did not blur the memory of the time when Efuah, the younger of her two children, had been so feverish that Marion had dared not leave her at the day nursery, so brought both girls with her to work. On the Friday, the woman had deducted what she considered the cost of the children's food from Marion's twelve-dollar-a-week wage. Five years had passed, but Marion still bristled at the injustice of it.

Lansdowne's hill ended at Sherbrooke Street, where the broad expanse of Westmount Park, with its Gothic library, greenhouse gardens, cricket pitch, and Philippa's favourite storytale duck pond, faced the handsome red-brick and stone building with the imposing double front doors that housed the Westmount Y. To bolster her flagging spirit, she pictured the residence wing on the top floor; its twenty-one single and five double bedrooms, with their five white-tiled bathrooms, were part of her domain. On the second floor were a teakwood indoor running track, two conference rooms, two dining rooms, and Amelia Hall's kitchen.

Amelia, born and bred in New Orleans, ran the Y's spacious kitchen as if it were her very own. Her Creole cooking skills had made the Y's lunch a must for businessmen, as well as Rotary Club and Lions Club members throughout Montreal. The lower-floor gymnasium and swimming pool, linked to the teakwood running track by an iron stairwell, were the fiefdom of Sven Svenson, a charming Norwegian who, because he adored Amelia's cooking, worked himself and everyone else into a sweat to keep their mutual weight problems under control.

Marion sprinted through the lobby – past its deep, maroon-leather chairs, oak reception desk, and lending library, which was watched over by the kilt-proud Thaddeus McGregor. The big hand of the clock over the information desk clicked to twelve fifty-five.

"G'day, Mister McGregor," she called to the reception desk as she raced up the second-floor stairs two at a time.

"God love us, lass. Why such a hurry?" But Marion had disappeared before Thaddeus McGregor could finish his sentence. "Such a bonnie lass," he said softly. "Make some man a fine wife." His smile hovered, then faded. He closed his lips firmly. Never do for a man who intended some day to become the executive director of the YMCA to marry a coloured lady. Yet she was powerfully attractive and winsome. He went back to his desk, his blue eyes sparkling.

Marion went directly into the kitchen where Amelia Hall was stirring a cauldron of Creole fish. "Good Lord, Marion, you musta run all the way from your morning job! Catch yo' breath, child. Working two jobs at your age! T'ain't right! Now jes' set yo'self down and sample this. Gatehouse delivered some Cuban shrimp and some red snapper this morning that cried to be part of a New Orleans gumbo."

"I only have five minutes, Aunt Amelia," Marion protested in vain. A steaming bowl of thick soup was placed before her and a finger poked in her ribs, with the remark, "You kinda skinny. No wonder yo'all can't catch yo'self 'nother husband." Amelia plonked in a spoonful of aïoli croutons when the bowl was half empty, scolding, "Don' woof it down so! Them rooms upstairs can wait. 'Sides, Vashti Dobson in a eee-vil mood. Ah don't understand those Geechee wimmen. They's so sometimey." While Amelia fussed, Marion marvelled at the food being dished up for customers. Delicious odours from Amelia's sugar-bronzed yams, roast pork with herb stuffing, string beans and braised celery, as well as her New Orleans fish chowder, permeated the kitchen's warm air. Obviously, Amelia knew how to circumvent the government's ration program. Little Clara, who was serving a Rotary luncheon, came in, complaining that everyone was asking for roast pork.

"Wha's de matter wid those social worker men? Ah ain't heard any calls for seconds of my creole chowder," Amelia complained.

"They prefers the roast pork, tha's why," Clara informed her.

"Well, they's only gettin' two slices apiece. What they 'spect for forty-five cents?"

"They's kinda 'fraid of the pow'ful smell of yo' garlic," Clara suggested. "They still gots to do they social work dis afternoon."

"That's not it at all." The prim voice of Gertrude Martin, the senior waitress, cut through the speculation. "They prefer the pork so they can wrap one piece up and sneak it home for their supper. For some, this is their only decent meal. We may be working in hoity-toity Westmount, but there's many a poverty-stricken member of the gentry living here, too." Gertrude's broad bottom pushed against the swinging doors to allow her string-bean figure and four-plate tray to go through. "As I see it," she concluded, "in Canada, poverty's colour-blind and the Depression's not class-conscious." The three women chuckled sympathetically. Had Gertrude not been a Negro, she might have been a school teacher or a social worker. As it was, she was a vigorous "Letters to the Editor" contributor.

Amelia moved her ample frame about quickly, for there were two dining areas to serve and both were crowded. Marion slipped out and went upstairs. Her afternoon job was to help the housekeeper, Vashti Dobson, make beds, dust, clean rooms, and sort linen. An outside man came to clean the five showers, the toilet rooms, and polish the building's brass. All the Westmount Y housekeepers, their assistants and the kitchen staff were drawn from Montreal's Black community. Any openings on staff were carefully stage-managed by Vashti to ensure the inclusion of only those she described as "the right people." Diminutive in stature, Vashti was meticulous about her work, yet usually so full of good-natured gossip about the Y residents, the church, and the local community that Thaddeus McGregor could hear Marion's tinkling laughter whenever he came up during the afternoon to check on their progress and receive Vashti's understated report on any irregularities among the residents.

But there was something wrong that afternoon. Vashti, although sparing with words, was generous with those sounds of tooth-sucking disapproval employed by the West Indian segment of the Montreal community. Marion was not an integral part of that earthy community, any more than she was of Amelia's circle of elegant American ladies who had begun an active, busy-bee-like social group in 1902 called the Coloured Ladies Club. They were mostly wives of Pullman porters, relocated from the southern United States because their college-educated husbands could only find respectable, well-paid jobs on the railway. Highly educated and very literate, with charmingly genteel upper-class pretensions and concern for the well-being of "the Race," many of these women did not have to work outside their own homes.

Marion felt herself a hybrid, neither American nor West Indian. Her ancestors had been whalers, bold men whose home port was Bermuda. "Black Richard" and his brother "Yellow Richard" landed there in 1802 seeking freedom. Having fought slave owners during the revolution, when France would not give Haiti the same equality, fraternity, and liberty that Napoleon proudly boasted of, they escaped in a fishing boat, sailing skillfully into Bermuda's hidden Tobacco Bay. For generations afterwards, they roamed the "Seven Seas," following the blue whale. They fell in love with women from Fiji to Finland, from Mombasa to Martinique, and brought them home to Bermuda each season to breed another sailor for the clan. They served as pilots, guiding ocean liners and other vessels past Bermuda's treacherous coral reefs, occasionally indulging in looting when an arrogant foreign captain, ignoring their warnings, grounded his ship.

In the 1880s, her grandfather skipped ship in Halifax, responding to Canada's call for workers to level more roadbeds and lay rails for the expansion of the Canadian Pacific Railway, first at Wolfville, Nova Scotia, and later at Sault Ste. Marie in Ontario. Her father and Uncle John had joined the polyglot railroad crew as they dug through Kicking Horse Pass in the Rocky Mountains of British Columbia.

In 1910, in Montreal, waiting for the last ship to sail back to the Islands before the port froze up, Marion's father was introduced to the dewy-eyed daughter of an exiled Haitian poet. Immediately, he surrendered his wanderlust for the joys of Clothilde's homemaking. Having apprenticed during his youth as an electrician in the Royal Navy Dockyards in Bermuda and now flaunting a Creole-tinted French, he had no trouble getting a job in Montreal's east-end shipyards. Clothilde presented him with a little daughter, but both parents died of tuberculosis before the child was four. The tiny Black community rallied around and somehow Baby Marion grew into adulthood surrounded by an extended family of uncles and aunts she had to obey and honour, but who in turn loved and protected her. Vashti Dobson was one of those "kissing cousins" or token aunts, as was Amelia Hall, who had taught her how to cook.

To pacify Vashti's grumpy hissing, Marion sped through the bed-making, hoping the older woman would go down for tea and perhaps relax. "No good you tryin' to get 'round me, child," Vashti said as they met in the linen room. "I don' approve of the way you carryin' on with Edmond Thompson and tha's that."

The pillow cases dropped from Marion's hands. "What?"

"Huh. Not much is hidden from those who have eyes to see."

"Aunt Vashti, what do you mean? Mr. Thompson has been a friend for years, but no more than that."

"Then why he nephew livin' in your new house, eh?"

Marion breathed a deep sigh of relief. "Oh, that! Otis is a nice young man and the children adore him. And now that I have a three-bedroom house, he'll pay rent for a room to use when he's in town. Goodness knows, we need the money – you know that. Aunt Vashti, why are you attacking me?"

The eyes of Vashti Dobson rolled twice. "Play with puppy, puppy lick you mouf," she murmured.

"Aunt Vashti, how can you be so crude? It just happens that we both belong to the Marcus Garvey Debating Society, but Edmond Thompson has his own home and his own life. We're only friends."

"No, child. No longer. I hear tell he done packed up Mistress Torrie Delacourt's overnight knick-knacks and returned 'em to her own abode."

Marion froze. Hearing Vashti mention the Delacourt woman was like listening to a serpent about to strike. She tasted fear.

"I wouldn't mess around with those high-yella, high-steppin' ladies if'n I was you. They know more voodoo tricks than a Yoruba market woman."

"But I don't even know her. And she can have Edmond Thompson for all I care! Why are people talking?" Horror released her tears. "What have I done? I had to have someone sign the rental lease and he did it, that's all."

"Hush now, child. I believes you."

Vashti, chastened as Marion's normally proud shoulders cringed pathetically, dug into the pocket of her coverall apron and pulled out her hanky. "Hush, I say. Next thing you know, ole Highland McGregor be trudgin' up here. Nothin' to cry about. You too proud, girl. You should marry and let some man take care of you. Deacon Stevens been interested in you since your husband died."

"Ralph Stevens is a ninny," Marion hiccupped. "He thinks just because he's got an office job at Canadair, he's the cat's whiskers. He doesn't even read hard-cover books!"

Vashti's arms circled Marion's shoulders. "Child, I don' blame you, but you too proud. Those carry-go-bring-home folks goin' to destroy you. Rock stone at river bottom never feel hot sun."

Marion sniffed. "What does that mean?"

"Means, only those who have suffered know how to sympathize. Most women in your position go on welfare."

"Welfare! Me? Never! There's no need. I work, I could earn as much as any man if the system was fair. I could be a dietician, but when you're coloured, they call you a cook."

They each returned to sorting the linen. Ironing the last of the pillow cases, Marion tried to mend fences with Vashti. "Now that I've rented a bigger place, I could run a lovely rooming house and stay home. You know, a bed and breakfast. I even have a dining room. Now, when it's my turn to entertain the Coloured Ladies Club, we can have a proper tea sitting around a table."

Vashti's grunts abated as Marion's enthusiasm grew.

"It would be perfect for tourists in the summer, or for our folks who come to the Royal Vic for medical treatment. Best of all, I could cater to those nice African and West Indian college students who can't find rooms around McGill. It would pay."

"Need licence for that, don' it?" asked Vashti.

The zephyr breeze evaporated, the chill set in again. Vashti was right. Marion couldn't get a licence in her own right, any more than she could borrow money to buy extra furnishings – no matter how sound a business proposition she had. Denise Laroche was right about the inequality of women. The Napoleonic Code reigned supreme in French Canada. Women, widows, and cripples were not persons under the law. Images of Mademoiselle Laroche preparing her male colleagues law briefs at home made her wince. She hit her fist against the cupboard shelf.

"There has to be a way. I won't give in."

"Honey, they a lot of orphan children in Montreal needin' homes. Now, if'n you'd board two or three, they pays fifteen dollars a month, I hear, and all they clothin's provided. That way you could stay home wif yours. Don' need no licence for that. City too glad to farm out mulatto babies. Nobody's goin' to adopt *them*. They fly-by-night fathers was Black."

"I say, am I intruding?" Thaddeus McGregor's raised bare knee pushed open the door. His kilt flipped down again. "Wondered if you'd care to join me in the kitchen for a spot of tea. Miss Amelia baked some scones."

Vashti sucked her teeth. "Um, must finish this list first."

"Come, now. Tomorrow's a special day. May the twenty-fourth — Victoria Day, you know."

"Special?" Vashti mocked. "Don' we havta work? Ain't there always beds waitin' to be made up?"

"Certainly, certainly. That's why we should celebrate Queen Victoria's birthday today while we're all here. It's a national holiday on Sunday."

"Huh. Go 'long! We soon come."

"Right-o. Don't tarry." Thaddeus backed out of the room and marched down the hall in step with an imaginary bagpiper.

Vashti suppressed a laugh. "Never call alligator 'long mouf' till you pass 'im," she advised, as they finished putting the clean linen away.

Pushing Marion ahead of her, she hobbled down to Amelia Hall's kitchen. Seated at the large central worktable, McGregor was holding forth, touting the achievements of Queen Victoria's reign, doing his patriotic best for King and Country against a battery of sceptics.

"That Victoria. Didn't she allow slavery?" Clara hissed as she buttered one of Amelia Hall's cornbread scones.

"No," McGregor declared. "She abolished it!"

Marion was not listening. Having foster children in her home instead of a male boarder might just help solve her money problems. A month before she had moved from the small flat on rue St. Antoine, a social worker had approached her to ask if she could accommodate Emily Capriccio, a little almond-hued, freckle-faced girl who had gone to the same nursery school as her own daughters. "Couldn't consider it," Marion remembered telling the social worker. "I have neither enough room, nor the time to give her." Racing home in the late afternoon after a full day's work, collecting her two girls, feeding and mothering them – that was worry enough. "Impossible," she decided.

Why should she penalize Otis? He was proving such good company for the girls and was always willing to fix things around the house. No, he was an ideal boarder. Edmond Thompson had done her no harm. Her resolve to ignore the community gossip propelled her through the rest of the day's work.

She left the Y shortly after four, still agitated. Arguing with herself as she walked briskly down des Seigneurs hill, she noticed in the distance a bright yellow convertible parked in front of her section of the street. Could that be her daughter Pippa, talking to someone in the car? She quickened her pace, a sense of foreboding tightening her stomach. The girls had been told not to talk to strangers.

The house was still so far away. She began to trot. Suddenly, the yellow convertible moved forwards. Pippa, balancing her load of books, moved back to join her younger sister, who was spinning a yo-yo on the front steps. The convertible glided into the lane and out of sight. With a relieved sigh, Marion broke into a run. Seeing her, the girls sprang down the steps to meet her.

"What treasures you are," Marion murmured as she knelt to hug them. "Now, tell me about your day," she coaxed, as they walked hand in hand into the house.

Pippa's recital at the supper table did not include the yellow car, and even at bedtime, her "God bless" litany did not include its occupant. "Maybe it's nothing, but I'm sure I've seen that car in the neighbourhood before," Marion thought, as she monitored her daughter's endless chant. When it seemed to be winding down at last, Marion asked, "Pippa, who was in the yellow convertible?"

Pippa hastily ended her prayer, not with an answer, but with a fervent plea: "God, please bless Emily and help find her a home."

"Amen," little Effie echoed.

Marion forced herself not to respond to the panic that began to build anew, but tucked the girls in bed, blew them a kiss goodnight, turned out the light, and went downstairs. Fretfully, she ignored the unwashed dishes. What did they matter, when something was going on – something she couldn't put a finger on? Pacing the floor did nothing. Wearily, she climbed back upstairs. Little Effie's pillow was on the floor. Tucking it under her daughter's sleeping head, she went over to sit in the window seat. Pitti-Sing, the Siamese cat, jumped onto her lap. "Do you remember Emily?" Marion murmured, but the cat ignored her question.

Emily Capriccio – had it been four years since she had last seen the child, and the wonderful old Italian fruit peddler who had taken such good care of her? He seemed to believe she was his child, poor man. Perhaps if I agreed to be Emily's foster mother, it would solve both our problems. Old Dominic must be ancient by now – far too old to bring up a half-coloured child. If Emily could live with a coloured family, at least for a year or two, she would perhaps learn how to cope in a world that punished people for being Black, or even half-Black – to say nothing of being illegitimate.

Marion's inner fear spoke aloud. "No, I just can't." She forced herself to relax by breathing deeply, counting slowly to ten. Pitti-Sing, sensing turmoil inside her normally calm mistress, purred more loudly and massaged Marion's stomach with paws, claws carefully withdrawn. "Pitti-Sing, what should I do?" she asked the cat. "The girl needs a stable home, but I can't provide one – at least, not right away. I still have to get over the nightmare of moving."

A soft, almost wistful smile slowly lit Marion's high-cheeked, café-au-lait face, as she continued to talk quietly about her children. "You know, Pitti-Sing, only little Effie found moving to a new house exciting. At eight, her world is still wide open. Everything enriches it. But Pippa has hidden fears. I think perhaps she remembers her father too vividly, and resents that both her father and grandfather have died. She doesn't talk about it; she has such forbearance. But I know she'd rather I marry her godfather Poppa Dad. What a silly name to call Edmond Thompson! He's such a Rock of Gibraltar."

Marion found herself withdrawing, even from the cat, as she reminisced. Pippa had not yet found a friend like young Trevor Wilson on rue des Seigneurs to make her feel proud about being different from other children, about being Black. Who would she find to share a love of poetry with her? "Why," she asked Pitti-Sing, "why is it so easy to develop an inferiority complex when you're from somewhere else? What should I do to make sure my girls grow up with self-confidence and pride?" The Siamese cat made no attempt to share her feline philosophy. Purring contentedly, she survived, as cats have for centuries, by being inscrutable.

Marion raised her head and looked up into the sky to help check the self-pity that was threatening her equilibrium. "Dear God, how can I prepare them to defend their moral values. Is teaching them the Ten Commandments enough, when so few people feel they apply to everyone? Tell me, how does one stay whole in this crippling society? How?" There weren't any stars to provide a divine signal, but the tree outside waved its bare branches in sympathy. "Dear Lord," she pleaded: "give me strength." Unbidden, the words of "Mother to Son" came into her head.

> *Life for me ain't been no crystal stair*
> *It's had tacks in it*
> *And splinters,*
> *And boards torn up;*
> *And places with no carpet on the floor —*
> *Bare . . .*

Along with Tennyson, Langston Hughes was one of her favourite poets. "*But all the time I'se been a-climbin' on,*" she continued, reciting the lines in her mind.

*And reachin' landin's, and turnin' corners, and sometimes
goin' in the dark where there ain't been no light. So don't
you turn back. Don't you set down on the steps 'cause you
find it's kinder hard. Don't you fall now — for I'se still goin',
honey, I'se still climbin'. And life for me ain't been no crystal
stair.*

She breathed deeply. "Amen. Come on, Pitti-Sing. Time for bed."
Disdainfully, the Siamese cat refused to leave Marion's warm lap
with its faint scent of Yardley's lavender. Scooping the cat up,
Marion carted her down to the kitchen, explaining that she
had to heat a kettle of water on the kerosene stove for both a
cup of tea and a sponge bath. Easing her slight body into the old
wooden rocker in front of the squat tube of liquid fire, Marion
glanced at the calendar on the wall. It had been almost three
weeks since May first, moving day in Montreal.

CHAPTER II

When the streetcar had passed her street-level window of their damp two bedroom flat on St. Antoine, Pippa followed the shadows it threw along the ceiling and over the cardboard packing cases at the foot of the bed. Tomorrow her whole life would change and they'd be in their new house on rue des Seigneurs. Slowly its rattle had receded; the darkness dropped silently down again. Ruminating under her tightly braided hair and silk stocking cap, Pippa had conjured up portraits of people on that midnight streetcar run. What did they do after dark in those tall grey towers facing Notre Dame Cathedral on Place d'Armes, near the streetcar terminus? Were they night watchmen, or Italian cleaning women, or were some of them bank tellers?

Her imagination isolated one as that mealy-mouthed, clean-shaven bank clerk who surreptitiously watched whenever she counted out the coins in her portable metal savings box before depositing them into her Christmas account at the City and District Savings Bank. Did he stay at work late at night, making double entries to cover up embezzlement of clients' funds? Did he steal to support a secret family? Was he madly in love with one of those beautiful brown chorus girls who worked at Rockhead's Paradise?

Rockhead's, the jazz cabaret on lower Mountain Street, was the "den of iniquity," Otis explained, that Prohibition had made irresistible to American sportsmen and gamblers. At night, with its pulsating yellow and red neon sign, it marked the halfway point of the streetcar run along St. Antoine. When the last streetcar before morning arrived at Mountain Street, how many of those Black musicians, who wore mysterious dark glasses while entertaining white folks at Rockhead's, would climb aboard for the long ride home to their own families in the respectable working-class districts St. Henri and Verdun?

After tomorrow, Pippa had noted in her diary, *I'll never have to listen to the late-night streetcars again*. But then, she'd realized, she probably wouldn't see the butcher's niece again either – her friend, tall Alice, who could rollerskate backwards all the way down Fulford Hill. "Some day," Alice had confided, "some day, I'm going to run away and join the Roller Derby." Pippa had realized that she might never know when that day came, for tomorrow she would be living in a new neighbourhood. The Willow family would still be wedged between the Canadian Pacific and Grand Trunk railway tracks, and the girls would still go to the same school; but at least they would be living in a house with an upstairs, as well as saving five dollars a month in rent – and, best of all, there was an extra room for Otis.

Will Otis be back from his job on the railway in time to help us move? she'd asked her diary. *I hope he remembers. Everybody in Montreal moves on May the first, so he can't forget*. But what if he did, she'd worried? Imagining herself carrying each cup and saucer, and each chair separately to their new home four blocks down and six streets away, Pippa had finally fallen asleep.

The yeasty scent of cinnamon buns drifting across the street from the Aberdeen Bakery Shop had heralded the arrival of morning. The McEwan sisters, who owned the bakery, didn't have to move every May the first, for they lived with their brother, the stern "Thou shalt not" minister, at the Presbyterian manse near Dorchester Street, eight blocks away.

Each and every dawn, long before the milkman's wagon came

along, they walked shoulder to shoulder, wrapped in tassled grey shawls, down the hill to their shop on St. Antoine. After lighting the ovens, they mixed the dough for the cakes, wholewheat breads, scones, and hot currant-filled cinnamon buns, which came from old family recipes. Later, at precisely five-thirty, half an hour before closing time, they hung a notice in the window: ALL BAKED GOODS HALF PRICE. That sign signalled the highlight of Effie's day. Even at eight years old, she hadn't lost her baby fat because the Aberdeen ladies awarded her with an extra cinnamon bun for her penny allowance whenever she managed to memorize another verse by the Scottish poet, Robert Louis Stevenson.

To Pippa, the highlight of her day was when Trevor Wilson came home from technical high school. To be precise, her happiest time was the half hour spent with him each Monday and Wednesday before he left for cricket practice, and again on Saturday mornings when he walked with her to the Westmount Library on the way to his cricket match at Greene Park.

⚔

"For very young he seemed, tenderly reared, like some tall cypress in the Queen's garden," Pippa had written in her diary, remembering the lines from the epic poem, "Sohrab and Rustum." "Yer nuts," tall Alice had informed her when Pippa used the quote to describe Trevor. "He ain't at all like a cypress tree; he's chocolate brown. Tall like a tree, maybe," she'd conceded, "and just as skinny. Anyways, he's older than you by six years. Yer not twelve till Hallowe'en."

"There's no poetry in your soul," Pippa had retorted. "Trevor really listens when I read chapters from my novel to him. He even suggests ways that Princess Aurora could react to various situations. And, furthermore, he knows a lot of things." But Alice had not been impressed.

Pippa had shivered inside her nightgown, not from the cold

16

of the late spring or the damp of her street-level room, but from the fear of not having a kindred soul to guide her in the new world that was about to begin. When they moved away, who would replace Trevor? Who would borrow books from the Westmount Library, since the downtown Children's Library had nothing about Black children except *Uncle Tom's Cabin, Elsie Dinsmore* and *Tom Sawyer*, in which the word "nigger" was used over and over again? In one of his books, the author Mark Twain had a character report that "Twelve niggers were killed, but no one was hurt." *Tom Sawyer* was one of those books Pippa regularly hid behind others on the shelves so that no one would find them. The librarian, not understanding her difficulties, barred Pippa from the library for a month.

Seventeen-year-old Trevor was deeply involved in race pride. Since his uncle lived on the only stretch of St. Antoine that was technically in Westmount – the three blocks of four-storey, post-Victorian dwellings that Vashti Dobson referred to as "Strivers' Row" – Trevor used his uncle's residence as an address for his library card, and took advantage of the superior schooling and athletic activities offered to Westmount residents.

When Pippa moved away, who would be there to reinforce her sense of racial pride by pointing out that both Dumas, author of *The Three Musketeers*, and the Russian dramatist Pushkin had African ancestry? Oh, there would always be old Professor McDowell, who used to corner them after Sunday School, wagging one gnarled, oak-brown finger ominously, warning that, "The half has yet to be told!" According to him, when the mighty King Solomon finally met the beautiful Ethiopian Queen of Sheba, he was overwhelmed. "Thou art Black and comely," Solomon said. Centuries later, King James the First of England, who had commissioned a new version of the ancient Greek Bible, read Solomon's glowing description, and ordered his scribes to strike it out. His scholars argued, but eventually had to compromise: "She is black, BUT comely," the Good Book records. It was that word 'but,' Professor McDowell contended, that was the beginning of colour prejudice.

Pippa needed to know that Trevor was near, just in case Jean Jacques ever tried again to wash off her colour with a snowball. Although it was tall Alice who had beaten Jean Jacques up for his curiosity, it was Trevor who had insisted that Pippa continue to walk right by Jean Jacques's house on Fulford Hill, her head held high. "Ignoramus," she would repeat in as dignified a manner as she could muster. She dared not add Trevor's "poor white trash" phrase, for tall Alice usually walked with her to school and, being white, might not understand that the epithet did not include her.

❧

"Pippa, wake Effie up and get dressed. Otis is here." She recalled how the warmth of her mother's voice had comforted her, and brought an end to her restless night. All was well when Mother was near – although, whenever her mother sat quietly at her desk in the front room doing sums, Pippa knew that all was not perfectly well. She sat up in bed and began unbraiding her hair.

Since the new house would be even farther away from the Westmount Y, Pippa wondered if, once they did their after-school chores, they would still be able to meet their mother halfway up des Seigneurs hill and play guessing games as to what treat she had tucked away in her tapestry carry-all with the cedar handles. None of the kids on the street had a mother who was as much fun as theirs.

"Come on, lazy bones – stop dreaming," Otis's deep voice threatened immediate action. "Get up or I'll come and get you."

Pippa climbed out of bed, but Efuah burrowed deeper under the covers as Pippa tugged at the quilt. "Effie, we have to get up. You can't dress under the covers today, it's not winter now. Come on, we have to hurry. Today is May first. It's moving day."

❧

Since dawn, the enamel kitchen table had been piled high with pots and pans wrapped in newspapers, the counters obscured by neatly stacked rows of serving platters, plates, cups, saucers, and cooking utensils. Pippa and Efuah took their bowls of steaming cream of wheat, sweetened with dark Demerara molasses, outdoors to the bench in the backyard.

"I can't imagine what's keeping your uncle," Marion called to Otis. "He promised to bring the car so that we could start moving at eight."

"Don't worry, he'll be here," Otis reassured her. "He always keeps his word, but the Chicago train might have been late out of Toronto last night."

Another green and maroon train clickity-clacked by on the tracks above.

"That's just the Dorval commuter train," Pippa explained in answer to Efuah's puzzled look. "Poppa Dad won't be on that." Fine cinders from the train engine filtered down into the backyard. Hunching protectively over their cereal bowls, they rushed back indoors.

More black soot, for Otis had begun to dismantle the kitchen stove. The stove pipe, where it U-turned in order to heat the back bedroom, was hanging from its wire, separated from the circular upright portion that funnelled the warm smoke from the coal stove on a circuitous route to the outside chimney.

Tiptoeing, the girls tried to pass him. "You can take these plates with you and wrap them," he suggested. "You won't be in anyone's way."

The Guaranteed milkman's cart stopped by the front gate. His bell jingled. Marion rushed out to settle her bill and give the driver the new address. The two horses, happy that winter was gone, waited patiently, munching grain in bags attached to their muzzles.

Otis handed the girls plates to wrap, and launched into his "hurry up" song:

One man and his dog
Went to mow a meadow.
One man, two men and their dog
Went to mow a meadow.
One man, two men, three men and their dog
Went to mow a meadow.
Three men, two men, one man and his dog
Went to mow a meadow.
Four men went to mow . . . .

Efuah could never keep up with the number of men who went to mow, and couldn't count backwards, yet somehow all the dishes were wrapped and put carefully in boxes, and the stovepipes banished to the backyard, before the twenty-third man and his dog went to mow the meadow.

When the kitchen cupboards were bare, and the kitchen table was moved into the hall, the full extent of the kitchen floor's dirt revealed itself. Marion tucked an old towel into her waistband, sprinkled Old Dutch cleanser and, with a pail, knelt down to begin scrubbing.

"No, Mrs. Willow. See here, don't do that. I'll do it. Though why you're cleaning the house for the next tenants I'll never know. Betcha they wouldn't do that for you," Otis added, as he looked for the mop. "A mop will clean it just as well," he insisted, anticipating Marion's protest. She smiled slowly as she shook her head at him. "You're more like your uncle than either of you will admit."

"You mean, we both admire pretty ladies," he teased.

As she left, Otis thought, "She really is a beautiful woman. When I marry, it's going to be someone like her. Someone with class." Pondering the complexity of marriage, he realized that he'd never be able to bring the girls he usually flirted with home for dinner if Mrs. Willow rented him a room in her new house. He might even have to keep his evening involvements at Rockhead's a secret.

Pippa tiptoed into the kitchen and around his mopping.

"I thought everything from the kitchen was packed, young lady."

"Oh, it's just that there's a secret hole in that cupboard up there and I wanted to make sure I hadn't left anything in it."

"You mean in that hole where the ole grey mouse lives?"

Pippa froze. Grimacing, his eyes squeezed shut, Otis plunged his hand into the cavity and swivelled his wrist around: "Ouch!" Pippa cringed. Clutching a square, enamelled Mackintosh's Toffee Deluxe tin, he withdrew his hand. With a flourish and a bow, he presented it. "Always at your service, milady."

Arching up on her toes to kiss his cheek, Pippa confided, "I keep my novel in it. Oh Otis, I'm so relieved you came to help us." She added earnestly, "It's very difficult not having a father, you know." Otis tilted his chin up to check the flow of compassion that threatened to moisten his hazel-flecked eyes, and hastily reached for the mop again. "Run along now and help your mother with the books. Your Poppa Dad will soon be here with the car."

Alone in the kitchen, Otis took out his handkerchief and blew his nose. Another passenger train went by on the half-hill at the back of the house. Otis watched as cinders from its engine filtered down on the newly washed floor. "Those goddamn trains," he growled, shaking his fist at the receding clickity-clack. "They don't have respect for people like us. I swear, someday. . . ." He stopped in mid-sentence, recognizing the honk of his uncle's car as it lurched to a halt at the front door.

The hallway, packed with cases, obscured Edmond Thompson's view of the kitchen and of Otis, who was furiously throwing water from the pail into the backyard. "Otis here yet?" boomed the baritone voice.

"Yes, Edmond, he is, and I don't know what I would have done without him."

"My dear, you shouldn't be lifting those books. Otis should have done that."

Marion smiled fondly. His brusqueness was a cover-up for a rather compassionate nature. She realized that, drawn taut by the ceaseless demands of his job as a Pullman porter on the railway that he'd served faithfully and with dignity for twenty years, Edmond Thompson, at the end of a trip, would sometimes unleash his frustration onto Otis, the nephew he'd brought to Canada from his homeland of British Guiana.

She was aware that sometimes his cricket-playing teammates felt the sting of his tongue as well, as he urged them to join the American J. Phillip Randolph Movement to form a Pullman porters' union. "There's never been any advancement for us and never will be, unless we stick together," he predicted, but the widespread Depression in Canada during the thirties had weakened their resolve. At least Black men had the priority for jobs on the sleeping-cars and in the narrow galley-kitchens of Canada's railways – where others had none.

Proud, a man of few words, Edmond Thompson did not haggle. He threw his lot in with the few West Indian porters who understood the issue. Like him, they were chameleons, living two lives. Their subservient jobs, catering mostly to the whims of inebriated travellers, did not injure their egos. They knew they were men of substance. They played cricket as a hobby, joined secret lodges, tolerated their wives being active in social and church affairs, and firmly encouraged their children to do well in school.

When Edmond had first met Marion, he'd told her how he'd come to Canada early in the twenties, after serving as a corporal in British Guiana's colonial army during World War I. A chemist by trade, Corporal Thompson had a clear vision of setting up his own chemist shop, and then eventually buying a farm for his retirement.

The farm was no problem. Marion remembered his description of how, while he was being demobilized in England, someone had placed an advertisement in *The London Times* offering a partially developed farm of a hundred and fifty acres in the Laurentian highlands northwest of Montreal. Sight unseen, using his mustering-out pay, Edmond had purchased the farm; unfortunately, after arriving in Canada, he never managed to find it, lost as it was "a hundred miles behind God's back" somewhere in the rockstrewn backwoods north of Montebello.

Arriving as an immigrant to Canada, with taxes to pay on the farm and a bitter winter to survive, he'd taken the only job offered to a Black chemist – that of a Red Cap porter carrying travellers' bags in Montreal's Windsor Station – just as Marion's African husband Kofi had while studying dentistry at McGill University.

Starting as an unpaid Red Cap subsisting only on tips, Edmond qualified as a Pullman car porter after six years. Working city to city on the trains, making up berths, shining shoes, preparing morning tea or midnight snacks, he attended to the demands of people who could afford to travel in style across Canada or into the United States. Booze was the primary demand of Prohibition-weary American sportsmen headed for the northern lakes and hunting lodges.

Edmond was sustained by his dream that someday he'd locate the farm and modernize it with his savings. The Sunday afternoon when he'd first met Marion at a Back to Africa rally in the old UNIA hall on Fulford Street, he had decided that if the Widow Willow was interested, he'd build her and her children a house there. "That would make a lovely retreat for the summer," she'd responded casually, not taking his offer seriously. "It's far away from the heat and idleness of the city children. Perhaps we could rent it for school holidays."

But Otis knew they'd never make that promised voyage of discovery, at least not in his uncle's Chevy. "It'd never make it off the island of Montreal," he'd commented to no one in particular. Yet now, the old Chevy seemed to be holding up under the weight of Mrs. Willow's flowered chintz chesterfield strapped onto its roof, and her rosewood writing desk wedged against the back seat.

The butcher had offered his cart. It was ideal for the odd-shaped blanket-wrapped bundles and kitchen pans that did not fit into boxes. Otis suspected tall Alice of engineering the offer. "Thanks, but no thanks," Otis snarled when Alice proudly pushed the three-wheeled wooden cart to the curb in front of him. "We don't need it, we have a car. Furthermore, who do you think is going to push that donkey cart all the way to des Seigneurs Street?"

"We will," volunteered Pippa and Alice together.

Otis turned twice. Slapping his forehead, he counted slowly, "One, two, three, four, five, six, seven, eight, nine, ten." He knew his class-conscious uncle would never allow the Willow girls to push that cart along the busy St. Antoine thoroughfare. So what did *that* signify? *He'd* be drafted, of course. All week, he had imagined himself driving the Chevrolet. He would deliver and unload the furniture promptly, leaving his uncle and Mrs. Willow to rearrange it. Then, on the way back for the second, third, and fourth loads, he'd circle by Rockhead's Paradise on Mountain Street so that his chums and the pretty chicks working the streets could see him driving the Chevy. Even some of his old pals in uniform didn't have cars to drive.

"Lay the mattresses on the bottom of the cart," Poppa Dad ordered. "I'll transport Mrs. Willow and the cat. You and the girls follow with the cart."

Pippa tugged at Otis's sleeve. "We'll take turns riding down in the cart if you'd like – to keep you company, and help unload at the new house."

Otis sighed. "Okay, little lady, let's alley-oop. But leave that giraffe friend of yours at home."

The pitch of rue des Seigneurs, below St. Antoine, was as steep as Fulford Hill. Their new home, the upper half of a three-storey red-brick building, was near the foot of the hill. Otis had to hold the cart back, digging in his heels, while Pippa and Efuah clutched the packages to prevent them from falling forwards.

A proper moving van, backed up to a house, forced them onto a high curb. Halfway down the hill, a boy, pretending to help, tried to steal the long hall mirror. Then a pale girl with bright yellow corkscrew curls came out of the grocery store on the corner near their new house and offered Efuah half of her popsicle. There and then, they decided to be best friends.

On the second trip, Otis reversed the cart and rode rapidly down the hill in dangerous but high style, using his shoe as a brake, and wearing out its leather sole. A discarded inner tube from a bicycle, cut to size and inserted into his shoe, gave him some protection until a shoemaker could be found.

The day passed quickly. Singing *One man and his dog went to mow a meadow* helped on the dull uphill trips back to the emptying house on St. Antoine. By the time the family stopped for dinner, Otis couldn't remember whether it was on the third or fourth trip down that he'd first seen the girl. She was young and slender, with creamy skin, very lightly tanned. She wore her almost black hair in a thick braid circling her head. She had been polishing the engraved brass plaque – with *The Russian Ballet Academy* inscribed in an elegant script – beside the door of the grey stone building only three houses down from the Willows' new home. "Great neighbourhood," he decided, then and there, whistling to himself.

To Pippa, who was taking books from the cart, he announced, "Mmm-hmm, this street has class!"

"Class!" Pippa echoed disdainfully, as she carefully loaded more books into her sister's arms. "Did you see those tacky window curtains across the street? Are you aware that there's actually a tavern on the corner? I don't see how we'll ever be able to live here. It's too common for words." She glanced critically around, pointing to the bold red and blue Kik-Cola sign advertising "L'Épicerie Vachon", the grocery store by the lane. Her brown eyes blazed at the shiny chrome and sagging velvet sofa being carted into the empty house opposite. Her heart sank at the sight of the eight raggedy, pock-marked, straggly-haired children who came to sit on its porch and stare at her.

Then she noticed the tall elm tree growing in front of her new home. Its bare delicate branches reached the third-storey windows where her bedroom would be. "When the leaves come out, they'll hide the houses across the street, and maybe a robin will build its nest there," she said to console herself.

Otis ignored her. Scooping up the kitchen chairs, he leapt the steps two at a time, his thoughts focusing on the lovely girl who had been polishing the brass plaque. Coming back out, he offered Efuah a piggy-back ride. "I'm too big," she giggled, hugging him. "Otis, are you really going to live with us?"

"Uh-huh, sure thing. 'Cept when I'm working on the train hustling bags, I'll be right here on this street. Yes sirree."

⁂

It took all of that Friday and most of Saturday to complete the moving and arrange the furniture at the house on rue des Seigneurs. Saturday evening, Poppa Dad treated them to dinner in Chinatown. On their return, a beautiful wicker picnic hamper greeted them. It was propped against the front door and wrapped in a giant yellow ribbon with a card that said *Welcome*. No name was given, but a line inside read *To help until things get back to normal*.

The gift thrilled Pippa, but embarrassed her mother. "Who would know that the gas is not yet connected, nor the lights turned on?" Marion asked Edmond once they were safely inside. "That's not your fault," Edmond insisted. "It's nothing to be ashamed of. You should have asked me to sign for those utilities when I signed the lease for you."

"I didn't have sufficient money then."

"You're too proud, Marion. No woman, not even the wealthiest woman in Westmount, is permitted to sign for utilities."

"Even when we're the breadwinners in a family?" she asked, clenching her hands. "It's scandalous. Women are treated like chattel here in Quebec – and we'll continue to be until we use our vote!"

"You have to accept it, Marion. It's a man's world," Edmond began to explain, but stopped as tears began to fall from Marion's lowered eyes. Her hands were still clenched. "Marion, why won't you marry me and let me worry about these things?"

She walked slowly to the window, examined the naked tree, then turned back to her constant suitor. "Edmond, you have enough to worry about, what with Otis, the union, your family in Guiana, paying taxes on the farm, and now the problems of Marcus Garvey's Black Star organization. They're in trouble, and you're one of the few people that Garvey trusted."

They were standing in the kitchen. Its two windows facing west, slightly above the backyard sheds, caught the setting sun's rays. They tinted Marion's white blouse a soft rose gold and lit her dark hair, revealing its russet glow. To Edmond, she looked as slender as a teenager, although he knew she would be thirty-two in a few months time.

"I have been a widow for three years now," she was thinking.

"Surely the hardest time has passed. And though I am tempted by Edmond's kindness, I don't want to belong to anyone. I cherish my independence." She realized he was waiting for an answer, but didn't quite know how to phrase her refusal. "When Kofi died, I vowed to bring up the girls myself," she said. "I'll manage somehow."

"But I could help you take care of them."

She reached out to touch his arm. "You're already their godfather and surrogate guardian. Why else do you think they call you Poppa Dad?" Her voice was soft and solemn, belying her warm smile. "Your life is full enough."

"Marion, I'd give it all up for you."

"Even Miss Delacourt?" Marion asked; her voice dropped low and trembled.

Edmond flushed; the deep brown of his skin took on a moist ruby glow. His Nubian nose flared. His slender six-foot frame seemed to grow even taller as he straightened his shoulders. For a moment, he and the woman he loved looked directly into each other's eyes. He backed down first, reaching for the folded linen handkerchief in the side pocket of his Harris tweed jacket.

He was tempted to say, "I have to have someone," but one didn't put it that crudely to a lady. Not to a lady who, despite having to work as a domestic to earn a living, kept the standards Marion Willow did – no breath of gossip, no asking for charity. "Yes, even Torrie Delacourt."

"Oh, Edmond. Don't promise a thing like that. I shouldn't have brought it up. I didn't mean it. I don't even know the lady. They say she's well-to-do and very attractive." Marion hesitated, flustered. "But that's not important – I mean, to me. It's simply that I'm not ready to marry again. I'm being unfair to you." She drifted to the kitchen table and began to unpack a box of dishes. Almost fretfully, she murmured, "There are so many things I want for the girls."

Edmond placed his hand gently on her shoulder. "I should go

now. I have to report in tomorrow at eight for the Chicago run, but I'll arrange for the gas and the electricity to be connected before I leave."

"Edmond, you're very kind. I wish . . . ."

Gently, he interrupted her. "Know that I appreciate your letting Otis stay with you. It's a load off my mind. But make sure he pays you rent each week." In an exasperated tone, he added, "He's so pig-headed. I don't understand him anymore. When I brought him to Canada, after he completed his O levels, I intended that he apply himself and go to McGill University. But the young don't consider education as we used to. They just want to go out and dance all night."

"Perhaps . . ." She searched for words. "Perhaps it's because they've seen educated men refused jobs for which they were eligible. They've lost faith in education. Edmond, think of all the coloured men with trade skills or superior education who have to work, the way you do, on the railway or on the steamships, simply because this is a prejudiced society. Neither Canada nor the States are willing to hire Negroes for professional jobs."

"Was it really so different back home in the West Indies?" Edmond asked. "Or was it just more subtle? Yet, we did have our own lawyers, teachers, doctors, and policemen. *Some* people made it."

"Yes, but acceptance was defined by class – and by shade."

Edmond lifted his hands in a futile gesture. On his little finger was an unusual, raw-gold, snake ring with a diamond eye. His long slim fingers, even after moving house, were clean, his nails neatly trimmed. "A job's a job, Marion. At least Black men are not on welfare."

Marion's response was edged with bitterness. "Not physically, at any rate." Edmond frowned, troubled by the subtlety of her reply. He shrugged, his shoulders indicating that he didn't intend to probe. He followed her into the hallway. "Must go. Where are the girls?"

"Upstairs reading, I imagine. Trevor brought Pippa a new *Anne of Green Gables* book, *Rilla of Ingleside*. I'll call them."

Pippa, followed by Efuah, came sliding down the banister. "Poppa Dad, even the front rooms have window seats," she announced. "Real window seats with cushions, just like English country homes."

"Always full of romantic imagery, this one." Her mother hugged her.

Watching Edmond put on his coat, Efuah asked, her lisp revealing her disappointment, "Will you be back soon, Poppa Dad?"

He nodded. "If I can." He produced two nickels. "Here, that's for the Sunday School collection plate." He bent and hugged each child in turn.

As he descended to the street door, Pippa called down, "Poppa Dad, please thank your friend for the can of lobster in the basket. Whoever she is, she has expensive taste." There was no reply; instead, the front door closed with a firm slam.

"Strange," Marion thought. "Why should Edmond lose his temper over Pippa's remark? *Sois gentille*," she cautioned herself silently as she scolded Pippa. "Mr. Thompson – I mean, your Poppa Dad – didn't provide the picnic basket. You should have thanked him for the Chinese dinner instead, or for helping us move. It's not correct to say thank you through a third person. We ought to thank the person ourselves, whoever it is, when he, or she, comes to claim the basket. That's the proper thing to do."

"But, Mother, Poppa Dad must know who brought it," Pippa contended, "because when we picked it up, he said, 'What the devil!' – as if it was a trick or something. And it couldn't have been there long."

"But whoever brought it didn't expect Poppa Dad to stay for supper. There's only three plates," Efuah pointed out, hoping her sister would realize how observant she was.

"Why, that's right, Effie." Pippa squeezed her tightly, so

delighted was she by the deepening of the mystery. After all, who could afford to give complete strangers lobster in a can? And six croissants, fresh cucumbers, bottled bean salad, preserved tomatoes, and raw carrot sticks? Family people didn't serve things like that. "Would the food last till the Victoria Day picnic?" she wondered. The basket even included peaches, six preserved spiced peaches!

As the girls searched upstairs for their nightgowns, Pippa speculated on the identity of the mysterious Lady Bountiful.

Bedtime. There were no lights to put out and it was too dark for a story. Together, they knelt down to say prayers:

Now I lay me down to sleep,
I pray the Lord my soul to keep.
If I should die before I wake,
I pray the Lord my soul to take.

"'Night, Mother."

"Good night, my dears. Sleep well."

The house was quietly losing its definition. From the back alley, cracks of light shone through loose boards in the shed. In front, the street lamp by their tree created stark bamboo patterns on the bare walls. The wicker picnic hamper sat provocatively on the kitchen table. Its ceramic-handled forks, knives, and spoons, red cotton napkins, and three red enamel plates nestled against a square red checkered tablecloth. The thermos, which had contained fruit juice, was draining in the sink.

"Pippa's right. You're a lovely hamper," Marion mused aloud. "Must have cost someone a week's wages. Obviously, ordered from Montreal's most exclusive grocery store." The sign scrolled along the side of Dionne's delivery van, she recalled, boasted, *Purveyors of fish, oysters, game and imported delicacies. Caterers by appointment to His Majesty.* "Who's your mistress?" she petulantly asked the basket. "Why do I consider you my *bête noir*?" The hamper refused to take the bait.

Seduced by its silent elegance, she eventually reached over to caress the wicker weave with its glossy patina. "Marion Willow, shame on you!" she lectured herself. "It was a kind gesture. Why are you so suspicious? Perhaps the person will call on us tomorrow. Oh Lord, I can't even offer a cup of tea – unless I find my Sterno stove. And one of my lovely Aynsley teacups broke in the move."

Exhausted, Marion put her head down on the kitchen table and finally allowed herself a gentle cry. It was almost dark when she sat up. She moved about looking for a candle, then a match. As she left the kitchen, she held the candle up to look again at the luxurious picnic hamper. "I wonder where Miss Delacourt lives?" she asked aloud.

Slowly, Marion climbed the stairs. Going into the children's room, she stopped to pick up clothes and tuck in blankets. Then, noticing that both of Efuah's blue wool socks had holes, she searched for her mending basket and wooden dowel. Sitting in the deeply cushioned windowseat, where the streetlight shone through the glass, she slowly darned the old socks, despite the warm tears dropping down her cheeks.

CHAPTER IV

The morning sun shimmered into iridescent jewels of dew that lingered on the new leaves outside the bedroom window. They triggered in Marion's sleepy mind lines from the epic poem, *The Green Eye of the Little Yellow God*, that McGregor had once recited in the Y kitchen. Pippa would so enjoy the sad adventures of its hero, Mad Jim Carew.

There's a one-eyed yellow idol to the north of Khatmandu.
There's a little marble cross below the town.
There's a broken-hearted woman tends the grave of Mad
  Carew,
And the Yellow God forever gazes down.

She should ask McGregor to copy it for her.

As usual, McGregor's weather prediction was spot-on. May twenty-fourth, the Victoria Day holiday, dawned as gloriously as he contended the old Queen's reign, as Empress of Britain's far-flung Empire, had been.

"Rise and shine . . . another day, another dollar," she murmured to herself. Still, she lingered in her warm bed, stretching long brown fingers towards the morning sun. Her beautiful pear-shaped breasts, the colour of ripe Julian mangoes, a throwback to her grandmother who had been lured from the South Pacific on her grandfather's whaling boat, made her feel as sensuous as Mura must have been. Consciously, Marion reined herself in. No, she couldn't afford to feel like that. "Not even for Edmond Thompson, and God knows, he's a powerfully attractive man." She shifted her thoughts to the day's chores.

In the three weeks since moving to rue des Seigneurs, the house had literally been transformed. Otis, sanding and scraping off old paint, had waxed the maple floors of the front parlour and hall till they glowed with the patina of old burnished brass. The banister and stairs were of maple, too, but the wear and tear on the step treads resisted restoration. Perhaps she'd find a decent, slightly used carpet runner for them at the Salvation Army store. Ruthlessly, Otis had ripped off old wallpaper, plastered cracked walls, and painted ceilings. In the bathroom, he and Pippa, inspired by an illustration in *The Ladies' Home Journal*, achieved the ultimate. He painted its walls a soft écru white. Pippa stencilled daisy patterns in a row above and on the iron sides of the antique eagle-clawed bathtub. Surely, Marion decided, the bathroom deserved gossamer curtains, and felt her lace wedding gown would probably provide sufficient material.

The lurching sound of the iceman's cart on the cobblestone street, accompanied by his high-pitched call of "*Glace! Glace! L'été s'approche. Glace!*", diffused Marion's reluctance to leave her warm bed. "Goodness knows, we need ice. We can't put food in the back shed any longer – it's getting too warm," she murmured. "I'll use some ice for the lemonade." She eased her feet onto the floor, reached for her bathrobe. "I just have to organize a better routine. Pippa, Effie, good morning!" she called. "Up you get. The iceman's here." No response. "Come on, sleepyheads. But do be quiet, don't wake Otis. He was late last night. Pippa, we're out of toothpaste. Come and get some baking soda to brush your teeth."

The iceman did not enter by the back door. Water from his twenty-five-pound frozen cube of river ice dripped all the way to the summer kitchen. Courteously, he waited until Marion wrapped it in newspaper before lowering it into the top compartment of the wooden icebox. Collecting his quarter, he promised his attractive new client to return Saturday. "*Pour vous, Madame, deux fois par semaine,*" he gallantly offered.

As usual, Marion extracted work from the girls in return for the promised Victoria Day picnic supper on Mount Royal. The kitchen cupboards needed brown shelf-paper liners; Pippa volunteered. The back shed had to be organized; a sleepy Otis was assigned. As usual, Effie helped with the family laundry. Singing ten verses of *One man and his dog,* she even managed to sweep the front staircase before lunch. But, in return, Pippa negotiated the use of the mysterious gift hamper for the picnic. The can of lobster, the last of the gift goodies, was reluctantly thrown in for good measure. "Why not?" Marion agreed with an impish smile, hugging her children. It would transform Pippa's potato salad from basic to sublime. It was almost two o'clock before they finished their work. Each chose a book and, armed with a blanket, they headed off up the steep slopes of Côte des Neiges to the mountain. Otis stayed behind; he had to stand by for work.

As the stone steps leading to the mountain path were near Mademoiselle Laroche's apartment, Marion slipped in for a moment to see that all was well with the crippled lawyer for whom she cooked and cleaned, and whose independent mind she so admired, as long as it was dealing with the rights of women. She resented Denise's blind racial attitudes disguised as liberalism, yet she enjoyed the stimulation of their endless discussions. There were times when she almost conceded that Denise was right about the nature of bigotry. Mademoiselle Laroche, touched as always by Marion's concern, gave apples to the girls, but voiced her resentment of the Victoria Day holiday by accusing Marion of being a royalist. Marion giggled to herself, but said nothing.

As they continued up the steep path past Beaver Lake and on into the dark pine forest, Marion lectured them on the importance of going to college. There were hardly any wildflowers to pick – the delicate three-petalled white trilliums were out-of-bounds, being rare and needing protection. Tiny, pesky flies infested the mountain dells, but a grassy knoll near the towering cross on the mountain's peak offered the pleasure of a sunny spot and a panorama of breeze-driven clouds.

Three blissful hours in the dappled sunshine slipped away, as they memorized poems, read books and made daisy-chains. Towards dusk, a light spring rain replaced the gentle breeze, forcing them to run half a mile to shelter in the mountain's massive stone chalet. Marion ordered milkshakes for the girls and tea for herself to ensure that they could enjoy the rest of their picnic supper without sarcastic, under-the-breath comments from the chalet waitress. When the rain ceased, they walked to the wide semicircular lookout. A lovely rainbow arching over the chalet hinted that a pot of gold was hidden just beyond the St. Lawrence River, but its colours dispersed as dirty grey spumes of smoke spiralled upwards from Lower Town.

Trudging home, shoes wet, fighting their flagging spirits with songs, they were accosted by fire engines clanging along the streets of Little Burgundy, putting out bonfires started by neighbourhood boys – boys who couldn't afford to celebrate with sparklers and firecrackers, and found emptying people's sheds of burnable furniture much more fun. The biggest Victoria Day blaze was leaping high above the Richmond Rink, where the wooden shack for changing ice skates was on fire.

⚜

Before the rain started, Maurice Vachon and his Victoria Day marauders had been on the prowl, but pickings had proved slim. Only a few mattresses and some broken chairs were stashed away for the festivities. Maurice discovered it was hard to steal in daylight, especially in the sheds behind the street where he lived, as his father had eagle eyes and his mother kept giving him chores to do. The residents of rue des Seigneurs were safe for the time being.

Across the CNR tracks, beyond the railway fruit depot, and deep into the Italian and Greek district, the gang ventured. Cautiously, they explored the back alleys of rue Notre Dame. In a cul-de-sac, hidden at the back of a stable, they found an old red cart mounted on bicycle wheels. Maurice was ecstatic. It was perfect for carrying all the little odds and ends they'd managed to swipe along the way.

At first, it wouldn't budge. Old Dominic, its owner, had not used his red cart all winter. He didn't feel strong enough to make his normal winter work transition to selling coal instead of fruit that year. When, years earlier, a neighbour had spoken to the priest about his daughter, Emily, implying that Dominic was too old and too poor to provide properly for her, he took her out of public school and created a home for both of them in the hidden attic above the stable. Uncalled for, a welfare worker had reported him to the police, hinting that it was dangerous to leave a little mulatto girl, just entering puberty, in his care. When the authorities finally took her away, he lost all incentive, only working when he had to. Although the Grey Nuns promised to take good care of her, he vowed that some day, when he was stronger, he would get her back.

What a terrible country Canada had proved to be. In 1918, as a displaced Italian prisoner of war, he had been released, spewed out of a New Brunswick lumbering camp. At first, the years passed quickly. Woodcutting winters, log-jamming summers, and always the incessant bitter cold or the insect-laden heat. Yet, the seasons rolled along. There was usually more than enough good food in the lumbering camps, casual friends, and always his mouth organ to help him while away the time, remembering the soft womanly nights of Brindisi on the Adriatic coast of his beloved Italy so far away. Then one morning, his best friend slipped between some rogue logs during a spring log drive on the Gatineau River. Dominic was mangled trying to save him.

Somehow, one New Year's Eve soon after the Great Depression had struck, half-crippled and alone, he encountered a sad sweet young lass from Scotland serving in a delicatessen on Main Street. He still wasn't certain who befriended whom, but for three bittersweet years he had a home, someone to fuss over him, and a little daughter to sing songs to. He lived in constant fear of the thugs who offered "protection," and of losing his young companion, for she was frail and tuberculosis was slowly sapping her vitality.

He was trying to remember how it had all ended when the ruckus in the stable below jolted him back to the present. They'd come again to steal his fruit stand. "Never! Jesu Christo! Was there no escape from the bandits?" Why must he pay a share of his earnings to them? They could break his legs again. "But never, no more ... there was the young bambino now to feed." Hallucinating, Dominic struggled against his fever. He had to get out of bed. Someone downstairs was stealing his cart! He pulled against the iron side of his single bed, but his back would not obey. He held his breath and tried again, but the searing pain of his collapsed left lung forced his mind to blank out. As he slipped into a soft oblivion, he heard the cart bumping away. Now there was nothing left.

⚐

Standing on a slight rise beside the Richmond Rink, mesmerized by the leaping flames, Marion became increasingly agitated. She was convinced that the rickety red cart, being thrown into the inferno by a muscular thug, was familiar to her. Wasn't that the cart of the old fruit peddler, Dominic? Those ruffians would steal anything! Distracted by thoughts of the old Italian and his kindness to her children, Marion realized that she'd better hurry home or her own shed would be rifled next. Pippa wanted to stay and watch the fire, but, as usual, Efuah was afraid. All the shouting and the clanging of the fire trucks made her hide her face against her mother's skirt. It was the only safe place.

Maurice Vachon poked his sooty face around at the height of Mrs. Willow's waist, trying to gain Effie's attention. "Hey! You Sylvie's frien', no? Why you 'fraid? Have fun!"

Incensed, Marion wheeled around. "Have fun! You've stolen an old crippled man's cart. Where did you find it? Aren't you the Vachon boy from the grocery store? Is this any way to behave?"

Maurice looked up. Bravado fought against inherent politeness as his friends appeared. "Ah, what's dat to you? Us, we celebrate *la maudite* Queen de way we wan'." They applauded. Mock bravado took over. "'Ere's to your Hinglish Queen!" Maurice turned his back, dropped his trousers and stuck his bare bum in the air. Shocked, Marion took a step backwards, then quickly pulled little Effie into the folds of her dress. Maurice hobbled off, laughing, with his gang.

"I must find Emily," Marion fussed. "If Dominic's gone, she has no one." Pippa had wandered over to the other side of the blaze to join tall Alice. "Let's go," Marion ordered. "Pippa, come. We're going home." With determination, she shepherded her children westward. Pippa, walking with Alice, was puzzled. "Mother, they're not destructive like this on St. Jean Baptiste Day. He's always shown as a gentle little boy with a lamb."

"Maybe them French kids don' like Queen Victoria, eh?" Alice suggested. "I don' know why. Gosh, her being dead gives us an extra holiday!"

"Perhaps it's because Queen Victoria is a symbol of Britain's ownership of two-thirds of the world, and people are beginning to resent it," Marion said rather sharply, feeling she should tell at least part of the truth.

"But, Mother, why? Britain's having such a hard time in the war and Victoria's been dead since 1900."

"She died in 1901, dear. But the French in Quebec feel she imposed a yoke on their province."

Efuah came to life. "What's a yoke?" she asked.

"Something heavy that's on top of people to control them, Effie."

"Like horses an' oxen have," Alice volunteered.

"Tell you what," their mother said, as they turned down rue des Seigneurs. "Let's hurry and I'll read you a poem on the death of Wolfe on the Plains of Abraham – that was the conquest of Quebec – before we go to bed. Would you like that?"

"Can Alice come?"

"Be seein' ya." Alice spun around and left. The fire would be more exciting than one of Mrs. Willow's endless poems, she reckoned.

Rue des Seigneurs seemed calm as they turned into it, but it was not. In the laneway behind the houses, chairs, mattresses, and wooden chests of drawers were being handed along by a chain of young hoodlums, stolen from the tarpaper back sheds of houses. Even second-storey storage sheds were being raided.

Preparing Ovaltine in the kitchen, Marion suddenly noticed a broad band of light from the alleyway shining through her back shed. She hurried across the walkway bridge into it. It had been broken into and looted! The maple rocker, Kofi's Ghanaian stool with its *adinka* incisions, and the mahogany china cabinet from the few happy years of her marriage were all gone. The shed's lock had been forced.

As she searched for something to wedge the door shut, curses in some unrecognizable tongue rent the air. "Dogs! Sons of bitches!" the voice then shouted in guttural English. "Thieves! Bloody peasants! May your children be born with no hands." Timidly opening the door, Marion peered along the line of tarpaper and wooden sheds until she saw a full head of silky black hair thrashing desperately from side to side, jutting from a small window in the all-wooden shed three doors away. The Russian Ballet

Academy had obviously been robbed as well. "*Yebout tvoya mat!* . . . *Yebout tvoya mat!*" But boiling oil! was the only curse Marion could decipher. She tiptoed back indoors, hoping the children had not heard. "I fear that woman at the Russian Ballet Academy hasn't got a husband either," Marion lamented as she wedged her shed door shut.

⚜

The owner of the husky voice that had screamed obscenities lived south of the Willows in the only authentic stone house on rue des Seigneurs. The words on the engraved brass plaque to the left of her front double door, always polished to perfection, read:

Dame Tatiana Orlova
The Russian Ballet Academy
By Appointment Only

The deep bevelled glass panels in the wooden doors were covered by iron grillwork, sensually scrolled in patterns which lent a certain elegance to their burglar-proof function. The inner wooden doors had stained glass windows. On reading the plaque for the first time, Marion wondered if perhaps Dame Orlova had sent the picnic hamper. "No, not her," Marion decided. Obviously, Dame Orlova didn't wish to be bothered by neighbours unless they could afford to pay for ballet lessons. Still, Marion had to agree with Otis, it was the most aristocratic house on the street.

Over a dozen years earlier, when New York's Wall Street Crash of 1929 had turned into the Great Depression worldwide, Tatiana Orlova, known then as Mrs. Cyril Braithwaite, was living in England, wreathed in a long black veil, in mourning for her handsome West Indian husband. As the Depression deepened, tradesmen in the ancient university town of Oxford showed less and less tolerance for a Russian emigré, who seemed to have very little money of her own and whose husband was no longer alive to lead their cricket team to victory.

In 1934, protesting "ingratitude" to whomever would listen, Dame Orlova packed what was left of her family treasures and, with her six-year-old daughter, set sail for the Caribbean island of Barbados. In Christchurch, St. James Parish, Cyril Braithwaite's family welcomed them with warm Barbadian hospitality. For two months, they fussed over little Marushka. Eventually, growing bored and increasingly annoyed with Tatiana's endless stories of a more civilized society, they presented her with two tourist-class tickets for passage on the S.S. *Lady Rodney* bound for Canada, along with the promise that Marushka would always be considered a member of the Braithwaite family.

The S.S. *Lady Rodney* eventually docked in Montreal. For three months, Dame Orlova searched for a suitable residence. Finally, in Little Burgundy, a "salt and pepper" district on the eastern fringes of St. Henri, she found a house large enough to realize her dreams of opening a Russian ballet school, while providing a safe haven for her little half-caste daughter, Marushka.

When first she sighted those rococo doors on the only stone house on rue des Seigneurs, Dame Orlova decided that, no matter what the place was like on the inside, her store of Russian tapestries, triptychs, icons, and mirrors, and her mother's samovar, would transform it into the magical home she had once lived in, before the Revolution on Pateimonouskaya Street near the Summer Gardens in St. Petersburg. Her hunch was right. Soon she had sufficient pupils, mostly from the petit-bourgeois French families in the neighbourhood, to support herself.

Twice, the Willow girls ran up the stone steps, fingers poised to ring the brass bell, for they had decided that Dame Orlova was still the leading suspect in the case of the mysterious picnic

basket. But the words *By Appointment Only* stopped them both
times. What if Dame Orlova herself deigned to answer? What
would they say? They didn't have the hamper with them. Their
mother had put it away somewhere where they couldn't find it.

"We'll go back home and make ourselves some calling
cards," Pippa decided. "I'm sure that's the correct way to introduce oneself to a stranger."

Dame Orlova's daughter, Marushka, dusting the piano that sat
behind the lace-curtained windows of the front room, watched
the girls, wondering who they were. It was rare in the neighbourhood to see such well-behaved children, who actually seemed to
discuss things with each other. When they left without ringing
the bell, Marushka felt a keen sense of loss. Why should two little
brown girls interest her so? The tall one was probably no more
than twelve. Although her face was alert and delicate, her eyes
were dark and very large. "She probably reads a lot," Marushka
thought. "She's looks intelligent." But the younger one made her
smile; she hadn't yet lost her little-girl tubbiness. "Perhaps seven
or eight, but what a happy face."

"Did I ever smile like that during my childhood?" she asked
herself. Her perpetual sense of loneliness returned. Marushka
had no brothers or sisters, or any relatives she could be with. At
eighteen, Marushka's world was still made up of her widowed
mother, her mother's absorbing stories of White Russian society,
the beautiful icons and artifacts of that era which she had been
taught to cherish, and the ballet school her mother ran, using the
double parlour on the first floor as a studio.

Mondays to Fridays, nine to five, and again for a half day on
Saturday, Marushka was a different person. Her name was Maria
then. Being Maria was a recent development in her life, and she
wasn't yet comfortable with it. She almost preferred the
anonymity of just being the pianist for the ballet classes. She had
deliberately given up a scholarship to the Conservatory of Music
in Toronto in favour of a job in the quiet music section of

Ogilvy's department store. Was she afraid to leave her mother alone, she wondered, or didn't she trust the world outside?

Idly, her long, slim fingers picked out a melody on the piano. She looked around the room. The entire length and height of one wall was mirror, with an exercise bar at waist height. Other than the piano, the only furniture consisted of four gilded chairs with velvet seats and a small Chippendale desk. No pictures decorated the white walls for, as a teacher, Dame Orlova was a stern disciplinarian and tolerated no distractions. Forest green velvet curtains covered the back windows, blocking out the sheds in the lane behind the house.

With a curious smile, Marushka stared at herself in the mirror. Even sitting, she seemed tall. Her too-thick dark hair was tamed into a long braid, which she wound around her head when doing housework, or looped into a low chignon like a Russian ballerina for her job as a saleslady in Ogilvy's music department. The white walls brought out the duskiness of her complexion, and her eyes, she noticed, were equally as large and dark as those of the taller of the two little girls. She turned back to the piano and began a Chopin polonaise.

Otis, carrying a club bag and his grey porter's uniform, slowed his pace as he passed the open window. Hearing the music, he stopped. Marushka saw him looking up curiously, his face revealing at first astonishment, then bewilderment. Slowly, his strong features eased into a look of utter contentment. She tensed momentarily; then, aware that he could not see her through the lace curtains, she relaxed. Her playing became less demanding, more exploratory. The young man listened for a while, but, as if suddenly conscious of the picture he presented, he picked up his bag and walked on.

Marushka ended the polonaise, closed the piano, and looked out at the street again. It was an ordinary street. Most of the buildings were red or brown brick with narrow iron stairwells leading from second- and third-storey flats down to the street. There was no room for gardens, except under the clotheslines at the back, between the houses and the storage sheds. Theirs was the only single-family limestone house on the street.

There was no sign of the tall, dark young man with the strange hazel eyes who had stopped to listen to her music. He must be new to the neighbourhood, Marushka decided. "Perhaps he belongs to the little girls. Maybe he's their father," she speculated. "No, he's far too young." The realization brought a smile. Every year, May the first brought so many new families and took familiar faces away. "We don't move — moving must be a peculiar Canadian habit," she thought. "No matter, I never seem to meet them anyway."

Reaching down, she pulled the louvered shutters together, then patted the lace curtains into place. It was almost dark; the room was shadowy. The door of the studio led into the main hallway. Locking it, she turned on a lamp that threw jewelled shafts of light against the high ceiling of the lobby, creating a cathedral glow.

A third door led to their upstairs living quarters. Marushka never failed to be struck by the difference between the cool, almost stern patrician environment of the ballet studio on the ground floor, and the lush rococo disorder her mother had made into comfortable living spaces upstairs on the second and third floors.

The large front room contained the elegant marble fireplace moved from the main floor to provide more practice space. Above it was mounted a hauntingly beautiful triptych of the Holy Trinity, oil-painted in glowing amber, sapphire, ochre, and indigo blue. Oil lamps nestled in blue and red glass cups hung in front of the icon, creating mysterious radiations in the gold-leaf crowns of the Saints and Virgins in the three-part painting.

To the left of it, centred in an ornate wooden frame, two young girls smiled from a faded sepia print. They were bundled in furs, seated in a graceful monogrammed sleigh drawn by a pair of horses. It was a photograph of her mother and her Aunt Natasha, who had died during their escape from Russia after the Revolution. Another photograph, in a simple silver frame, was a traditionally posed group of Caribbean cricket players, taken on the MCC cricket ground at Lords in England. Their captain, her father, stood proudly in the front, dark and tall, wearing immaculate white doeskin trousers, a straw boater, and, on his blue blazer, the crest of the West Indies Cricket Club. Marushka went straight to the photograph and looked carefully at him.

"How tall was my father?" she asked Dame Orlova. Her mother was startled.

"Why how tall? Why do you ask? So much has happened. I don't want to talk about him."

"'Captain Cyril Braithwaite,'" Marushka read. "He's handsome. I wish I looked more like him. What was he like?"

"What's to know?" her mother answered.

"I need to know," Marushka insisted.

Dame Orlova shrugged. "I was an immigrant." She sat down in a straight-backed chair, wrapping a fringed Spanish shawl around her shoulders as though she were cold. Marushka leaned on the mantelpiece patiently. Moments passed before her mother continued, almost in a monotone. "When I met your father in England, I was at my wits' end. I was so alone. Mama had retreated into a world that no longer existed. Uncle Anton drank the days away. Natasha was dead."

A long pause. When she spoke again, it was as if she were speaking to someone else of a time that still haunted her. "It was so cold in the train. No food – not even for drachmas or a small jewel. No food, nothing." Her tone changed again; she spoke petulantly. "Why were we so afraid? We were not nobility, not aristocrats. Why did we flee from Russia?"

Marushka put a hand on her mother's shoulder to calm her. The monologue went on. It did not and would not include her father, Marushka realized. She had heard it all before, many times.

"Uncle Anton was a fool, I tell you. Yet he managed to get us safely out of Russia by train, through the border checkpoints at Verjbolovo and past the danger point at Eydtuknen. He knew all the backroads to Berlin and eventually delivered us to England. Always, he protected Mama because of her beauty. He starved himself and we had very little. Soon Natasha was beyond needing food, but he pushed on. What he did not know was that Count Wassilikoff did not want his former mistress in England. He had married an English wife who was not as tolerant as the old Countess had been. He dared not show his love for Mama and despised Uncle Anton for his foolhardiness, for complicating his new life. 'I left you safe in Russia. No one would have bothered you at Lake Ilmen. The dacha was yours,' he kept insisting. 'Why did you follow me to England? Why?'

"Count Wassilikoff found lodgings for us in 1920 or '21 in a place far away from London, the old university town of Oxford. A pretty place, with historic buildings, but strictly divided between the arrogant undergraduate students and the tradesmen. The Count gave Mother some of his remaining family jewellery, his ruby cufflinks, and his diamond dress studs, then abandoned us. All Uncle Anton's bravado had been expended by then, and he took to quaffing vodka as if it were black tea." Turning to Marushka, she suddenly held out her arms. "Yes, I must tell you as it was. You're old enough."

Marushka backed away. "I just sometimes wonder about the men in our family," she said, trying to lead her mother to talk about Cyril Braithwaite. She looked again at the picture of her father, then gave a futile shrug. "It doesn't matter. It's just that we never meet any men like my father here. I mean, most people in Montreal are white – French or English, but white like you and Uncle Anton."

Her mother's eyes followed her as she moved around the room touching fabrics, picking up the tiny enamelled boxes as though seeing them for the first time. There was something infinitely sad about the way she carefully put them back. "There's nothing of my father here."

"He's dead, Marushka. He died." Something in her mother's tone that had never been there before startled Marushka. She turned. Her mother opened her arms in a gesture of such love and warmth that Marushka went to her, burying her head in her mother's lap. "Forgive me, Mamushka."

"You have his hair, his thick, soft curly hair. You have some of his colour and his grace. He was a prince, your father. Not a real prince, Marushka, like we had in St. Petersburg, but a gentle man who knew how to keep his word.

"Tall, yes. My, how he was tall. I saw a man on the street yesterday helping some little girls. He reminded me of your father – dark, erect, full of humour, and as graceful as Nijinsky."

Emotionally, but without words, Tatiana Orlova Braithwaite focused on the tall, dark West Indian cricketer who had loved her, and his Barbadian family who had rejected her. Smiling and slowly shaking her head, she cupped Marushka's face in her hands. Then she began to rebraid her daughter's thickly textured hair, and returned to her story.

"I was about your age then, eighteen. No one to introduce us into society. Most of the White Russian emigrés lived in London, or with English relatives in Sussex or Kent. Many were related to the British Royal Family, but we had no connections, no money, no skills. Oh, I could play the piano and the mandolin, and I could dance. Natasha and I had studied folk and classical dance during the summers at Lake Ilmen, but Mama did not understand English, and because of the Count's perfidy and his wife's intolerance, Mama hated the English. She pined away, became very ill. Can you imagine it, Marushka? She willed her own death.

"Mama had made Count Wassilikoff so happy in the days before the Revolution. She had been so cherished. He had provided us with everything. For him, she left the Imperial Ballet,

brought Natasha, me, and Uncle Anton from the country to live
with her in St. Petersburg. And, for almost ten years, we lived well,
very well.

"I still don't quite understand how it happened. The autumn
of 1917 was a terrible confusion. The Czar and his family were
interned at Tsarskoe Seloe. Armed workers, soldiers, and sailors
took the Winter Palace in St. Petersburg by storm. After
Christmas, the Count took us for safety to Gatchina. I remember,
as we crossed the bridge over the Neva River that night, the double heads of the Imperial Eagles lay demolished on the pavement,
half-covered in snow." Marushka's braid was finished. "The Count
escaped from Gatchina with the retreating White Army. It was the
last train west, a freight train full of wounded officers – but I've
told you about that before. Let's have some tea now, and then I'll
prepare borscht."

"But what about my father?" Marushka would not let her
mother rise.

"Marushka, enough," she said darkly.

"I don't want any tea, Mamushka. I don't want ritual. I
want . . . I want reality."

Dame Orlova stood imperiously. She was not tall, but her
erect back suggested a dignity denied by her old-fashioned clothing. Conflict moved across her face. Her hands fluttered against
her heart, mist filled her almond-shaped eyes. "What do you want
to know, Marushka?"

"You've never told me much about him before. Not like you
do about St. Petersburg and Babushka."

"Perhaps I shouldn't be telling you now," her mother replied,
her mood slowly changing. "Marushka, tell me. Why do you
demand to know about your father now? You have never insisted
so much before."

"I guess, because . . ." There was silence between them for a
moment. "In all these years, and now even at work, I've never
met anyone whose father was the colour mine was. And because

he's not here, no one thinks I have West Indian blood."

"What they don't know doesn't hurt."

"It does hurt, Mamushka. It does, constantly. You should hear what people at work say about coloured people. They despise them. They don't know them, yet they look down on them. It's like at Victoria School, when they used to gang up on my friend Ivy, and if I defended her, they'd say it was because I was different, too. 'Your mother's a Commie,' they said. The principal suggested that Ivy's mother send her to Royal Arthur School below the tracks where there were more coloured students. After we graduated from public school, Ivy stopped associating with me. She said it was for my own good. She was the last true friend I ever had. There were one or two her colour at Montreal High School, but they ignored me."

"Bosh. You have that nice girl Grace and that strange creature Monique, at work. They seem to like you." Her mother poured tea into two glasses.

Marushka took one, put lemon in it, and, holding a square of sugar, went to the window. "Grace's brother wants to start dating me."

"Dating you? Dating you! But you have never brought him home," Dame Orlova protested haughtily, regaining some of her old arrogance. "What's his profession?" she asked. "Be careful, my child. Men are deceitful."

"Don't worry. When I marry – " The doorbell rang, interrupting her. "If I marry, Mamushka, he'll have to be prepared to live with both of us." They laughed together. The doorbell rang again.

The meek-eyed man standing outside the door had a series of booklets fanned out in his freckled hand. "Are you saved?" he asked.

Marushka suppressed a smile. "We're Russian Orthodox."

His amazement made him stutter. "Armageddon is at hand," he warned.

"What a pity," she replied. "I hope spring comes first." With a sympathetic smile, she closed the door.

The man rang bells that did not answer until he reached the Willows' door. When he asked Pippa, after his introduction and the gift of a booklet, if she was saved, she told him how, in her novel, Princess Aurora had been saved by a prince. "Maybe this Armageddon could be the scene of a battle. Do tell me more about it," she invited.

Hastily, he retreated, deciding that there was no desire for salvation on rue des Seigneurs. Most of the people on it spoke French or had strange accents. The woman at L'Épicerie Vachon had fearfully responded to his warnings by offering to light a candle. One man, who looked as ancient as a Jewish patriarch, listened patiently at the door, his wife crocheting silently at his side. When the "messianic avenger" stopped for breath, old Sam Cohen offered him a dime, saying *"Danke schön."* The evangelist doggedly trudged down the street. At the corner, confronted by a massive tavern door, he took out a tract and, with chewing gum, stuck it on the haunch of the *Black Horse Beer* sign. He turned east along St. Jacques to continue his quest.

⚜

Almost two weeks passed before Otis caught sight of Marushka again. The tree outside the Willows' window had swelled with a mass of tender green leaves. It was eight-thirty in the morning. Efuah had forgotten her school bag, but had remembered to take her lunch box. Otis waited to lock the front door and walk with the girls to the corner.

"Good morning," Pippa called out as Marushka walked by, a knitted tam on her head, a blue mackintosh raincoat wrapped around her.

"Good morning, Pippa," Marushka answered, smiling at Otis without breaking her stride.

Otis called up the stairway to Efuah, "Hey, Fatso! Get down here, pronto."

"Coming." Efuah appeared, school blouse turned the wrong way round.

Pippa dashed into the house. "It's going to rain — I have to find an umbrella."

"Forget it, let's go." Otis barked. Collecting their hands, he firmly steered the girls in the direction Marushka had taken.

"No, not that way — this way." Pippa tugged at his sleeve, pointing towards St. Jacques.

"Ai-yai-yai!" His palm slapped his forehead. He watched Marushka disappear among the dozens of other women walking up the hill towards uptown. Reluctantly, he turned in the opposite direction. "What's her name?" he asked Pippa, feigning casualness. "You seem to know her."

"I don't, but Effie and I feel we ought to call on her out of neighbourly politeness. We want to find out what a Russian Ballet Academy looks like."

"When do you plan to go?" Otis asked.

"Maybe tonight, after school, if you'll go with us."

The idea grew on Otis. "My pleasure — see you after school then. Behave yourselves," he added, as he watched them cross the street. When Efuah began to hopscotch, he cupped his free hand to his mouth and called, "Pippa, take Fatso's books before she drops them. Ai-yai-yai!"

But Pippa didn't hear him. She was daydreaming again. "Surely," she reasoned, "the Russian Ballet Academy would be a chance for the Princess Aurora to be catapulted into the limelight of the stage." Maybe she should write a ballet for her. The clanging red light at the train intersection, a block from their school, reinforced by the noisy group of children waiting there, forced Pippa back to the present. Taking Effie's hand, she discussed a strategy for the proposed visit to the Russian Ballet Academy after school.

The freight train was long. It shunted to and fro, manoeu-
vring its boxcars into the freight sheds on the south side of the
main line. Obviously, she and the other children would now be
late for school. If their teachers kept them after school to atone,
Pippa realized with a sinking heart, the visit to the ballet school
could not take place. "These stupid, spiteful trains," she said angrily. "Otis is right – the railway has no respect for people."

O tis hoped he would arrive too late to be assigned stand by duties, should there be sufficient sleeping-car tickets sold by three o'clock to merit putting on an extra Pullman car. He didn't intend to be noticeably late, for he had promised his uncle to turn over a new leaf and be dependable. Otis had to give the appearance of appreciating his job, Edmond Thompson insisted, for although thousands of young men had already gone off to war, hundreds of others would welcome the chance to work on the railroad, rather than serve as cannon fodder in North Africa or on the Second Front.

Otis remembered the tail end of the Depression years. Assigned as a trainee on the Pullman car run from Toronto to Vancouver, he had seen many family men who didn't have jobs. In his mind's eye, he could still recall those exhausted, thin, shallow-faced farmhands from the earth-eroded wheatfields of the midwest, who jumped onto freight trains as they shunted through apathetic prairie towns, or hung around the dining-car kitchen when the transcontinental trains stopped for water. They gave him the willies. How could white men, who didn't have colour to hold them back, be so destitute? Often these same ragged drifters had the gall to contemptuously refer to the Negro cook as "coon."

A streetcar came ricocheting along behind him, but he didn't sprint to the stop. "Better walk. It's only three miles. Gives one time to think." Thinking about the day ahead chased away images of those faraway hobos, but did nothing to mute the reality of those young men his age whose choice was either living on one meal a day from a charity soup kitchen, or entering the army. Already dozens of his contemporaries were overseas, most serving in the Royal Canadian Signals Corps. Factories and war industries discouraged able-bodied men, as women were proving more than adequate and didn't demand union wages. Otis swung his leather club bag and long legs into action. "Better not be too late."

On St. Antoine, near Fulford, he passed the house where the Willows used to live. The door of the Aberdeen Bakery Shop opened, wafting out its warm scents of honey, yeast, and raisins, behind a smiling customer, clutching a brown paper bag. Otis hurried past the Perrier Funeral Parlour, with its garish maroon-and-white awning over the front steps that was supposed to provide the illusion of dignity and privacy. Unfortunately, the weight of the winter's snow had buckled its spine. "No one notices," Pippa once explained. "They're too busy weeping." On her way home from school, she often made a detour to visit the Perrier Funeral Parlour to see if there was anyone lying in state who had had no mourners. Whenever she discovered no names in a guestbook, she would dutifully kneel down, shed a tear, then write, in her most ladylike script, *Mourned by Philippa Clothilde Willow.*

Otis, recalling her compassion, smiled. It was good having little sisters again. He remembered, as a boy in that far-off bush village near the sugarcane plantations in British Guiana, having two sisters and two older brothers. His parents, with the older boys, cut sugarcane for a living, but his grandfather, who would work for no man, stayed home and fished. A sluggish red-brown river meandered through the village. Old Amos, his grandfather, told everyone that he owned that river. In his mind's eye, Otis could still see old Amos, very grizzled and very black, with dark eyes that missed nothing. He knew which plants and leaves cured which ailments, which snakes did not bite, and which roots lowered a fever.

He also knew where gold nuggets could be found. "Way inland, it was, far past where the mighty Orinoco River plunges, roaring loudly, half a mile downwards. A four-day walk through underbrush and jungle to where the Amazon River flows, but not there – just *near* there. That's where the richest gold fields lie." Amos owned a hidden bag of gold nuggets. One he wore as a substitute for a tooth he'd lost.

Otis's grandmother, Amos explained, was from that same jungle river area. She was Amerindian and, like all of her tribe, had green snake-hazel eyes and a constant silence. Her skin was always moist and as golden as a baked yam. She wore two gold nuggets as earrings and one as an ornament on the lower part of her nose. As Otis remembered, she was continually cooking – baking fish in banana leaves, grilling yams, or making cassava pone – stirring her clay pots and chewing coca leaf. It was one of her gold nuggets that had made it possible for Otis to go to boarding school in Georgetown.

The sharp honking of a horn broke his reverie. Otis jumped back onto the curb and waited for the light to change. A familiar hand clamped him on the shoulder. "Hey, man. How's things? You sure look busy thinkin' 'bout something." Rodney Brown extended a slim, olive-brown, manicured hand. "Put it here, man." They shook hands, then threw their arms about each other.

"Cool. You's a sight for sore eyes," Otis responded. "What's new? How's things?"

"Copacetic! Can't complain. Where you heading?"

"To the Glen. Got to report. Supposed to stand by for the Detroit–Chicago train."

"Hey, lucky you. It's a mean run, but you could make a pile of money! They's hungry for reefers at the club, so stash some away – bring it back."

The light changed. They crossed the street, Otis protesting against the sound of traffic. "No, man. I'm not into that stuff. No smuggling cocaine for me. Nor marijuana. Nothing!"

"They's dozens who do. You gettin' religion or something, eh? Or have you found some sweet pidididdy gal that's got standards?" Rodney laughed; his wide mouth emitted a guttural donkey sound, but his steely eyes examined Otis coldly.

Otis decided he might as well laugh, for Rodney pretended never to take anything seriously. It was always "Let's catch the action at Rockhead's" or "Let's inspect the chicks at Club St. Michel." He revelled in the nightlife around Montreal's Mountain Street, with its jazz entertainers and brown-skinned chorus girls imported from New York's Harlem. Both nightclubs were owned by former railway porters who, gossip contended, had made their initial nest eggs rum-running, in the decade when Prohibition in the United States made smuggling liquor across the border profitable.

"Come on." Rodney gave Otis a nudge with his elbow. "I'll walk with you. Was going to hop the tram, but every dime counts. I mean, for some folks, that's the extent of their tip!" They walked west along St. Antoine through St. Henri, parallel to the Canadian Pacific rail line and away from centretown Montreal with its mammoth passenger terminal and its handsome Sun Life Assurance building facing Windsor Square.

"I mean," Rodney explained, "there jes' ain't as many bucks smugglin' as in the old days when Americans would do anything for a drink. I 'member my old man tellin' me 'bout a porter who would hide a whole case of Old Moll bourbon under his mattress. Then, when the train reached Rouse's Point, he'd begin to fuss an' yell, 'Inspection! Inspection! Open all your bags for the custom inspector!' – all the while keeping the Man so busy inspecting luggage he didn't have time to look under the porter's bed."

"That's nothing!" Otis countered. "They say there was a

high-yella woman in Windsor who used to wheel her baby carriage onto the ferry that crossed to Detroit, every single day. 'Going to visit the reverend, my father,' she'd say. After about a month of this, the U.S. Customs officer got suspicious. That was the sleepiest baby he'd ever seen. Well, sir, under the blanket he found twelve bottles of Seagram's whiskey! And in the baby's bottle? Rum!"

"If the truth be told, m'frien', all kinds of ruses was used. They say even the Chinese in Windsor was involved. Froze bottles of booze in large blocks of ice and floated them across the St. Clair River to Detroit."

"For real? That's not possible."

"Cross my heart. Liquor don't freeze. I was born in this country, I oughta know," Rodney insisted. "All them fences on the American side had to do was let the ice melt. Lots of Canadian people got rich because of Prohibition. They say that's how the Bronfman brothers, out of Winnipeg, made they fortune, and look at 'em now. Seagram's! We the basis of it. We did the work, and got nuttin' to show fer it."

"Still, it ain't worth taking a chance," Otis argued. "Now it's pot. That's more dangerous, and it's against all the rules – you could lose your job."

"Since there's nuttin' in it fer you, wouldn't you rather be a Red Cap?" Rodney asked. "Porterin', bein' away from town five, ten days, tha's for married folks. Gets 'em away from their wives. Me and you, we need F-R-E-E-D-O-M!"

There was music in Rodney's body language, rhythm in his flowing zoot suit, and such a promise of the good life that Otis felt tempted. But he resisted. "My uncle doesn't agree with you. He wishes I had stayed in school and qualified for McGill. He doesn't even want me to go in the army. I told him, if I join the Engineers, they'll pay for my education after the war's over."

Rodney's exuberance turned sour. "Christ, what good does education ever do? Look at your uncle, or Patterson – or

Mr. Mills. Came from Trinidad with a good education and where
did it get *them?* Na, they don' really want no immigrants here to
give 'em competition." He suddenly broke into a conspiratorial
grin and nudged Otis as an attractive redhead looked back at him.
"That is, they *men* don't."

His mood changed abruptly again. "You know, years ago they
actually recruited West Indian mechanics to come work in that
big Argus machine shop near Viau in the east end. There's plenty
of 'em livin' there still. Now, mos' is unemployed. When the war
was over and white men came back, bang! Las' hired, firs' fired.
No jobs, no transportation back home. They was skilled workmen
from Bridgetown. They built boats, and them from Bermuda
came from the navy dockyard – 'lectricians, fitters, boilermakers.
We was professional! What we all now? Day labourers, tha's all."

"Oh, knock it off! Alex Williams works as an outdoor lineman for the power company."

Rodney stopped abruptly. He faced Otis, his grey eyes blazing. "Yeah, a lineman who hasta climb them high-voltage poles
and could get 'lectrocuted any time, when he's a qualified – an' I
mean, England university qualified – en-gin-eer!"

"Well, what about Doctor Beaubien, that dentist from
Haiti?" Otis said, feeling he ought to be more positive, for
Rodney stressed the negative every time, whatever it was –
putting down girls, discussing jobs, anything. It depressed him.

Rodney's finger was jabbing back. "A doctor's a doctor. And
the French are different. But do you ever see any Black nurses?"
he challenged.

"Yes!" Otis shot back. "Doris Mills works at the Royal
Victoria Hospital on the wards."

"And d'you think the hospital authorities know she's
coloured?" Otis was silent. Rodney sucked his teeth and walked
on. "No. She don' look like no Negro, so she's passin'. Tha's how
she got her job. D'you think she told her boss her daddy is from
Jamaica? No sirree! She's passin', and I say three cheers for her!

Personally, if I was her, I'd drop a bit of arsenic in them medicines." Rodney chuckled. "'Specially for those early Gothics from Westmount. They be's the wors'. They scared of Black mens, but they work our wimmenfolk to death in they kitchens – and they love, love, *love* to tell you 'bout they Black mammy when they was children."

Otis walked without responding. His thoughts had moved to the girl from the grey stone house on rue des Seigneurs – the girl with the long braid, who lived at the Russian Ballet Academy. She didn't look much like it, but he was sure she was coloured, maybe like Doris Mills – only half-coloured, perhaps. Someone had told him that before the war, there were about three hundred coloured families in Montreal, but he was certain there were many more. If a person was only dusky and perceived as being country French with a bit of Indian blood way in the background – or Middle European with a gypsy ancestor – they crossed over.

In the eighteenth century, a number of slaves were imported to Quebec or brought back from the French West Indies as prized possessions. Some eventually intermarried or lived in isolated communities as oddities. Yet, now, to have just one Negro parent seemed a stigma. If you were all Black, at least they knew where you were coming from.

What about this Dame Tatiana Orlova? Was she the girl's mother? Did a father live behind those massive bevelled-glass doors? Pray God he was Black. The Chopin melody she had been playing hovered in his head – "white folks' music," he labelled it, but instantly felt ashamed of his discrimination.

If only he didn't have to serve on the Detroit train that evening, he would be free to go back to rue des Seigneurs and escort Pippa and Effie on a visit to the lady in the grey stone fortress. He quickened his step.

"You suddenly in a great hurry to go to work for Charlie," Rodney remarked, as they climbed the hill towards Westmount Station.

Otis felt expansive. Conjuring up images of the girl pumped energy through his entire bloodstream. "Yes sirree! I'm ready to work and earn a whole lotta money. But not tonight. Tonight, I've got a date with an angel," he crooned. "At least, I intend to."

"You!" Rodney chuckled, slapped his lean thigh. "You? You couldn't give up those devil-may-care chorus gals even if you wanted to. I warn you, m'frien', those angel types don't let they mens hang out at Rockhead's." They crossed into the train yard. "Jes' wait till the boys hear 'bout this – Otis Thompson smitten. What's 'er name?"

But there was no reply. As Otis disappeared into the assignment office, Rodney heard the dispatcher's jovial voice greet his friend. "Thompson. Just in time. Need you to complete the Chicago run tonight. Report at three."

Sucking his teeth as a sign of disgust, Rodney turned back towards the Westmount commuter platform to catch a train headed to Windsor Station and his duties there as a Red Cap.

CHAPTER VII

T wo weeks passed before Otis's dream of seeing Marushka again had even the slightest chance of happening. From Chicago, through the twin cities of St. Paul and Minneapolis, north around the windswept shores of Lake Superior, and then west into Winnipeg, with only three hours of sleep, he made up berths, carried bags, served coffee, cleaned toilets, polished shoes, fetched ice, and, with all the charm he could muster, avoided tipsy grass widows who demanded tucking in. In Winnipeg, the dispatcher ordered him to lay-over for forty-eight hours, or until the special Vancouver-bound troop train was ready to roll. For the first time in his life, Otis envied those married Pullman porters who were given the preferential, and usually more lucrative, short runs to the States.

Nothing managed to interest him in that flat, sprawling prairie town. Located halfway between the Atlantic and Pacific Oceans, Winnipeg boomed when the railway spewed out immigrants from Eastern Europe, religious dissidents from Russia, and farmers from the Ukraine, who created farms of wheat and barley large enough to feed even those left back home. Not even the cheerful exuberance of the second-generation Polish waitress who insisted he try the spicy goulash soup and pointed out the onion-domed spires of Russian Orthodox churches, nor the expansive openness of a Jewish merchant who marketed zoot suits as outrageous as those in Chicago, broke through his ennui.

Only the strange, sad bewilderment of some lanky native Indians lolling about outside the railway station disturbed him. They seemed so battered by their constant rejection in a country they had once called their own; their hunters' eyes had gone dim, reminding him that, for these earth-dark men, as for so many of his own people, the Depression lingered on. Then, a slim sloe-eyed lady, standing in the doorway of a souvenir shop, directed her gentle half-smile at him. To his surprise, he found himself following her into the untidy shop. Slowly, he became aware, as he faked interest in the ashtrays, miniature Red River carts, and tomahawks, that his response was triggered because she was dusky and dark-haired, like the girl from the ballet school.

"Postcards?" Yes, he could send the Willow girls a card. He handed the salesgirl a dime. "Thanks. Keep the change." As evening replaced the strange, almost iridescent clarity of the Winnipeg sky with the stark drama of a full dome of stars, Otis retreated to his room, longing to get back to Montreal and rue des Seigneurs so he could see his beautiful neighbour again. When sleep came, he dreamt he was holding her in his arms, the music of Chopin echoing in his ears.

⚓

Pippa, late because of a rehearsal for a play at school, turned the corner onto rue des Seigneurs and spotted the postman climbing her steps with his satchel of letters. Racing ahead of Efuah, she was able to thank him before he moved on to the next door. "*Merci.*"

"*De rien,*" he replied gallantly. "*Il y en a deux.*"

Yes, there were two, an electricity bill and a postcard from Otis. The card had taken a week to reach Montreal.

June 15, 1942. Dear Family: En route to Vancouver. Train bulging with raw army recruits. Many my age. They tell me about fathers and brothers wiped out when Japan overran Hong Kong last Christmas. Feel sorry, so being specially simpatico, but it's an exhausting run. Rocky Mountains still have snow. Miss you. Love, Otis.

Sitting on the stairs, encouraging Efuah to read the card aloud, Pippa hardly heard Marushka's softly spoken words: "I hope it's good news."

"It is! It's from Otis," Efuah replied, proudly ready to share her joy with anyone who asked.

"Otis?"

"Yes. You know, our Otis. He's taking care of soldiers."

Marushka looked bewildered. Pippa, suspecting that their neighbour obviously didn't know who Otis was and was only being polite, explained. "It's just a postcard from a friend who works on the railway." With a nod and a good-bye smile, Marushka walked on, wondering if she had intruded.

The girls watched her climb her outside steps, take off her beret, and search in her purse for her key. Suddenly, Pippa realized they had missed a golden opportunity to introduce themselves, but it was too late to call out. Efuah felt cheated. "Now we'll never see inside the 'cademy." Pippa decided to be philosophical. "Call it kismet, Effie. It just wasn't in the stars. When Otis comes home, we'll call on her, you'll see."

They didn't have to wait for Otis. The very next day Marushka, looking as cool and lovely as a lady on a chocolate box, wearing a navy blue linen dress and high-heeled shoes, stopped at L'Épicerie Vachon on her way home from work to buy lemons for tea, and came face to face with little Effie. She and her best friend Sylvie were minding the Vachon store, playing at being salesgirls, while Madame Vachon stocked the shelves. "We have some nice bubbly home-made beer. Wanta buy some?" Efuah asked, her lisp sluring "s" into "th," her wide smile creating dimples while revealing a missing front tooth. She wasn't a pretty child, Marushka realized, but curiously appealing.

Madame Vachon waddled over, wiping her hands on her large flowered apron. "She means spruce beer. Sylvie, *donne-moi trois citrons et deux bières.*" In addition to the three lemons her customer had offered to pay for, Sylvie's mother tucked two corked-top bottles into the bag, suggesting she try the spruce beer. "Oh, don't worry, ma'mselle. You won't get drunk. We make it ourselves from our own trees." Giggling, the two little girls opened the screen door to let Marushka out.

Crossing the lane between the store and the next block of buildings, which contained both her home and the Willows', Marushka noticed Pippa curled up on her top step, reading. Again, she slowed down, for she sensed the little girls were special to her. They might be the only neighbours she would ever get to know, and knowing them might tell her more about herself. She slowed to a halt, but Pippa didn't notice, so completely absorbed in her book was she.

"Is it a good book? What's it about?" Marushka had time to study the distinctive way the girl's dark brown wavy hair framed a widow's peak on her forehead, for Pippa deliberately finished the page before she put the book down and looked up.

"Oh!" she gasped. "I'm sorry. I didn't know it was you. I thought it was just one of those curious passers-by."

"I am curious, but I'm not just passing by. I'm your neighbour."

Pippa unwound her long legs and started down the stairs, extending her hand in greeting. Her face was serious, as though trying to resolve a problem. "I don't think I should curtsey to you, should I?" she asked, "'cause you're not a proper grown-up lady yet. Are you? My name is Philippa Willow. Otis calls me Pippa."

Marushka's heart flipped. Was it because of this precocious

child, or was it because she now knew that Otis had to be the name of the tall, moonstruck young man who had listened to her play the piano? "You're right. I'm not a proper, full-fledged lady yet. I'm only eighteen. My name is Marushka, Marushka Braithwaite."

"That's a lovely name. You belong to Dame Orlova, don't you? Is your father dead?"

"Why do you ask?"

"Well, because you look so quiet and sad, like a lonely lady in a poem, like 'The Lady of Shalott.'" Pippa retrieved her book. "Here, it's what I'm reading. Imagine . . . ." She thumbed through a few pages, struck a tragic pose, then read:

> She left the web, she left the loom,
> She made three paces thro' the room,
> She saw the water lily bloom,
> She saw the helmet and the plume,
> She look'd down to Camelot.
>
> Out flew the web and floated wide;
> The mirror crack'd from side to side.
> "The curse has come upon me," cried
> The Lady of Shalott.

"Then what happened?" Marushka moved closer. "Why was she cursed?"

"Don't you read poetry? You ought to. I'll lend you my copy. It's written by Alfred Lord Tennyson. It's wonderful, it's so tragic."

"Tell you what." Marushka shifted her packages of lemons and spruce beer to search for her house key. "If you read 'The Lady of Shalott' to me, I'll read my favourite tragedy to you. It's called 'Sohrab and Rustum.'"

"Isn't it about Russia?" Pippa's large, dark eyes became intense, revealing her hunger for things exotic. "I know it! At least, I know a line from it." Again, she struck a dramatic pose: "*For very young he seemed and tenderly reared.*"

"Yes, that was Sohrab, from a Persian epic of long ago." Marushka bent over to kiss her new friend's cheek. "I'm glad we've met."

"May I bring the book tomorrow?"

"No, I'll be working late and my mother has students in the afternoon. But why not come Sunday at three for tea? Bring your sister."

An invitation, a real invitation to the Russian Ballet Academy! Pippa didn't even notice Marushka go into her own house, or Efuah arrive, her pinafore soiled with chocolate candy stains. "Can Sylvie come and play?"

"'Fraid not, Effie. We'd better go in and tidy up. Mother will be home soon. You'll play with Sylvie tomorrow."

At six, when Marion Willow arrived home, instead of finding her daughters waiting impatiently on the front step, they were inside washing their socks, gloves, and bloomers in anticipation of having tea at the Russian Ballet Academy. Pippa was determined that their manners would be impeccable and they'd act as elegantly as Mrs. Maude Jones or Mrs. Angela Brock did at the Coloured Ladies Club's Annual Rose Tea. Out of the china cabinet came Marion's precious Aynsley teacups. Milk, cocoa, and even lemonade were served in them so that the girls would learn to use their wrists to lift their teacups and not stick their pinkies in the air. For the next three days, including Sunday, all lunch meals were prepared as tiny sandwiches.

Otis arrived back in Montreal too late to accompany them. But, on discovering where they were, from a note left on the icebox by Mrs. Willow, he hurriedly took a shower, put on his grey flannels, and went to pick them up. It was five o'clock. The tea party lasted until almost seven.

⚜

Marushka began to make a difference in their lives. As her mother's summer ballet classes for beginners started when school closed the last week in June, she was able to persuade Marion to enroll little pigeon-toed Efuah. Otis insisted on paying the fee and, after winning money in the Chinese lottery, bought her a beautiful rose-coloured tutu. Sylvie Vachon's mother, not to be outdone, enrolled her child, freshly coiffed with Shirley Temple curls, and contributed second-hand black ballet shoes for both girls from the Salvation Army store on Notre Dame. Marion thanked her lucky stars. Earlier, when Pippa had been invited by Mrs. Brock to study elocution on Saturday mornings, Marion had demurred, worrying lest Efuah feel left out. Now, she could accept, using the time to earn extra money working at the Westmount Y.

At least once a week, Marushka came over to read, and on Monday evenings invited Pippa to the Russian Ballet Academy for piano lessons. When Pippa's friend Trevor, having received his conscription notice from the army, began to pare down his belongings, she persuaded him to let Marushka borrow his dog-eared book on Negro poets. Proudly, he informed Marushka that Pushkin, the Russian author, was also partly Negro. Marushka hadn't known. "How does it show in his poems?" she inquired. Trevor had no answer, so they spent several evenings critiquing his work. As the day of his army induction drew near, Trevor shyly suggested that Marushka join the girls and Otis at the Saturday cricket practice at Greene Park, after which they could all troop to the Y to be fed by his godmother, Amelia Hall.

Marushka was embarrassed when Otis sniped at the hapless Trevor and became competitive at cricket. Slowly, it dawned on her that Otis just didn't know how to adjust to the reality of having someone he coveted treat him almost like a relative, or a big brother. Amazed at her own naïveté, she recalled that the first time he'd suggested that they go somewhere together, she'd automatically included the girls. Pippa had chosen Belmont Amusement

Park and, despite her producing two-for-one tickets, their fren-
zied activities had wiped out Otis's "mad money." Not knowing
quite what to do or how to handle it, Marushka began to with-
draw, to focus only on the girls.

Otis's one consolation was his uncle's glamorous friend,
Torrie Delacourt, who lived quietly, but in great splendour, farther up the street from the Willows. Often, when Otis was in
town, around the time Marushka was due home from work, he
would stand by Torrie's window, watching impatiently. When
Marushka appeared, he'd throw his arms around Torrie in a
'thank-you' bear hug, then race down the winding iron staircase
to walk the rest of the way beside his dream girl. Torrie, although
amused at Otis's platonic yearnings for the little Russian filly,
wisely gave him no lectures. She knew he didn't dare meet
Marushka at Ogilvy's staff entrance, for that would blow her
cover. Torrie's mothering instinct reached out to Otis – he had no
idea what he was in for, she suspected. However, she was also
deriving a vicarious pleasure from gaining insights into the life of
the Willow family, which now seemed to revolve less and less
around Edmond Thompson – the man for whom her own passion smouldered.

Edmond had tried to discourage Marion from renting the
house on rue des Seigneurs. He hadn't told her why, because he
himself was in denial of Torrie's claim on him. "There's nothing as
dead as a dead love affair," he protested to calm himself. Torrie
bided her time. From her fourth-floor observation post, she
watched Marion come and go, and listened with a jaundiced ear
to Otis's praises of her. "Bloodless," she judged, then corrected her
assessment. Inhibited was a better word. Yet Marion seemed a nice
enough person, and her two children were unpolished gems.
Torrie coveted them. "*Tant pis!*" Torrie shrugged. "We'll just have
to live separate lives until Edmond tires of her."

Working nights, Torrie's days seemed incredibly long. Going
uptown to movies, like those featuring the "stiff upper lip" of

Greer Garson as Mrs. Miniver, bored her. The woman had no gumption. To combat ennui, Torrie let her imagination run rampant. Invariably, it focused first on her years in Harlem and then, more vividly, on her ten-year sojourn in Europe – the Europe before the war, not the pitiful, battered Europe that was now enduring relentless air raids and a stifling mid-summer heatwave after a long Arctic winter. Its only blessing had been that its bitter cold grip had helped defeat the Nazi troops at Stalingrad. All summer, both *La Presse* and *The Montreal Gazette* continued their daily litany of buildings destroyed in the relentless "Battle of Britain" air raids.

She muted the horror of Hitler's European occupation by following the crushing defeat of American troops in the Pacific in 1942. Yet, for news of what was happening to her own people, Torrie had to depend on the weekly Afro-American papers brought into Canada by porters and entertainers.

The *Amsterdam News,* from Harlem, reporting on the oppressive heat drying up the Black sharecroppers' cotton fields in the southern states, compared it to the withering hot fury of singer Lena Horne when she discovered, during a free concert she'd agreed to give in Arkansas for the troops, that the army had put German prisoners-of-war in better seats than Black enlisted men. Lena's ultimate triumph came when Joe Louis, the "Brown Bomber," knocked out the "Great White Hope," Max Baer, in the first round at Madison Square Garden, before he was inducted into Uncle Sam's segregated army.

Torrie was aware how very much she still resembled her old friend, Lena Horne, in both temperament and stature. Lena's torrid love affair with Joe Louis had begun at the Cotton Club, where she and Torrie had both worked in the late twenties, as had Torrie's with Lars.

Montreal's high-summer humidity was enervating everyone. Even though she was pampered by the fine furnishings and velvety quiet of her flat and did little more than daydream, Torrie had to admit that no matter how often she indulged in cold showers, her skin did not feel tinglingly clean and cool, with that sense of sensual well-being that she had nurtured to a fine art during those halcyon pre-war years with Lars in Norway. Oh, how she missed making love in the afternoons, cross-country skiing through the midnight forests north of Oslo to hidden cabins, meandering endless mornings on the arm of her lover down the long, dim corridors of Danish country museums, followed by a smörgasbord lunch with Aalberg aquavit and Tuborg lager at a quiet *krol* in Liseleje.

Ten years in Europe, and where had it taken her? Into exile, even from the flat Kansas prairie land of her birth. And now, to add insult to injury, here in Canada, in this cultural wilderness, she was being subtly rejected by women she could easily run circles around, economically and intellectually. Those snooty biddies in the Coloured Ladies Club had turned down her application for membership with one cryptic comment: "Source of income unknown." They knew damn well where her money came from, from their own husbands' pockets, that's where! Well, at least partly. Not because of physical favours – she was certainly above that. She, Torrie Delacourt, simply functioned as a hostess at Café Michel where, after their demanding chores on the railway, Pullman porters and Red Caps came in for a beer – to unwind, shift gears, and wipe submission off their faces, exchanging gossip while listening to the legendary neighbourhood pianist, Steep Wade. Then, they generally headed home to Verdun or St. Henri in time for family supper – that was all.

Now, her job working nights and weekends at Rockhead's Paradise, that was the icing on her cake! Those hungry out-of-town business tycoons, suddenly-shy salesmen, and penny-pinching college students who came slumming downtown for the night she handled easily with flip banter and slick jazz phrases. But with aggressive Americans and sanctimonious provincial politicians, she often lost her cool. What they needed were the "ladies of the night" who plied their trade along Berri and de Montigny streets, not the more erotic but esoteric pleasures of simply admiring fine brown frames, never quite in step in a chorus line.

Still, everyone made a living the best way they could, and
Torrie was relieved that she didn't have to hustle as Marion
Willow did to make ends meet. Increasingly, she speculated
about the Willow family, but only to herself. True, she often
served as confidante when Otis felt derailed, and she was more
than confidante to his Uncle Edmond. But she was discreet; she
never discussed her conviction that, if Mrs. Willow were not so
over-protective and did not set such impossibly high standards
for her children, her life would be so much simpler.

Living on the same street as the Willows, Torrie was aware
that the girls had to stay indoors after school, while their mother
was at work, or, at most, sit on the top steps just outside the front
door, pretending not to envy other children allowed to play outdoors in the early evenings. The eldest Willow girl usually scrib-
bled furiously in her notebook, stopping only to read back to
herself whatever it was she was writing. The little one, who had
such a wistful smile, would look enviously at the undisciplined
McDonald children playing hopscotch on the sidewalk across the
street. Even when all eight McDonald kids had measles, their
mother didn't keep them indoors.

Occasionally, on Saturday mornings, Torrie would spot the
Willow girls playing marbles with the Padowlski boys and the little Vachon girl, but only right in front of their own doors.
Obviously, Marion Willow was very strict. She meant well, Torrie
supposed, but her girls must often have felt isolated. Torrie made a
point of waving cheerfully to them whenever she drove by.

She had arranged to park her 1939 yellow Buick convertible
in the backyard of l'Épicerie Vachon, just a block from her apartment. Since the Vachons' son Maurice wouldn't let the neighbourhood thugs steal what he couldn't, he was her best insurance
against theft, she reckoned. Torrie only used the car on weekends.
She much preferred to walk to work, not intending to lose her
figure now that she could no longer afford a masseuse. One of the
musicians usually walked home with her, past the dangers of the

rambunctious blind pigs, the gambling dens, and the roustabouts lounging along rue St. Antoine in the wee hours after work. Rue des Seigneurs was relatively safe. True, there were often whistles as she climbed the winding outside staircase to her top-floor apartment, but they were mostly the admiring calls of local adolescents or tradesmen. She wished Edmond Thompson had learned to whistle.

⚓

Torrie adjusted the electric fan to wind-bathe the lower part of her honey-tinted brown body. "Thank God it's Thursday! Don't have to work tonight." She stretched, extending her long legs beyond the blue damask chaise longue and returned to her daydreaming. "Torrie, you gorgeous thing," she said to the image reflected in the mirror that ran the full length of the room. "You'd best plan for the Sunday picnic. You'll be on show. Can't wear these Japanese pajamas, now, can you?"

Her long slim legs were encased in Oriental dragon-patterned silk slacks. A blouse of the same material, scooped low at the neck, flowed loose to below her hips. Flung across a Queen Anne chair was a matching jacket. It had been her last couturier purchase in Paris before the war ended her life of ease as the mistress of a wealthy Norwegian commercial traveller. Torrie gurgled her low throaty laugh as she thought about Lars. In the United States, he would have been referred to as a travelling salesman. In Europe, where he was judged a fine physical specimen of Viking superiority and was safely ensconced in the Nordic upper class, Lars was considered a distinguished representative of a leading Scandinavian manufacturing firm; as such, both economic and social doors were open to him during the thirties.

He had a wife for the social season in Oslo, a rather attractive woman who was obsessed with producing Ibsen plays, leaving him free to have Torrie accompany him on his European working

trips. They always bedded down in wonderful little hotels in
ancient towns far from the industrial capitals where he did business – the walled city of Bruges, instead of Brussels; Avignon
rather than Lyons; Honfleur instead of Paris; Heidelberg en route
to Düsseldorf. While he conducted his never-discussed business,
Torrie learned to fill in the time alone with train travel to Paris,
Rome, or Amsterdam. In the late thirties in Berlin, she experienced the haunting bittersweet music of Kurt Weill, but felt too
ill-at-ease with the endless shouting of a *sieg heil* and the steely-
eyed, black-booted youth to ever contemplate returning to
Germany. Torrie winced involuntarily, remembering the anti-
Semitic signs and the first serious argument she'd ever had with
Lars. He had tried to placate her with a Russian sable coat.

In Paris, she discovered a talented *midinette* who could copy a
couturier original in less than a week; spent afternoons arguing
about social justice, freedom, and political reform with Franz
Fannon and his Communist friends from Martinique, who frequented Les Deux Magots café in Montmartre; and even signed
up for a series of cooking lessons in French cuisine, she remembered.

No one bothered to ask how she met Lars, for no one except
a few close friends in that long-ago Europe knew about him.
Josephine Baker did, and approved. Ken "Snakehips" Johnson, the
tall, slender, ebony-hued leader of London's all-Black orchestra,
who played only in the best clubs in Mayfair, didn't approve at all.
Red-haired "Bricktop," whose supper club on the Via Veneto in
Rome introduced the aristocratic Europeans to jazz, proved an
invaluable friend, who schooled her in the fine art of social survival. The famous Black baritone, Paul Robeson, who spotted
them both in the audience while on a concert tour in Russia,
seemed to know about Lars and gently warned her to keep an
independent bank account and her distance from his business
friends.

In 1936, without Lars, Torrie joined Robeson and his charm-

ing wife Eslanda for two incredible days in Leningrad, exploring
the Hermitage Museum. She regaled them with tales of growing
up in Kansas City, Missouri, under the stern thumb of her grandmother, who prayed to her Baptist God that little Torrie would
not love life, jazz, and trifling Black bucks as her young mother
had. At sixteen, having had to dodge trifling older men for almost
six years, Torrie headed east to New York City's Harlem and,
within weeks, was hired as a stand-by for the Cotton Club chorus
line. "I know that routine," Essie Robeson said with a laugh. "You
were declared 'lithe enough and light enough.'"

With the Robesons, she reminisced about the glorious years
of the Negro Renaissance in New York City, when poets, actors,
artists and writers began to be recognized for their talents. Bessie
Smith entertained downtown, Cab Calloway made Park Avenue,
and the Fisk Jubilee Singers were booked for a European tour.
Paul Robeson discussed the shock waves his interpretation of
Othello had created in London. Europe and America were alive
with Black creativity in the early thirties.

During those lonely first years in Canada, Torrie often
thought back to her initial encounter with Lars. Was there such a
thing as destiny? In New York City, a month before the disastrous
Wall Street crash of 1929 ushered in the Great Depression, everyone in café society was dancing the Charleston and the Black
Bottom, and exploring the jazz scene in Black Harlem. At nine-
teen, Torrie had finally made it to the front chorus line at the
exclusive Cotton Club on Lennox Avenue, where Cab Calloway
held sway onstage, but folks of colour were hardly welcome as
patrons.

Early one smoke-filled dawn, a gentleman, no longer young,
ash-blond, arrow-tall, and Nordic-looking, who had sat quietly
and alone through a week of Cotton Club show-times, politely
invited her to join him for breakfast at the Waldorf Astoria hotel
on Park Avenue. She did, and by that evening her clothes were
packed and she was off to Europe with him.

Torrie thought proudly of the ten years their romance lasted. With clarity, she remembered that day in 1940 when he suddenly disappeared. In September 1939, the Germans had invaded Poland and a full-scale war had broken out in Europe. The following April, German storm-troopers marched into Denmark and occupied that little peace-loving country within a single morning. Across a narrow strip of the North Sea, on the Norwegian coast, resistance was mounted, but quickly crushed. Too many Norwegians believed the invasion was the *Ragnarok*, the "last day" prophesied in *The Edda*, an ancient Norse saga Lars had often recited to her. "It is the time," he would quote, "when man will forget the laws even of brotherhood – axe time, sword time, wind time, wolf time – when flames will leap down from heaven itself."

Every detail of the German campaign had been meticulously planned, she realized in retrospect. Their commanders had been sent incognito on holidays to Norway, equipped with excellent maps, to become familiar with every bit of the country. The Germans had also carefully organized their Norwegian support through the *Nordische Gesellschaft*, a society for the "propagation of Nordic culture and ideals" that had contacts in nearly every Norwegian village and town. One of its members, Vidkun Quisling, used to ski with Lars and Torrie.

Within days of the invasion of Denmark, Lars was suspected of being part of Norway's fifth column. Torrie hadn't believed then that Lars could be a Nazi sympathizer, and still couldn't understand it – he who for almost eleven years had taken her all over Europe, taught her to appreciate the influence of the Moors in Spain; to read Pushkin; to admire Picasso's "Guernica." How could he – who had encouraged her to challenge her mind during the long weeks away from him, then gently fed her desire when he returned – how could he have been an evil man? It took her years to face the fact that, although he didn't sell guns, as a supplier of industrial ballbearings he was in the same league as an arms dealer.

Deserted in her hilltop chalet in the ancient market town of Kaupang on the Oslo fjord, an hour southeast of Norway's capital city, with German panzer troops moving ever closer, Torrie came to the conclusion that she'd better head back to the States. The American Embassy in Sweden, deluged with expatriates trying to get home, could only put her on its long waiting list. Bewildered and frightened lest the U.S. military attaché suspect she had connections with the Nazis through Lars's friend Quisling, Torrie decided that her best chance would be to seduce the cultural attaché, Miles Cabot-Lowell.

Inflamed by a passionate affair for the first time in his long, hidebound career, Miles cunningly arranged to ship Torrie back to the States, passing her off as a curator accompanying a precious collection of drinking horns, deer antlers, fourteenth-century Trøndelag wooden panels depicting the martyrdom of St. Olaf, and rare medieval silver pendants, destined for his family-owned museum in Boston, Massachusetts. Torrie found Boston dreary beyond belief, however, and insisted on living with him in Washington. But they soon ran afoul of the draconian Mason–Dixon segregation laws that forbade Blacks and Whites to mingle, let alone copulate. When she refused to pass as his housekeeper or hide out in the Black ghetto like some kept tart, the distinguished Boston gentleman became vindictive. He confiscated her passport.

New York City in the winter of 1940 wasn't as welcoming a place as it was in the twenties. The years of good living in Europe had turned Torrie's litheness into mellow curves. She was almost thirty. Her Sorbonne French and intimate knowledge of Old World cuisine were not marketable. The Harlem Renaissance was over. No one, in what little café society was left, made a fetish of having Negro friends any longer. Torrie realized that she was suffering culture shock at the hostility of racial segregation and the shabbiness of Harlem. And, owning a really fine sable coat, she missed the cleansing snows of winter.

"Try Montreal," her friend, the comedian Redd Foxx, suggested. "It's the Paris of the New World. They speak French, play hockey – and it's got a great Negro nightclub! Canadians didn't suffer during Prohibition – they prospered. It's a racy town – you gotta see those de Montigny Street bordellos. Whoo-ee! Not many coloured folks there, though," he warned her, "and the few that live there are kind of hoity-toity."

That Christmas, the Will Mastin trio, with their little nephew Sammy Davis Jr., planning to drive north for a gig in Montreal, convinced Torrie to come along for the ride. On New Year's Eve in Montreal, Torrie found herself invited by Rufus Rockhead, the Black impresario who owned the Rockhead's Paradise nightclub, to accept a job as his bilingual hostess. Proudly, she invested in a yellow Buick convertible and frugally rented a small upstairs flat on rue des Seigneurs, within walking distance of the club. The winters of '41 and '42 passed quietly and coldly, warmed only by an on-again, off-again affair with the slightly repressed but wildly handsome Edmond Thompson.

Until one Saturday early in May, while driving up rue des Seigneurs, she offered a little brown-skinned girl, loaded down with books, a lift up its steep hill. Politely, the child refused, explaining: "I'm not allowed to talk to strangers. But the next time you offer, I might say yes, because you won't be a stranger then."

Eventually, they became friends, for Torrie loved books and haunted Montreal's few avant-garde bookstores. She found Pippa's fertile mind as much of a challenge as Lars had found hers. What she suspected was that Pippa, like many children with a sixth sense or a high IQ, had decided not to explain the lady in the yellow convertible to her mother. Sensing that Pippa's mother would not be comfortable with so glamorous a person, she felt that Pippa would refrain from discussing her new mentor with anyone except Trevor. "Like Trevor, you're curious about the world outside, and not too many grown-ups are," Pippa informed

Torrie. Trevor acted as a go-between, borrowing books for both of them from Torrie's extensive collection of Black authors, not found in Montreal's public libraries.

Torrie replaced the soothing Rachmaninoff album with a recent recording of Billie Holiday's haunting *God Bless the Child Who's Got Its Own*, provoking thoughts of Edmond Thompson and starting juices she didn't want to flow. Damn him! Why was he so reluctant to admit she was his woman? "Because he hankers after that pure upright widow, Marion Willow," her conscience taunted her.

It was after six o'clock. She'd been daydreaming a long time. There was laundry and shopping still to do. Rockhead's chorus line had decided to attend the Union United Church's picnic on Sunday, August the first. The dancers convinced Rockhead that Reverend Lorenzo West, the church's minister, was right – they needed to spend more time in their own community. Feigning reluctance, he cancelled the Sunday matinee, knowing, in his wily mind, that they now owed him one.

Torrie had offered to make *poulet galantine* for the picnic, as well as gingered pears *en croute*. The Jewish butcher had promised to reserve five brooder chickens for her. She trusted his standards, but on Fridays he closed before sundown.

Reluctantly, she rose from the chaise longue. Humming along with Lady Day's haunting lament, she turned off the Victrola, then the Chinese porcelain lamp. Knotting her luxurious long hair into a bun, she changed into a light tweed skirt, white cotton blouse and low-heeled Oxford shoes. Now, she thought, she looked like all the other women in the Coloured Ladies Club when they went out shopping.

Perhaps she'd even join the church choir. She might kill two birds with one stone: discover if the divine Reverend Lorenzo West was "worth the candle" and, using her fine contralto voice to enrich the choir, gain acceptance into the community. "Torrie, you old rascal. No need to advertise your hunger," she murmured, as the door clicked shut behind her. She descended the circular outside stairs as if entering a ballroom. Her long legs extended gracefully, step by step, down the forty-three stairs to rue des Seigneurs.

CHAPTER IX

G lancing out of her bedroom window, Marion chuckled. The Reverend Lorenzo West and God must have struck a deal, for the morning sky was cloudless. Otis had been up since six, getting ready for the picnic. "Shoes must be whiter than white, dresses starched to stand-out perfection, hair braided – Pippa's tied with ribbons – and an extra pinafore packed for Effie to wear when eating," Marion mimicked him fondly.

At seven, Marushka appeared with a hot prune and poppy-seed cake for their breakfast. Even Dame Orlova had finally entered into the spirit of what Pippa boasted would be the biggest community event of the year by contributing a dozen carefully packed, elegantly decorated devilled eggs with capers. Only the day before, had she finally given Marushka permission to accompany the Willows. Wanting to have Marushka to himself, Otis sent the girls over to thank Dame Orlova. Pippa almost charmed the "dear ogre" into putting on her Sunday-best frock and coming along. "There'll be lots of women just like you. Not all coloured people are coloured, you know," Pippa informed her.

Dame Orlova, who'd been secretly yearning to join the Coloured Ladies Club – after all, her late husband had been Barbadian – began to search through her hat boxes until Poppa

Dad pulled up in the green Chevy, honking proudly to announce his arrival. Hearing him, Dame Orlova suddenly developed a case of the vapours and shooed the girls back home.

"Perhaps the palpitations started," Pippa suggested, "because Poppa Dad reminds her of her late husband."

By eight-fifteen, the Willow party was *en route*, squeezed cheerfully into Poppa Dad's noisy Chevy, greeting community people, mixed families, and friends from all over the Island of Montreal as, in their hundreds, they converged on foot, by bus, street car, taxi, bicycle, and private car on old Victoria Pier below Viger, near rue St. Denis, from where the boat *S.S. Belle Isle* would sail.

Church posters had advertised nine o'clock as the departure time, but at nine-thirty Professor McDowell, hurrying along the cobblestone quay, was still calling, "Wait up! Wait up! Detain departure. The choir ain't all here yet!" Since the captain didn't seem to appreciate Minister West's explanation of "coloured people's time," the good reverend, as a delaying tactic, resorted to quoting biblical platitudes about Christian patience and fortitude. Fearing he was losing the battle, Amelia Hall rounded up as many members of the church choir as were on board to belt out an old spiritual from the days of the underground railroad;

> *On my journey now, Mount Zion.*
> *On my journey now, Mount Zion.*
> *Well, I wouldn't take nothing, Mount Zion,*
> *For my journey now, Mount Zion.*

In heartfelt harmony, the choir repeated the chorus after each of Amelia's solos:

> *You can talk about me, just as much as you please,*
> *But I'll talk about you, when I get on my knees, Mount Zion.*

Clapping gaily, their bodies moving joyously, the choir and Amelia Hall continued singing until almost everyone seemed to be on board. Reverend Lorenzo West had kept pace, marching up and down the quayside in time to the music, hurrying his flock along. Inwardly, he marvelled at how much the spiritual community had grown from when he had arrived in the late thirties, a fledgling divinity school graduate of Ohio's Wilberforce AME College – American Methodist Episcopalian in name, Baptist in orientation – to this polyglot Montreal church called the Union United Congregational.

The years had mellowed his flamboyance. Now he restricted his seductive Southern charm to the lifting of a second, or if need be a third, collection from the congregation for worthy causes. His inspired rhetoric, delivered almost as a sermon in verse, made folks weep at the death of each church member as though it were a personal loss, reinforcing the code that they were their brother's keepers. Sometimes, his descriptions of "the sweet bye and bye" were so rewarding, those left behind felt momentarily short-changed.

His vitality, social conscience, and discreet good looks endeared him to his far-flung parish, which extended many miles from the church's centretown location, where its mortgaged organ pealed twice on Sunday, north to Rosemount and east to where the Island of Montreal joins Quebec's mainland. Along the wharf his parishioners came, stylishly dressed, beautifully behaved, quite prepared for a glorious outing.

Safely ensconced on the upper deck, Pippa identified the arrivals for Marushka. There were her kissing cousins, the Scotts from Bermuda, who lived in Montreal North. Then came the pioneering Frazer family, with their five tall sons, who owned so much real estate that their district near Bout de l'Isle was called Frazerville.

"Look, that tall man is Dr. Gibson, with his Mrs. Dr. Gibson. He's a real McGill University professor, you know," Pippa pointed out proudly. "The Gibsons, along with only three other Black families, can really afford to live in Westmount – that's apart from the musical Spenser sisters whose mother owns the best doll hospital on Sherbrooke Street." Marushka had never seen so many people of colour in her adult life. It brought back fading memories of her short stay in Barbados as a child.

Jogging along like boxers in training, hustling their brothers and sisters ahead of them, George and Hugh Selwin, from the lane behind the Vachon store, waved mischievously as they slyly presented four tickets for the six of them to Deacon Stevens.

Pippa's voice suddenly became conspiratorial as she explained to Marushka how "those proud, colour-conscious, pale-beige Valcours – those people just boarding now – won't admit their ancestors were slaves in Quebec City in the 1780s, yet boast of their kinship to one of Quebec's leading poets, whose poem on Marie Angelique, the slave who burnt old Montreal down, they'd probably never read."

Interrupting Pippa's stream of gossip, Marion presented Marushka to her dear friends, the Chinese Lam family from Trinidad, and their cousins the Woos, who had walked all the way to the pier from Chinatown. May-Ling and Simon Lam, considered Efuah's kissing cousins since kindergarten days, trotted off behind her to explore the boat, leaving Pippa to her "town crier" duties. "Here come the Petersons – the pretty one with dimples is Miss Daisy – she teaches piano – Chuck plays the trumpet, and Oscar, their younger brother, plays 'boogie-woogie.'"

"That accounts for only two hundred and fifty tickets," Deacon Stevens calculated, as he monitored the gangway. Montreal was reputed to have almost three hundred families of colour. "Where in the world are they?" Ignoring him, Reverend West continued to smile benignly, shuffling his shoulders in time to the music, hurrying his flock as they ambled along the pier.

Vashti Dobson joined Pippa just as the Halifax contingent boarded. Pippa didn't need to explain who they were, for, with a tooth-sucking cackle, Vashti immediately launched into her usual diatribe against the fair-skinned Nova Scotians. According to her, their "high yella" colour betrayed their reason for leaving Africville's solid community in Nova Scotia, a province where African heritage had put down roots when they arrived as British Empire Loyalists during the American Revolution in 1776.

In Vashti's view, their rich, dark strain of West African blood had been rejuvenated when the fierce Maroons, refusing to remain enslaved in Jamaica, were shipped to Nova Scotia. Those intrepid few who were willing to brave the wild North Atlantic were sent by Methodist missionaries to colonize Sierra Leone, but most Black Scotians tried valiantly to farm the barren and rocky hinterland allotted to them.

Some found work in the Stellarton and Cape Breton coal mines, others enriched the Annapolis Valley with their craft skills. They were a God-fearing people, with high moral standards. Those few who misbehaved and produced "high yella" children, courtesy of the endless supply of randy sailors in the port city of Halifax, left quietly to begin a new life in Montreal.

Vashti's history lesson, delivered in a patois that Marushka could barely understand, was interrupted by Pippa's breathless "Who are *they*?" as twelve attractive but theatrically dressed ladies swished by.

"Wouldn'chu know," observed Vashti caustically, "the very last to arrive. Those high-steppin' gals from Rockhead's chorus line gonna get the choice seats." The captain, it transpired, was delighted to invite the "gals" up to the bridge. Reverend West was equally delighted – they would be, as it were, out of sight.

Just as the boat pushed off, already one and a quarter hours late, a taxi skidded to where the gangway had been. Mistress Hattie Turner, lugging a big brown leather suitcase, struggled out. "Alas, too late! There'll be no floating crap game at the picnic this year," Reverend West exulted under his breath, but he smiled graciously, waving his regrets across the ever-widening divide of water, acknowledging in his soul that the Lord did indeed work in mysterious ways.

Impishly, the *S.S. Belle Isle* chugged down the broad St. Lawrence River, passing under the tall, arched girders of the new Jacques Cartier bridge. Over two hundred and eighty-two members of Montreal's multicultural community were now on board.

Amelia Hall made certain Reverend West knew that she had, on behalf of the church and through the proper channels, invited the ten West Indian and two Nigerian Royal Air Force officers, training in eastern Canada, to join the community picnic.

Gertrude Martin, with barely concealed malice, informed Amelia that the Trinidad and Tobago Society had offered to sponsor any coloured servicemen not included in the Club's "hoity-toity" invitations. The cricket team had made certain that all Caribbean and African students from McGill were included, while the church choir had sold tickets to just about anyone who could afford a dollar fifty, no matter their colour, faith, or creed.

Reverend Lorenzo West beamed with beatific approval at the groups of adolescent girls, their sashed flower dresses starched stiff, their thick black braids restrained by ribbons, gathered demurely near their Sunday School teachers. With younger children like Efuah held in check by mothers or grandmothers, those old enough to attend high school or secretarial college demurely walked the decks. "But," he mused, "where are all those new immigrant girls who simply work as domestics, nannies, or such? Has no one informed them?"

On the foredeck, he noticed a closely knit group of rather good-looking young men, who lived far away from Little Burgundy, St. Henri, or Verdun, comparing notes. These were the exotic young bucks who excelled in sports, whom the nuns referred to as "*les Beaux Sauvages.*" In the sparsely settled white working-class suburbs of Rosemount, N.D.G. and South Shore, their sisters, being the only girls of colour in their neighbourhood, felt socially isolated and didn't integrate. "Alas," Reverend

West lamented, "it's those boys who are going to marry out of the race."

Two and a half hours down river, the ship's captain tootled a series of blasts to warn the picnic island of Petite Madeleine: its guests were finally arriving. At its wooden wharf, the gangplank was lowered. Marion and Marushka repacked the picnic basket, put on floppy Panama straw hats, and, in spotless white shoes, daintily descended the gangplank, helped by handsome men proudly wearing blue blazers, white doeskin or grey flannel trousers, and straw boaters – men whom, Marushka suddenly realized, most people only saw as subservient Pullman porters in grey uniforms, or Red Caps toting baggage.

Half the island of Petite Madeleine was taken up by a large baseball diamond and band shell. Its shoreline was far too rocky for much swimming, but inland was plenty of shade, ample room to spread blankets, and enough flat land for a cricket pitch. Deep earth barbecue pits were quickly dug and fuelled with broken branches of maple trees and salty driftwood, for there was no way Amelia Hall would tolerate Cajun spareribs or blackened fish that weren't freshly and slowly barbecued over natural wood. Nor would Steep Wade's mother serve her family and guests *roti* that wasn't freshly browned on hot stones, just the way her grandmother used to prepare it in Trinidad.

Pippa and her best friends, the Williams twins Myrtle and Minnie, decided to inspect the feasts as though they were food critics. Intrigued at the subtle competition going on between the American and Caribbean women as to whose simmering pots emitted the most irresistible aromas, the girls tasted everything, giggling endlessly.

They discovered that the Jamaicans used fire pits to keep their curried goat and escoveitched fish bubbling, while they passed around steaming black-eyed peas and rice in coconut shells. Under Amelia's organization, the Coloured Ladies Club offered their military guests peppered and brown-sugared yams, along

with slices of savoury pork and ham farina pie, platters of fricas-
séed chicken, and spicy apple-ginger cobblers. The picnic table of
the high-spirited Nova Scotian McKyntire ladies, wearing their
frivolous best, sported a beautifully decorated picnic ham,
mounds of potato salad, and curried macaroni salad, as well as
Spam sandwiches.

They noticed that most uncommitted young men weren't
certain which group to patronize, once they'd arrived at the picnic ground. On board ship, dancing and flirting with the provoca-
tive Rockhead demoiselles was acceptable, but eating with them
was another matter. The forty-two men in uniform took advantage of everyone's hospitality. Having sampled like scavengers, the
girls decided that Molly White's Kentucky "recession ribs," made
from finger-sized, budget-priced cuts of lamb, won the day. Pippa
then recorded it all in her ever-present diary.

Otis Thompson was in seventh heaven – Marushka was there.
Even his uncle's gruff orders to see that the Willows had the best
spaces under the shade trees, the best seats for cricket, and endless
supplies of fruit punch couldn't quench his spirits.

Edmond Thompson was in purgatory. He noticed that
Marion Willow seemed hard-pressed to be even icily polite, for
on a grassy knoll not far away sat Torrie Delacourt, demurely
attired in a white eyelet Edwardian blouse and long flowered
skirt, lounging in one of the ship's deck chairs, looking fetchingly
serene under a Japanese paper parasol.

Marion was indeed discombobulated. Yet Torrie maintained
such a graceful, unobtrusive air though occasionally smiling gently, as if surpressing a poignant regret for a lost totality – a hunger
to be one of the people casually socializing – that Marion was
forced to examine her antagonism. Could it be based on jealousy?
Hardly, for Edmond was making clear his preference, hovering
faithfully around the Willow picnic table. He'd acknowledged
Torrie only with a courtly bow as they'd embarked.

Imperceptibly, as the golden day galloped along, Marion's

feelings shifted from irritation to admiration, then secret envy. "Now there's a truly independent woman. No man would ever be unfaithful to a woman like her," she sensed. But that very articulation suddenly unleashed a fear she had hidden deep in her subconscious – that Edmond, having once been Torrie's lover, might find Marion too tepid. She wished she had the courage to do as Kofi would have done – poured a libation to the gods to keep Torrie's spirits from interfering with her. Voodoo practice or not, Torrie had to be held at bay.

Beside Torrie on the grass, on leave from his gig at Rockhead's Paradise, lounged the irrepressible comic, Redd Foxx. He joined dapper Will Mastin, strumming a banjo, and his talented young nephew, Sammy Davis Jr., as they vied for her attention by singing the American entertainer's lament:

> I'm going away for the summer,
> Won't be back 'til fall.
> Good-bye, Broadway.
> Hello, Montreal.

Marion watched apprehensively as the three entertainers mimicked the antics of the community folk, much to Torrie's delight. It was obvious that their caustic comments could never be repeated in polite society. Her full antagonism crept back. She wished the woman and her rowdy admirers were on an island far away.

Reverend West could hardly keep up with the demands to adjudicate. There was a cricket match organized for gentlemen and softball for the military guests. Not needing or wanting his services, a surreptitious poker game was in full swing in a small grove of trees near the wharf. After lunch, the church's gospel choir took over the band shell – "to make," as the good reverend suggested, "a joyful noise unto the Lord." On the way to the band shell, he took the precaution of negotiating with the lead singer of Rockhead's chorus line not to offer her jazz version of "Oh

Mary, Don't You Weep, Don't You Mourn," but the truce held for only two verses. Soon, everyone was swinging up-tempo, announcing happily: *Pharaoh's army got drownded. Oh Mary, don't you weep!*

"Hope springs eternal," Pippa whispered to Marushka, as the reverend suggested that the choristers try the more classic Negro spiritual, "*There's No Hiding Place Down Here*," but the song soon ran to twelve verses, most of them improvised and full of innuendo. Mid-afternoon, the choir was replaced by a male quartet of rich bass and vibrant tenor voices as finely tuned as instruments, explaining in song how "the hip bone's connected to the thigh bone."

That's when the children were sent off to the potato-sack races, for the verses were becoming increasingly risqué. Sammy Davis tap-danced on a picnic table to raise money for the church organ fund. Gertrude Martin won the ladies' race when little Clara's egg fell off her teaspoon. Old friends caught up with news. Grandparents reminisced about other picnics, other times, and the moonlight boat excursions of old, while young men of Otis's vintage invited young ladies of Marushka's beauty for rowboat rides.

The picnic was not without a few nasty incidents. Despite the fact that the Secret Fraternal Society of Elks and members of the Household of Ruth tried valiantly, and almost succeeded, in preventing whiskey drinking on the island, small silver hip flasks surfaced on the long boat ride home. People became impolite. One raucous argument was only resolved when Reverend West confiscated the contested poker game profits for the church's organ fund.

On the return trip, from the safety of her seat on Otis's shoulders, Efuah only half-believed him as he tried to convince her that those stumbling people were just seasick. Sensing she was tired and frightened, Marushka suggested they find a quiet spot on the ship's port side with its view of the narrow, riverfront farms on the southern shore. Rodney strolled by, intent on enticing Otis and Marushka down to the dancing, but Marushka demurred, preferring to watch the sunset alone with Efuah.

Just before dark, Torrie Delacourt came by and, tucking a Shetland shawl around Efuah's shoulders, introduced herself to Marushka, asking: "Does Ogilvy's have any of Scott Joplin's sheet music in stock?" Marushka immediately warmed to the elegant stranger. "Yes, it just came in. I ordered it on spec. But not many people know of his incredible ragtime piano compositions yet." Torrie pulled up a chair. They discussed music, the church choir, and why Schubert's *Ave Maria* sounded better with a gospel beat.

Efuah didn't understand the conversation, but could tell they liked each other. Once, through slowly closing eyes, she saw Otis lurking somewhere behind a lifeboat, but as Torrie and Marushka seemed to be getting along and not discussing him, he went back down to join the dancing and the Rockhead demoiselles. Efuah thought how wonderful it was that they'd met, for their interests seemed to range from names she'd heard, like Duke Ellington, to foreign ones like Schubert. They joked in a conspiratorial manner about Black folks' music that Ogilvy's wouldn't stock.

Marushka had never been close enough to anyone in the community to discuss her worries about working in an all-white department store. Torrie seemed to sense that the pressure was not just passing as white, but having to turn the other cheek when judgements were made or assumptions expressed about the lives and aspirations of non-English, non-French Canadians. Soon, Torrie had Marushka laughing merrily at a joke that suggested all Canadians were immigrants, except the Indians and Eskimos — but they too had trudged across an ice bridge from elsewhere long ago, she insisted.

Efuah tried to stay awake, but the warmth of Marushka's arms and the soft intonations of Torrie's voice, compounded by the gently rocking vessel, lulled her to sleep. The last topic she heard was Torrie's considered opinion that Effie's mother ought to adopt Emily Capriccio.

The *S.S. Belle Isle* steamed along through the quickening

dusk. The ever-increasing lights on the shoreline, and the sight of rusty ocean freighters docked by the grain elevators, alerted passengers that they were nearing home. Sailing under the high arc of the Jacques Cartier bridge, a series of warning whistles and a loud blast calling for the pilot tug woke Efuah with a start. Did she dream, she asked herself, that Torrie Delacourt had kissed her eyelids as she removed her Shetland shawl, leaving only a lovely lingering scent of perfume? Torrie was nowhere in sight when Efuah's mother, followed by Poppa Dad and Pippa, came down from the upper deck. The ship berthed with a thud.

"Pippa, come along. We'll get the car. Otis, stay and protect the ladies," Poppa Dad ordered. Pippa raced over to say good-bye to some new friends, tapped the twins a last tag, then skipped back to Poppa Dad, holding his hand tightly as he made his way along the pier towards the parking lot.

Slowly, loudly, but regretfully, the crowd dispersed. The Reverend Lorenzo West stood by the gangway to wish each family God speed and a safe trip home, while reminding them how delighted God would be if they attended church more regularly.

I n both Europe and North America, the summer continued to be unrelentingly hot. The Netherlanders, locked in the vise of German Occupation, sweltered in Gestapo-imposed silence and privation as families, suspected of hiding their Jewish neighbours, were grilled. Chafing, they took advantage of the calm North Sea nights to smuggle their young sons abroad to train as fighter pilots in England.

Smarting from the Japanese conquest of Hong Kong, the prison internment of over fifteen hundred Canadians and the slaughter of almost three hundred others, Mackenzie King, prime minister of Canada, finally repealed the restrictive clauses in his Mobilization Act and, with ambiguous reassurance, promised: "Not necessarily conscription, but conscription if necessary."

More Canadian troops, secretly referred to at high levels as "zombies," were shipped off, but never to Britain. In bomb-strafed England, the top brass were troubled that Canadian troops, chomping for something to cut their teeth on, were playing havoc with the ladies in the Aldershot pubs. Others, idling their time away in at Camp Borden in Surrey, wondered when the Second Front would kick in.

Lord Louis Mountbatten, Britain's Chief of Combined Operations, decided to schedule a gruelling mock military exercise, code name Yukon, to cool down the irrepressible Canucks. The Cameron Highlanders of Winnipeg, the Calgary Tanks, the Royal Regiment of Toronto, and the crack Québec Fusiliers Mont-Royal were among those selected as part of the promised invasion of Nazi-occupied France, sixty miles across the English Channel.

Storm warnings were circulating in Montreal, too, but of a different velocity. Thaddeus McGregor, signalling Amelia Hall to refill his teacup, listened without comment as the ladies described how things were going from bad to worse. In fact, to hear Vashti Dobson tell it, the picnic at Petite Madeleine was the last nice thing that had happened in the community that long hot summer of 1942.

Thaddeus absent-mindedly fingered his ear, trying to recall the incident that had seemed to change the dynamics of their afternoon tea breaks. Was it the Tuesday right after the picnic when, as he had arrived for afternoon tea, he'd heard Gertrude Martin declaring, "It's racism, pure and simple racism"? "Don't back away, Mister McGregor," she had said, clearing a space for him at the table. "You might as well know what's going on."

It seemed that Susie Combes's brother had been arrested and sent to reform school for stealing a car, despite the intervention of Reverend West, who had claimed that the youngsters simply had gone for a joy ride. "The car wasn't busted up!" Gertrude had exclaimed. "It was racism, pure and simple! If not, why were the other boys with him, who happened to be white, simply remanded into their parents' custody?"

"The fact that the other two boys weren't driving and had fathers in the army made the difference. Wrong is wrong!" Clara had contended.

"Nonsense," Gertrude had insisted.

Thaddeus had refused to adjudicate.

Later that day, Vashti Dobson had received a sad long-distance telephone call through his office. Her nephew in Jamaica had accidentally chopped off his left hand while cutting stalks during the fiercely competitive sugarcane harvest and now wanted her to sponsor him as an immigrant to Canada. "Would Mister McGregor help fill in the forms?"

Clara's contribution to the litany of community calamities had come a week later. It concerned her nieces Myrtle and Minnie, the Williams twins, enrolled in the Good-Will summer camp in the Laurentian Mountains north of Montreal. They had returned home in triumphant disgrace ten days early. Clara had described how the swimming teacher, amazed that the girls' hair grew shorter and woollier after each swimming session, would not let them wear the bathing caps their mother had bought.

Thaddeus hadn't seen anything to laugh at, though the others had. But even their titters and murmurs of "I know it's the truth" had turned to silence when Clara had hissed what the instructor had said to the twins: "'Youse nigger kids probably have lice, eh! Why else do you keep putting grease in your hair, eh? Here at camp, you gotta wash your hair before every swim.' To make matters worse," Clara added, "de ignorant cook serves rice as a puddin' for dessert – good Demerara rice mixed with tapioca to look like frogs' eyes!"

But the really galling part, according to Clara, had been that, apart from having to sing endless verses of the popular "Way Down Upon the Swanee River" about homesick darkies, the girls had had to endure the camp's ritual rhyme for choosing leaders for each day's sport activities:

Eenie, Meenie, Miney, Moe,
Catch a nigger by the toe.
If he hollers, let him go,
Eenie, Meenie, Miney, Moe.

And the twins were never "Moe."
That did it! One morning before daybreak, Clara's nieces had

untied all the camp's wooden rowboats, pushing them out to drift into the misty grey half-light that hovered protectively over the lake. Piling their belongings into the remaining boat, a birchbark canoe usually reserved for counsellors, the girls had paddled to the far shore. Finding no visible path to the main highway and knowing that the camp was the only habitation on the lake, Myrtle and Minnie had trekked through the pine forest until they had discovered another lake and a well-stocked fisherman's cabin beside it.

For three wonderful days, they had camped out, singing songs they liked, catching and cooking fresh fish over an open fire, collecting wild plums, blueberries, and flowers. A grey owl had hooted warnings when raccoons had come foraging for food. Some beavers had shared their watery cul-de-sac for morning baths.

Unfortunately, the girls had missed the lecture on recognizing poison ivy and had been oblivious to the three-leaved plant growing in the gully they'd selected as an outdoor toilet. By noon of the third day, raw itching skin had driven them back to the camp nurse to face the furor caused by their disappearance. They had been sent home.

Their father, the church organist, who had promised God that he would join the army if his children were found safe and sound, did just that, leaving his tone-deaf wife to lead the choir, deal with the energized twins, and find an organist to replace him.

"Well, at least there'll be a regular army paycheque to compensate for his absence," Clara had concluded. "And now, the reverend will be able to gospelize the church choir to his American heart's content."

"Hear tell Miss Torrie Delacourt's joined the choir. 'Magine her in choir robes!" Amelia had chuckled. "Sweet Jesus! Ah reckon, Lorenzo West's body is in mortal danger."

After these troubling events, their daily tea break for scones or gingerbread had almost returned to normal when news of the

Dieppe disaster reached them. Hundreds of Canadians had been slaughtered on the beaches of France. Marion asked Thaddeus what it all meant and how it had come about. As a reserve officer in the Black Watch Regiment, he rose to the occasion as the ladies waited in expectation, sitting around the kitchen table.

"The newspaper reports are conflicting, don't you know! But now it seems that on the morning of August the eighteenth, airmen from Britain, Canada, Poland, the United States, France, Norway, New Zealand, and Czechoslovakia, making up about seventy squadrons, took to the air in what was probably the mightiest single day of air fighter battles since the war started." Thaddeus paused.

"They were supposed to provide cover for a land invasion of Europe's French coast by our Canadian infantry battalions and their allies. Now, from what I can piece together from the BBC's radio reports, our Canadians heading for Dieppe ran into a German merchant marine convoy, preventing them from chugging full-steam ahead to France. Most were able to hide in the fog, so didn't think they'd been detected as an invasion force. But when they finally touched down at the two small beach towns flanking Dieppe, the element of surprise was gone."

Warming to his story, Thaddeus cleared his throat. "Try to imagine those soldiers landing on the beach, facing a relentless hail of German bullets. Those who managed to get to shore tried to scale the cliffs, while others huddled beneath them for safety. But the Germans had planted machine gun nests in the upper cliffs. Dieppe was a death trap. Exploding grenades from above tore through our brave Canadian lads. It's rumoured that two hundred and twenty-five died, and God knows how many hundreds are being marched to German prison camps." The five women sat in silent amazement and horror.

"Mind you, that's not the story they'll tell you in the newspapers. Propaganda!" Thaddeus warned. "'A glorious victory.'" He mimicked Churchill, putting two fingers in the air. "We

Canadians were just patsies," he concluded sadly. Eyes glassy, throat dry, he left the room. McGregor didn't return for his tea break the next day, or the remainder of the week.

Gloom haunted the Y's corridors for the rest of August and September. Vashti Dobson kept trying not to weep. Captain Gordon, who had lived for years at the Y, and Lieutenant Lefevbre, who had regularly sent her slightly wicked postcards from overseas, were among the missing, and presumed dead, at Dieppe.

Marion learned from a depressed Otis that one of those captured in the raid was the only son of their railway porters' union organizer. Another community son was reported killed in Poland. He was one of the four Phillips brothers, the one who had made it into the RCAF petty-officer ranks, shot down while serving as a radio operator.

"Thank God," Marion thought, "Trevor Wilson is still in training at Petawawa." Marushka was teaching Pippa, who missed him terribly, how to knit a pair of socks.

On the very last day of that tragic August which had brought the war so close to home, Marion pulled open one of the massive double doors of the Y to begin her one o'clock sprint through the lobby and felt strangely alone, as though an air-raid drill had left the building deserted.

Reaching the kitchen, she pushed through the swinging doors, only to sense again an emptiness. Frightened, she called out for Amelia Hall. From far away, a comforting voice replied: "Coming, child. Set yo'self down. I'se coming." Entering from the pantry, Amelia moved slowly to the stove. There were few pots bubbling. "No one's eating much. The war news takes they appetite away. Here, drink this tomato soup."

Gertrude Martin entered sullenly, took a tray, ladled out soup, buttered two hot rolls, and then took them down to Thaddeus McGregor's office. "He don' want to socialize," she explained. "His cousin is missin' in action."

"And presumed dead," little Clara added, as she entered the room. Amelia cut her green eyes at witless Clara.

Arms akimbo, she spat out, "Who you to talk, girl? Leaving us to work in a munitions factory! Reckon you Rosie the Riveter? Who going t'replace you?" Exhaustion replaced exasperation. "Who I gonna get to replace this foolish girl?" she asked her cooking pots.

Chastened, Clara went back into the almost empty dining room. Amelia slumped down heavily into her chair. Marion's arms went around her sagging shoulders. She nuzzled her nose against the wrinkled brown neck. "Don't fret, Aunt Amelia. I'll try to come a little earlier till you find someone. And I could work here Saturday afternoons."

"And, pray tell, who's gonna take care of yo' piccaninnies when you work yo'self to death? Why you so scared of marrying Edmond Thompson?" Amelia's voice was full of honest concern.

Marion straightened up, looked around to see if anyone else was in the kitchen, and bit her bottom lip. Perhaps she'd better be frank; after all, Amelia had known her all her life. "I really don't know why. Yes, I do . . . for one, he's too set in his ways. He's too judgemental. You know . . ." She hesitated.

As Amelia began to stroke her hand, Marion found the courage to continue. "After that Victoria Day fire – remember when they rifled our shed? Well, I tried to inquire about old Dominic's child, Emily, since Edmond works on the railway and porters always seem to know what's what. In fact, Amelia, they gossip worse than women."

"Ain't that the truth!"

"Aunt Amelia, his response was so brutal. He referred to Emily as having bad blood. As though she is responsible for being illegitimate." Marion's voice wavered. "For all I know, she could be his or any railway man's child! I don't feel safe with Edmond."

"She ain't his child! Believe me, he ain't that kind."

Clara came in – and went right back out again.

Marion, ashamed at her need to explain, as much to herself as to her beloved surrogate aunt, backed down. "I didn't mean that. Dear God, forgive me! Oh, how can I explain it? I know he's a good man and I know we depend on him. But he's so damn hidebound. I'm afraid I won't be able to bring my girls up with grace. They need to have his strength, but not his rigidity, nor his colonial acceptance of class. He thinks they'll be lucky if they qualify as a secretary or a nurse. My girls are not going to be anyone's lackey! They're going to go to college, girls or not. Besides, he has a mistress. He'll be unfaithful."

Amelia slowly shook her head, then indicated that Marion should pour them both a cup of soup. Slowly, sipping the spicy hot liquid, Marion began to soften.

"You know, Aunt Amelia, Kofi had such a delightful sense of the ridiculous. He was easy to live with. We laughed a lot. He had an innate sense of *noblesse oblige* that had nothing to do with having money or not. It had to do with standards and expectations. Being an immigrant didn't inhibit *him*."

Amelia chuckled. "Sweet Jesus, when you going to get over that African man you married! He was so black he coulda spit ink. But they do say, 'the blacker the berry, the sweeter the juice'!" She stifled Marion's indignant response with a hug. "He dead now, Marion, you alive. Hurry upstairs, child, before that Geechee woman starts at you."

Tucking in sheets with precise hospital corners, emptying wastepaper baskets, and stacking newspapers to take home kept Marion's hands busy, but not her mind. Obviously, the ladies at the Y knew more about Emily than they were letting on. Vashti Dobson, she was sure, had some inside information.

When Marion went to the linen room for clean towels, Vashti raised the subject herself: "Has you decided to adop' that Italian's chile yet? Ah thinks she's the best of that breed of them poor motherless children, if'n you ask me. She comes from good stock!"

"Aunt Vashti, how can you say good stock? No one knows who her father was. Wasn't old Dominic, that's for sure."

"Marion, don' look a gif' horse in the mouf. Reason your husband's Ashanti tribe choose they king from 'mong his sisters's sons is knowin' fer sure the wimmen who birthed 'em was his kin – if'n you know what Ah mean."

"No, I don't. I'm told Emily's mother was from Scotland and died of TB. That's all I know for sure."

Vashti sucked her teeth and continued counting bath towels. "Well, that child don' have her TB, but she is sickly. It's sickle cell, an' that's a coloured folks' disease. Ain't nothin' that a bit of love and good down-home vittles won't cure."

Marion drooped. "Don't think I haven't thought about Emily. But dare I take a chance? I may not have the energy to give her what she needs, or the wisdom." Her hands fluttered. The face flannels she was stacking fell from the shelf.

"You a bundle of nerves, honey. Best we go down for tea, though t'ain't three-thirty yet."

"No, you go. I can't face McGregor's unhappiness." She restrained Vashti's hand. "I'll restack them."

"Sickle cell ain't catchin', honey, but rejection is. Tha' pore chile's gotta find a home soon or she'll never know who she is. You the bes' person Ah knows to help her. 'Sides, she looks like you."

"I don't look half white!"

"You don' look all Black!"

For a split second, they glared at each other, then burst out laughing. They laughed until they had to hold onto each other for support.

"Oi!" Vashti giggled. "This old bladder of mine can't stand too much laughing." She hobbledy-hopped quickly into the loo. When she returned, the face flannels were stabilized, and Marion was willing to go down for tea.

❧

Seven weeks after the Dieppe disaster, just before Thanksgiving Day, Thaddeus returned to Amelia's kitchen to announce that he had decided to join up. His friends, hunched in uncomfortable silence munching cold bread pudding, couldn't dissuade him. Marion feared that the Black Watch Regiment wouldn't accept him, for he was too ruddy of complexion and, at forty, too heavy on his feet. He was almost portly. "Who will manage the Y if he's sent overseas?" she asked herself.

Their peaceful little island was falling apart. Sven Svenson had already fled, hoping to join the Norwegian air force in exile. McGregor was a fair and honest man, with no class or race prejudice that she could tell. None of the other Ys had such an efficient international staff.

Vashti Dobson suggested they pray. Gertrude Martin, before bowing her unwilling head, hissed: "Most wars is based on religion."

"Hush," Amelia said. "All blood's the same colour when it's spilt."

"Amen." McGregor's voice broke. "I'll miss you ladies so much. Now that my cousin's gone, you're all the family I have left."

Looking at him through her misty lashes, Marion suddenly realized why he spent so much of his time at the Y. Obviously, his job satisfied his need to be central to something and, in return, he made the Y a place where all the employees could give of their talents freely.

"Because of McGregor, it's never felt like domestic service," she whispered to Gertrude. "There's dignity in doing a good job well."

"Ain't it still jest peeling spuds and washing dishes? Don't yo' all still hafta make beds other folks a-slepted in?" Gertrude asked, imitating Clara. Marion could have argued the point, but the day had been too much for her. She simply wanted to hug McGregor and let him know they would miss him, too. However, the moment passed.

Down the quiet corridors, as she made beds and allotted thick white towels to each bedroom, Marion thought she heard McGregor's measured tread. But it was just her imagination – or was it her longing that nothing would change, that he would come to the kitchen each afternoon, eyes twinkling at the sight of her, offering to share his tea break with his favourite ladies?

She sensed that despite McGregor's strapping six-foot frame, Amelia could have wrapped him around her little finger. But she never did. Instead, she'd learned how to bake Scottish scones and serve them with bitter marmalade instead of raspberry jam, and how to keep the kitchen accounts in a proper ledger book.

When he went off to war, he would miss the smoked herrings he always found simmering on the back of Amelia's stove for breakfast. She had drawn the line at fixing porridge, though they shared a passion for a kind of blood pudding, called haggis in Scotland and *tripe diable* in backwoods Louisiana.

A half-smile lit Marion's pensive face. What about her? What about that extra jolt of feline power his admiration provided as she entered the building each day? Was he even slightly aware of the mischievous daydream she had once indulged in, wondering if under his kilt his hair was also sandy red?

Both she and Vashti worked quickly and in quiet harmony. They wanted to be gone before the residents came home.

Waiting on the kitchen landing for Marion to leave, Amelia tucked a large package into her tapestry carry-all. "It's the meatloaf from lunch and some greens for the children. I 'spect it will go bad if'n ah keeps it. Best I make some chicken noodle soup for tomorrow. Everyone's going to need it. Sweet Jesus, this is one useless war!"

As Marion turned to leave, after kissing Amelia on the forehead, Amelia reached for her hand. "You instincks are right on,

child. That little orphan needs you, more'n you need Edmond.
Take a chance!"

Only Marion's eyes said "thank you," for her lips had begun
to tremble. She needed air. Outside, the floral garden clock on
Sherbrooke Street by the Victorian glass conservatory marked the
hour with late-blooming marigolds. The tall sugar maples in the
park were turning yellow, red, and gold, while the water in Pippa's
favourite storytale duck pond was almost hidden by greying
water lily pads.

Passing the cricket oval, she wondered how Trevor, such a
private person, was managing in crowded barracks as a "buck private" in the army. Pippa had become more withdrawn and fearful
after he had been pressured to enlist. Frowning, Marion forced
herself not to think of war and young men dying.

But more women than usual, wearing crisp blue or khaki
uniforms, seemed to fill the main thoroughfares on the way
home. More women in slacks carrying industrial-style supper
pails stood at streetcar stops. More posters with fingers pointed at
the viewer covered the post office walls.

For the first time, Marion was intensely conscious that she, as
well as her country, was involved in a desperate, almost
unwinnable war. It was like having an incurable disease that one
hoped would go away. Her mind focused. It was like being Emily.

CHAPTER XI

"When the night is beginning to lour." At least, that's how Pippa pronounced the word in Longfellow's poem:

Between the dark and the daylight,
When the night is beginning to lower,
Comes a pause in the day's occupations,
That is known as the Children's Hour.

Since Montreal autumn days are short, their "Children's Hour" usually fell between the time when Marion arrived home from work and suppertime. But tonight, Emily was coming. The hour slipped away without homework, without poetry – the children simply watched and waited.

Suddenly, the streetlights came on, shining without brightness in the late autumn haze. Efuah wished Pippa would hurry and finish her bread pudding. It would be awful to be out back in the kitchen when Emily arrived. She wanted to be the very first one to count the number of suitcases their new sister would bring with her.

"Mother, how much longer do we have to wait?" Pippa asked, selecting raisins from the pudding.

"Almost an hour, dear. There's plenty of time. Do finish your

food. I put fresh milk and eggs in that bread pudding." Through
the window, Marion could smell the chill that comes before
Hallowe'en, and hear old Mr. Ferguson next door trudge upstairs.
Her new home had paper-thin walls. It would cost more to heat
in winter than she had budgeted for.

Watching Pippa toy with the warm crusted pudding, realizing that her daughter would probably never stop being finicky
about food, Marion felt it might be just as well to let her go into
the front room with Efuah to watch for Emily.

"Run along. It isn't every day that someone new comes to
live with us. But you must be very kind when she comes.
Remember, her mother is dead and she has no one to live with."

"What happened to Emily's parents?" Pippa asked, thoughtfully folding her napkin.

"Surely, you haven't forgotten Dominic, Pippa. The old man
who used to bring Emily to kindergarten in a red wooden cart
made with two bicycle wheels? Remember, he sold fruit at the
corner of Guy Street and St. Catherine, and every morning,
except in winter, Emily would arrive at kindergarten perched in
the very front of that wagon, surrounded by bananas, yellowing
pears, and slightly bruised apples which, I suspect, they'd salvaged
from the wholesale fruit sheds in the railway yards."

She nudged Pippa's memory. "You were usually the first to
run up and hug Emily when she jumped off the cart, don't you
recall? Miss McPicken didn't like it a bit. 'Get ye along,' she'd
scold, chasing you both inside. 'I'll no' have ye behavin' like street
urchins.'"

Hearing her mother mimic the Scottish kindergarten
teacher, who had what Pippa described as a romantic soul,
opened a floodgate of memories. Miss McPicken kept a brush
and hand mirror on a high shelf in the hallway, above where children hung their winter coats. Every morning, before Emily came
into the classroom, Agnes McPicken would take her aside to try
to smooth down her wildly tangled mop of black hair. She would

hand Emily her own beautiful bone-handled looking glass, hoping the little girl would be too preoccupied to complain if it hurt when the snarls were pulled out.

Usually Emily didn't complain about anything at all. Nor did she usually look at herself in the mirror. The two times she did, Pippa recalled, she would stare at herself soberly, turning her small beige face from side to side, wiggling the ginger-brown freckles on her nose, and examining her huge hazel eyes – eyes that were not the colour of most girls' eyes.

Emily was the only child the Willow girls knew who had skin the colour of unroasted peanuts. Most of the children in the school had pale skin (with red cheeks in winter), except for May-Ling and her brother Simon, who were Chinese and had warm, almond-coloured faces. Theirs were brown – a real brown. Like Effie's, Emily's hair grew thickly all over her head, a mass of tight curls that neither Dominic nor Miss McPicken could ever seem to uncoil. Effie's hair was brushed and braided very tightly every night, and both Willow girls slept with stocking caps on to keep their hair in place. But Emily had no mother to braid her hair.

Often, when their mother took time to listen, Miss McPicken speculated about Emily's mother while the girls were taking off their winter leggings. It seemed that the teacher and Emily's mother had come from the same lowlands in Scotland. Miss McPicken would repeat over and over, rolling every "r" as she spoke: "Her people were guid people. They had a dairy farm, a lovely dairy farm, and Rebecca took care of the sheep. She married a young ne'er-do-well from Glasgow, but he died, they say. How she came to Canada, I canna fathom."

Miss McPicken was very concerned about what would eventually happen to Emily. Pippa wondered if she felt half-related to her. But Miss McPicken did nothing about it – or did she? Someone must have squealed about Emily's living alone with Dominic as she suddenly didn't come to Miss McPicken's kindergarten anymore. At first, Pippa believed that Emily had gone on to a real school, being two years older. But when Pippa went to Royal Arthur School, and even two years later when Effie was old enough to go there, they couldn't find their friend. She had been missing for almost five years, and now she was coming to live with them.

The light in the street lamps grew brighter as the night dropped down. "Maybe she isn't coming after all," Pippa thought as she pushed the white accordion shutters all the way back against the sides of the window. There was nothing left to do but curl up on the wooden window seat and count the Ford cars passing below on the street.

"All the daddies are coming home to supper. Wouldn't it be wonderful if Poppa Dad were really our daddy?" Effie asked. Pippa didn't reply because just then a tall red-haired woman in a black coat, walking rigidly against the chill wind, stopped at their door. With her was a tall, thin olive-coloured girl with freckles, carrying a large brown paper bag. Pointing to the wooden front steps, the girl mouthed "seven-oh-eight" and, climbing the stairs, rang the doorbell, just as if she had always known the way.

"Mother! Mother! She's here!" Scrambling wildly down from the window seat, Efuah ran into the hall. Her mother came scurrying from the kitchen, primping her hair as she walked. Pippa flung open the door.

Emily walked in. "D'ya wanna see what happened?" Emily dropped the brown shopping bag by the door and threw her blue woollen mitten on the floor. "See? Look!" She stuck a slim finger in from of Pippa. "They stuck pins and needles in me!"

Marion Willow interrupted to introduce Pippa and Effie to the social worker. "My daughters. Philippa will be twelve on Hallowe'en, and Efuah is eight." They bobbed a curtsey, then hurried back to Emily, who had taken possession of the window seat in the front room. Marion led the red-haired lady down the hall towards the kitchen.

"Was you really born on Hallowe'en, when ghosts and goblins roam the streets?" Emily asked in awe.

"Uh-huh! On October the thirty-first. I'm really a mystery child, you know. I was snatched out of my cradle by an evil old witch . . . at least, they say I was."

Pippa was delighted that Emily had arrived. Effie was obviously too young to talk about serious matters like witches and witchcraft, while Emily listened avidly, her mouth wide open. Pippa decided to let Emily share her greatest secret. "Do you know what? I'm writing a novel. It's all about a devastatingly beautiful young girl, with stark raven-black hair, named Princess Aurora Philippa Felicia – that's me! I'm an orphan, you see. And in my book, I have all the adventures of a real orphan, like in a real novel. There are asylums, mean headmistresses in boarding schools, escapes, hunger, wanderings with gypsy caravans . . . everything."

Emily broke the spell, for Pippa had intruded on her special domain. "How kin you write about orphans, eh? You ain't one. You don' know what yer talking 'bout!"

"Yes, I do. I'm an orphan, too, you know," Pippa proudly announced.

"How kin you be a orphan when yer mother is gonna be my mother, 'cause my *real* mother is dead?" Emily's green-brown eyes blazed.

The explanation was simple, but Pippa decided to send her little sister out of the room before she divulged it. "Effie, run and get Winnie-the-Pooh. He hasn't met Emily yet." Efuah scampered out happily to collect her beloved teddy bear. Pippa clasped her hands and hung her head. "Our father is dead," she announced.

"Christ! Yer a orphan, too." Emily held out her arms. "At least, yer half a orphan. Ain't it tragic?"

Kindred spirits at last, the girls fell into each other's arms to console each other. Grown-ups always acted as if life would go

on, and so it might, but not without tears and sorrow. Effie came
back down the stairs and, introducing Winnie-the-Pooh to Emily,
asked what the matter was.

"You're too young to be burdened with such weighty problems," Emily replied, giving her a hug.

When Pippa noticed that tears were coming out of Emily's
eyes and her freckled nose was a little red, she breathed deeply and
began to sniff. After all, she was an orphan too. "Tell us what it's
like in an orphanage," she begged.

Emily delightedly provided the gruesome details. The more
Emily explained, the more Pippa cried. Emily didn't talk about
her mother; her mother had been dead for so many years that she
didn't remember much about her. But what she remembered well
were all the smooth-faced, straight nuns in long grey uniforms
who asked Dominic endless questions about her. They spoke a
very proper French; Dominic spoke only Italian. Emily had had
to translate.

She described how the nuns had turned her over to the
Protestant Home for Wayward Girls, who had sent her back to the
Catholic convent, where she lost the rosary Dominic had given
her. She told Pippa and Effie about the endless papers that had to
be filled in because they said she had no birth certificate, wasn't
baptized, and belonged to no one – so no one would sign. But,
most of all, she described the needles they stuck in her for diseases
she didn't have.

The more Pippa empathized, the sorrier Emily painted her
adventures, and Pippa began to suspect that the full orphan's lot
was, by far, the most interesting way of life. Here was authentic
new material to enrich her novel! When Efuah wrinkled up her
face, as if she, too, would start to cry, Pippa took Emily into the
bathroom and locked the door. There they could be miserable in
peace and not be disturbed.

Little Efuah and Winnie-the-Pooh watched the girls go into
the bathroom, heard the latch click, and knew they weren't

wanted. Pippa had never done that before. Effie wasn't so sure it was a good idea having an extra sister. From the bathroom came the muffled sound of whispering, followed by a fresh outburst of crying. Picking up Winnie-the-Pooh, Efuah trotted through the dining room and up the two steps into the kitchen. Her mother was busy listening to the lady who had brought Emily.

"Now, Mrs. Willow," the social worker was saying, "Emily's clothes are normally provided by the Protestant Children's Service Centre. We have to investigate whether the rules will let you select her clothing, but we'll try. You'll get vouchers to Eaton's or Ogilvy's with which you'll buy her shoes. I realize twelve dollars a month isn't very much, but we want you to know that we appreciate your taking the child in. She's far too old for adoption. And, as you suggested, we will contact her former guardian Dominic to advise him that you'll allow him to visit."

Since children weren't allowed to interrupt adults, Efuah knew she couldn't tell her mother what Pippa and Emily were up to. By the time the lady had finished talking, it seemed better not to tell tales in front of a stranger, so she just stood there, her nose buried in the good smell of her mother's hair. When the lady was ready to leave, Pitti-Sing followed them to the front door. Pitti-Sing didn't need to go out; she sat, nestled beside the teddy bear, and waited while Marion Willow finished saying goodbye.

"Time for bed, little one." Marion picked up the cat and the teddy bear. "Where are the others?"

"In the bathroom."

"What! Both of them? At the same time?" Efuah nodded. "Well, they don't have to see each other to the toilet. Whatever is that noise in there?" She listened, shook her head, and suppressed a laugh. "Effie, go on to bed now. Wear your blue bunny pajamas. I'll come and tuck you in and give you your cod liver oil as soon as I contend with these Sarah Bernhardts."

Sobbing tirelessly, Pippa couldn't hear much of what was

going on outside the bathroom. But the voice she finally heard calling her name didn't sound all that sympathetic.

"Now, stop this nonsense this very minute, young lady. Do you hear, Pippa?"

Pippa tugged at Emily's arm. "We'd better stop. My mother wants us. Oh, please stop, Emily. I'll cry with you some more tomorrow. Mother's calling us."

"But," Emily sniffed, "tell yer mother we ain't through yet. I ain't tole you 'bout the black veil I hadta wear." The handle of the door began to turn.

"Unlatch the door, Emily!"

Dabbing at her nose with her sweater sleeve, Emily got up from her perch on the rim of the bathtub and slowly worked the hook out of the latch.

"Are you coming out, or shall I come in?"

Those words left no alternative. Taking the time to dry her eyes, Pippa slowly opened the door. There were no windows in the hall. The light from the front windows travelled up as far as the bathroom door, but not much beyond. The light from the back door was all used up by the kitchen, leaving a part of the hall always in twilight. No one was in the hall.

Pippa cocked her head. She held Emily's hand tightly so that Emily wouldn't move or make a sound. She listened to Effie in the upstairs bedroom singing a lullaby to Winnie-the-Pooh. Pippa cupped her ear, still listening for the sound of her mother. "Why," she wondered, "didn't Mother wait for us to come out of the bathroom?"

Pitti-Sing, with her arrogant crossed eyes, padded by, mewing politely at the new guest. She was on her way to the front room. There she stopped, listened for a moment, and then, easing herself gingerly towards the edge of the half-open door, peered in.

Suddenly, she raised her long, black-tipped tail straight up in the air, let out a deep purr, and floated forwards into Marion's favourite room. Pippa heard her mother return the cat's greeting with a sweet rush of baby talk. Marion had never talked baby talk to her daughters, not even to little Effie when she was young. She always used what she called "the King's English." But with Pitti-Sing, she spoke a lovely language that cats understood.

Pippa knew that when her mother sat quietly in the front room, it meant she was in no mood to trifle with. It was better just to go upstairs and get ready for bed.

Quietly, the girls undressed and put on flannelette night-gowns. Pippa rubbed cocoa butter over her knees and elbows. "It removes the scars," she explained. Emily was persuaded to sleep with an old silk stocking covering her hair so that it would be smooth and straight in the morning. They knelt down together and prayed, Emily repeating what her new sisters said in unison:

Mother, Father, God, loving me.
Guard me while I sleep.
Guide my little feet up to Thee.

Bless Mother and make her well.
And all my dear uncles and aunts, cousins and friends.
And make me a good girl.
Amen.

"Goodnight, Mother," the girls called. Marion came up to tuck them in. Pippa snuggled down in the centre of the large feather bed, Emily on one side, Efuah on the other.

The room was softly dark — not the silent dark that hovered outside above the streetlights, nor the eerie darkness of the river canal at night. No, it was the kind of soft dusky dark that Pippa wrote about in her novel. Her heroine did not have a mother who had to work cleaning other people's homes all day. There were no draughty rooms in the castle Pippa intended to live in, no ashes to be sifted, no bread puddings made from stale bread. She, Effie, and now Emily would live in a world as lovely as her mother's

Regency desk, with teacups as delicate as the Aynsley china that appeared when the Coloured Ladies Club or the Bermudian cousins came to visit.

"Emily," Pippa whispered. "Emily, are you asleep yet?"

"No, I ain't."

"Emily, if I'm to share all my kissing cousins and aunts with you, will you share yours with me?"

Emily yawned. "How can I, Pippa? I ain't got none."

"Oh." Pippa was disappointed.

"Tell you what." Emily was prepared to meet her halfway. "We kin share my Dominic."

"Share Dominic!" The thought was exciting. Maybe he could be the one in her novel to bring golden mangoes and other exotic fruits to the green-eyed Princess Aurora Philippa Felicia when she was sent to an orphanage, or to bed without supper. Planning her heroine's next adventures, Pippa finally fell asleep.

CHAPTER XII

D odie skipped out, Emily jumped in.

House to let, apply within.
People put out for drinking gin.
Gin, you know, is a very bad sin.
As I go out, you go in ...

Emily skipped out. Efuah missed her jump in. The skipping rope stopped.

"Aw, she's too clumsy to jump rope. Can't even skip double-rope 'cause of her!" Dodie stamped her foot. "You're always draggin' that kid into everything we play." Dodie pushed Efuah away from the rope; her friend Yolanda giggled.

"If my sister can't play, then I can't neither," Emily announced. Her arms went around little Effie's sagging shoulders. "She's gotta learn."

"Well, she ain't gonna learn on my rope! She jes' ain't coordinated. Anyways, she ain't your real sister!" Dodie pushed a fine strand of corn-yellow hair away from her narrow face. Her cheeks were flushed pink with impatience.

"I am so," Efuah lisped.

"Yer not," Dodie insisted.

"Am so."

"Yer not!"

"Am so!" insisted Efuah defiantly, her eyes filling with tears.

"Dodie, you want a punch in the nose or something?" Emily's voice didn't sound angry, but her eyes had turned the green of a cat's.

"Yeah? From you and whose army?" Dodie retorted, backing away. Emily wasn't like the other Willow girls. She was always ready to fight.

Impatient to get on with the game, Yolanda pushed the skipping rope towards Dodie. "Oh, come on Dodie, stop it! Yer the one who started it."

Dodie pursed her lips. Another strand of hair slid onto her forehead. She blew it away.

A dried leaf drifted by the four girls standing in the empty lot under the gnarled old elm tree. It no longer had leaves of yellow-red and mottled brown to collect for scrapbooks. Indian Summer had come and gone long before Hallowe'en. Now, in the last crisp days of November, the children played in a clean, cold light that by four o'clock would flare in a brief burst of colour, then turn to dusk.

Emily, waiting for Dodie's answer, followed the single leaf as it drifted. Little Effie didn't know how to skip rope properly, but she had to learn. The other girls were willing enough to let her turn rope for them, so why shouldn't she have a skip once in a while?

In the days since she'd arrived, Emily had become quite wise to the ways of rue des Seigneurs. Most children who played on the street after school either went to St. Anthony's, the big grey Catholic school, or to Protestant Royal Arthur, the school she attended with Pippa and Efuah, beyond the CN railway tracks.

Crossing those tracks reminded Emily of Dominic and the old days when he used to take her down there to the fruit sheds in the railway's freight yards, explaining, as he selected discarded fruit for his wagon, how to pull the green spear at the centre of a pineapple to tell if it were sweet, how to pinch a pear without leaving a bruise, and how to judge which bananas would ripen slowly.

Emily knew that Mrs. Willow disliked living so close to the railway tracks. She complained that her life was bounded by the Canadian Pacific on the hill above and the Canadian National with its freight yards two blocks below. The smoke from the passenger trains above peppered her laundry with cinders, while the shunting of the freight trains held up her children on their way to and from school.

"I don't really mind the trains," thought Emily. "Nothing matters now that I have a family again." And nothing did. She faced Dodie, not wanting to, but quite ready to smack her to smithereens, even though her stomach was quivering, the soles of her feet felt itchy, and her freckles were beginning to pop.

"Come on, let's all be friends, eh?" she heard Yolanda whisper to Dodie. "You got no right sayin' she ain't Emily's sister. How d'you know? My Ma says Emily looks more like Missus Willow than Pippa or Effie." Yolanda grabbed for Dodie's hand and held it out towards Emily. Emily unhunched her shoulders.

"Yeah, well," Dodie offered by way of apology, "*my* Ma says you can't never tell with darkies 'cause they all look alike."

Emily froze again. Her head felt tight. She didn't think all dark people looked alike – she knew they didn't. Why couldn't Dodie see that they didn't? She wasn't blind.

She remembered the tight feeling in her stomach and the dark rush of fear when the nuns had told her they were unable to place her with the two little girls who were the colour her father must have been. "They're like chestnuts," they had tittered. "The tall one is golden, the other is sun-baked and brown. The mother has been here a long time, so she's blanched." Emily had continued to feel ill until the nuns had handed her over to the Protestant social worker, who had finally delivered her to the Willows.

Emily thought about the kids on the block. Dodie's buttercup yellow hair was a different colour from her brothers', but no one seemed to think that odd, while Yolanda was a redhead with skin the colour of eggshell. White people are peculiar, she concluded. "We're going home. Come on, Effie."

"Whatsa matter *now*?" asked Dodie. Carefully, she began to loop the ten-foot rope. "Whatsa matter with *her*?"

"You always spoil things," her friend replied. "You know we're not supposed to talk about colour 'round coloured people."

"Why?" asked Dodie. "She ain't really coloured, she's half-coloured. My Ma says her Daddy was Black, but her Ma was white, just like me 'n' you. What is, just is!"

"Well, yeah. But yer always sayin' things that get the French kids mad, too. I know you. You think 'cause your uncle's a priest, you kin judge people." She kicked a pebble into the street. Bending down, she rolled her black stockings back up her legs, straightened her skirt and walked off, leaving Dodie sulking.

Just before sunset, Emily came back onto the street looking for Pippa, who had gone down the lane to reclaim some library books from the Selwin children.

"Hurry up, it's gettin' dark. We're not ragamuffins, we can't be on the street after dark. We havta finish our work. Mother will be home soon." Consulting the list in her hand, Emily continued: "You still got the living room to dust and Effie ain't wiped the silver or put it away."

"I did the dishes," Pippa protested, "and you know we're not supposed to say ain't."

"You forgot the pots." Emily's voice took on the imperious tone it always did when she read out the chores. She was the mother when Mrs. Willow was at work and enjoyed the importance of being in charge. Imitating Mrs. Willow's walk, she shooed her sisters ahead of her, back into the house.

"Come, Pitti-Sing," she called to the cat, who was eating the last of the marigold leaves in the windowbox. "Him's muvver's itty pussy-tat, him is, but him must tum in now." Pitti-Sing gave

Emily a haughty 'who do you think you are!' look before padding back into the house, tail held high.

Just as she turned to close the front door, she noticed a muscular, copper-brown merchant seaman looking up at the number on their door. He lifted his pea cap. "Is this the Willow residence?" Emily nodded. "Your mother home?" Emily shook her head. "Well, when she comes in, please give her this package for me. It's the cassava your cousin in Bermuda sent," he explained, climbing the stairs to hand her the parcel.

"Oh, are you one of the sailors from the *Lady* boat that goes to Bermuda?" Emily asked, reaching for the fabric-wrapped package.

"Yep, but we're part of the merchant navy now – dodging submarines! You must be Marion's eldest. You sure do resemble the family."

"Do I really?"

"Yep, know you anywhere. Same hazel eyes, same riney colour. You're a B'mudian, all right." He handed her the package. "Got to run, be late meeting my mate. Nice town you live in. Give Miz Willow my best. Name's Simmons, Simmons from Somerset. She'll know," he said as he walked away.

Emily hugged the package. What a wonderful, wonderful feeling. For a moment, she just stood there, watching the last slim rays of the sun blaze, then fade. Its transforming magic made her heart beat fast. She wondered why she had never noticed how mercurial the last rays of the sun were. She closed her eyes, waiting for the dark.

A sound on the bottom steps made her open them again. "Mother!" For the first time, Emily leapt down towards her as Pippa and Efuah always did – hugged her, kissed her, and squealed without knowing why. When Marion tickled her to make her let go, she forgot the feeling of newness. She forgot everything, except that there were millions of things she wanted to talk about. Matching her tread as they climbed the stairs, she explained, "There's a good reason why our chores aren't finished."

Marion, turning to her with a smile that hid a laugh, replied, "My dear, there usually is."

Emily thought about the unfinished work and how her new mother never yelled at them, as some parents did. Tomorrow was Saturday, no school. She would work twice as hard because her mother would be home to show her how.

⌨

Marion spent the morning feeling guilty. There was no way she could stay home all Saturday. She had promised to have lunch with Thaddeus McGregor. "I'm afraid they're going to make changes in the staff at the Y, now that he's leaving and, being decent, he wants to warn us," she explained to Emily. Fidgeting as she helped Efuah put the laundry through the wringer, she wondered aloud: "What will I do? I can't go to work in a war factory. With those split shifts, how could I nurture my children, monitor them, protect them?" She managed to get the house spotless by mid-morning.

Hearing Marion continue to fret and scold herself as she peeled potatoes for oxtail stew, Emily offered to quit school. She didn't like it anyway, and preferred to take care of her sisters. "After all," she reminded her mother, "I'm almost fourteen."

Marion hugged her tenderly. "Never you mind. It's just me, my dear, full of foolish fears. Somehow, we'll cope. And you, young lady, will stay in school. I think in January they'll transfer you to Montreal High. You'll like it better there. Just imagine," she added, mischievously, "Oscar Peterson goes to school in the next building!"

Emily blushed. "Naw, he never hangs around outside after school. He's always practising piano. Besides, he's got a crush on Lil Frazer, 'though she's only fifteen. Didja know? Pippa's got a crush on Trevor," she added, "tho' she's just turned twelve."

"What a tattle-tale you are, Emily. Anyway, it's not a crush in the real sense of the word. It's perfectly natural, really. Pippa's just been so accustomed to Trevor being there for her that now he's gone to war, she misses him." Turning to face Emily, she added, "You'll have to help fill that void, Emily. That's what love is all about." They rubbed noses like Eskimos.

Emily, too full of emotion to stay in the kitchen, ran off into the bathroom, locked the door, and had a good cry. "I really belong," she told herself. "They need me." Down on her knees she went. "Mary, Mother of Jesus, protect my new mother." Having reverted to the old supplication Dominic had taught her, she thought of him and added to her prayers, "And if you find my Dominic for me, I'll say an *Ave Maria* every night."

"Emily." There was a knock on the door. "Emily, Mother's waiting for you," Pippa called. "She's ready to leave."

Emily joined her sisters lined up by the front door.

"I've prepared both lunch and dinner," Marion said, drawing on her best leather gloves. "Don't eat it all at once. I'll be at Mrs. Brock's for the club meeting by three if you need me, and I should be home before six. Now, Otis's train is due in this afternoon. I've changed his linen. See that he has supper.

"Pippa, would you like to walk with me as far as the library and return your books? Providing, young lady, that you promise to come right back home directly. No funeral parlour visits, promise? Effie, you have ballet this afternoon, and Emily, I expect you to have memorized your lyrics. It's "A Wandering Minstrel," isn't it? Did Marushka bring *The Mikado* music for you?"

"Yes, Mother," the girls answered in turn, their eyes wide, admiring the beauty of Mrs. Willow in her camel-hair, wrap-around coat from the Salvation Army. She sashayed around to show her appreciation of their adulation, since she knew she wasn't beautiful. Luckily, she'd inherited good bone structure and had a face that showed no tiny lines – no signs of the strain or fear that haunted her life.

"Come then, Pippa. Wrap up warmly. It's a thirty-minute walk and I mustn't be late. Effie, please remember, the Russian Academy does not operate on coloured people's time. Be there before one o'clock. And remember to rub vaseline over your elbows and knees."

"Mother, don't worry!" Emily scolded, opening the door for her. "We'll be okay."

"Maybe they'll be okay, but will I?" Marion wondered, as she climbed des Seigneurs hill to Dorchester Street. Pippa kept pace, but wasn't her talkative self. "Damn this war," Marion thought. The endless Allied losses were soul-destroying. She encouraged Pippa to talk about Trevor, but her replies were spasmodic.

As they cut across to the Westmount Library, Pippa suddenly asked: "Why don't you like Miss Delacourt, Mother?" Marion felt her heart seize. Why hadn't Pippa brought it up earlier, while there was time to discuss it, to explain? Now, she could only protest, "I don't dislike her. I just have little in common with her."

"That's not true. You're much alike in some ways. Only, you won't be friends. Why? Is it because of Poppa Dad?"

"No, it isn't."

Thank God, the Gothic pile of red bricks, limestone cornices, and Victorian bevelled glass that was the Library loomed ahead.

"But if it would make you happy, Pippa, we'll invite her to tea one day."

Pippa instantly hugged her mother. "That would be wonderful!" She added almost shyly, "I told Emily you weren't a snob."

"Does my acceptance of Torrie mean that much to her?" Marion fretted, watching her daughter run up the library stairs, her long legs taking them two at a time.

⚜

A cold westerly wind blew against her, forcing Marion to hold on to her felt hat and wish she'd worn a scarf instead. A scarf around her head, with woolen stockings and wool gloves would have been wise. But no, she had been invited to lunch at Rurphy's and she intended to be dressed as well as, if not better than, the middle-class matrons who frequented the restaurant. Her camel-hair coat was a rare find among the clothes discarded by the rich and sold by the Sally Ann to the poor. Remembering the joy of finding it reminded Marion that all three children would need new winter coats this year. They were growing so fast, and Efuah, although she didn't mind hand-me-downs, had never had a new coat.

The Rurphy's restaurant in NDG considered itself a cut above the others in the *rafiné* eatery chain that served a Canadian version of English food with a kind of Victorian gentility. Handy to his apartment, it was Thaddeus's favourite place for steak and kidney pie on a Sunday evening when the Y kitchen was closed.

"We could meet there for lunch. It would be easier to talk," McGregor had said, having returned to the Y to spend a few days supervising the new manager. He'd been wearing his Glen plaid suit, not a uniform, although Marion understood he was expecting to be assigned overseas duty with his Black Watch Regiment, after a short stint as a recruitment officer.

She stopped to catch her breath. Ahead was the restaurant, its multi-windowed front blandly reflecting the unruffled pace of tree-lined Sherbrooke Street. For a moment, she almost decided not to go in. A streetcar was clanging along the street heading east. If she sprinted, she could make it.

She shouldn't be mixing business with pleasure. If they wanted to fire all the coloured women who worked at the Y, they would. There were plenty of British war brides longing to take their places. But, damn it, they were the best working force the Y had ever had; and if Thaddeus still had some influence with the management, here was an opportunity to fight for them! Resolutely, Marion spun around and marched into the restaurant.

The clock above the hostess's desk pointed to just after one o'clock. The haughty peroxide-blonde hostess, who watched Marion unbelting her coat as she approached, suddenly disappeared. Marion looked around the half-empty room for the familiar, slightly rotund, tall figure of Thaddeus McGregor. He was nowhere in sight. Relieved to be first, she waited for the hostess to return and seat her.

It seemed an eternity filled with veiled glances from diners who looked briefly at her, then away, before a nasal voice behind her asked quietly, "Do you have a reservation?"

"No, I'm to meet a friend here."

"Sorry, but we can't seat you —"

"I'm waiting for someone and I don't mind waiting here, but it does seem unnecessary. There'll only be two of us."

The voice became a man — a tall, angular, pale man in a dark suit. Obsequious in manner, he moved to block her — presuming, Marion thought, that she'd simply barge her way in. Seconds passed. Holding up the restaurant's menu to prevent anyone except her from hearing him, the man said, "We don't serve coloured people here."

Shame — or was it humiliation? — rained down like a hot, full-powered shower, drenching her entire being. She couldn't speak, then dared not, for as his words sank in, rage replaced shame. An urge to smash the restaurant to smithereens, break the windows, and set fire to the tablecloths erupted within her. The man staggered back, unnerved by the flash of rage in her eyes. "It's not me. It's the management," he protested.

"Marion."

From the half-opened door, McGregor's voice floated between them. The undertone of delight in his enunciation of her name took away some of her rage.

"Sorry to be late." Tossing his navy mackintosh over his left arm, he cupped her elbow with the other. "What's the matter?" His voice was full of concern. "You're cold as ice." He turned slightly to speak over his shoulder. "Bring two sherries as soon as possible," he ordered, indicating with a flick of one hand that the man should seat them at once.

"Mr. McGregor, I can't stay," Marion stuttered, turning to face him.

"Nonsense, lass. You don't look at all well. You're probably catching a cold. Come, I'll order a hot chicken pot pie."

The man in the dark suit led the way to a window table as if nothing had happened. After the waitress brought their drinks, Marion's first sip from the glass of sherry calmed the pounding of her heart.

All during lunch, Thaddeus kept the conversation going as though they were sitting at the Y's kitchen table and he had been called upon again to explain the military decision that had led to the bloodbath of Dieppe. The second glass of sherry eased the throbbing in her temples.

"As I see it, lass, the Dieppe raid was more than a military disaster. It provoked a complex series of messages. For, don't ye see how a vulnerable Britain had to put pressure on Canada and her other colonies for more money, men and munitions? France, in submission to its centuries-old adversary, is now kowtowing to the Vichy government in order to survive, betraying its Jewish citizens and selling its African colonies down the river," Thaddeus explained.

Marion, rage still throbbing through her veins, thought, "So what else is new? Africans have been sold down the river so many times, they're like crabs. Here am I, rejected by Rurphy's because I look different from the other customers – just as I rejected Torrie Delacourt because she acts differently from most of us." Marion knew if she took another mouthful of that tasteless chicken pot pie, she'd gag on it, but still she said nothing.

Thaddeus continued to expound. "The United States, don't you know, who infused such energy into the Allied cause after Pearl Harbor, is now suffering defeat after defeat. Island after island, fortress after fortress have been lost, as the Japanese defeat them at every turn."

"Why should I care?" Marion's mind countered silently. "Why should I hate the Japanese, or the Chinese for that matter? Canadians refer to them both as the "Yellow Peril," and took their fishing boats in Vancouver. My father said they treated the Chinese like dogs when they were building the railway." She took another sip of sherry.

Thaddeus misread her frown as a sign of agreement with his political assessment. "Do you know why the Dieppe disaster bothers me so?" he asked. "As you know, I've enlisted – but not to become cannon fodder!"

Involuntarily, Marion reached out to touch his arm. Her gesture moved him. "Don't worry, lass. I'm part of the Frazer clan – I'll survive. The Frazers, my mother's family, took part in the Dieppe raid, yet came back unscathed. You see," he continued, "Simon Lovat – that's the current Lord Lovat, whose country seat is Beaufort Castle in Beauly, Scotland – well, since the sixteenth century, the Lovats have always raised their own army. Shimmie – that's what our family calls him," he explained carefully, not realizing she was engrossed in her own battle, not his, "Shimmie resisted Dickie Mountbatten's plan for Dieppe and took his own army, the Lovat Scouts, as commandos into France – landed, did the job, and returned to England without a single loss. Not a drop of blood for aught."

Marion winced. The word blood reminded her of another bitter rejection of her people during this war. She wondered if McGregor was aware that one of the most important medical innovations of the decade – the technology to bank blood and to take blood plasma onto the battlefield to save soldiers' lives – was pioneered by a Black doctor at McGill University, Dr. Charles Drew. Yet, in Canada, Black people weren't even allowed to donate blood to the war effort! Her eyes moistened with fury.

"What is it, Marion?" Thaddeus tried to make eye contact,

but she deliberately looked away. "You're not yourself, lass. Am I boring you? I'm so clumsy, forgive me."

"Forgive him?" Marion asked herself. "What has he ever done to hurt me?" Aloud, she protested, "It's not you. I just promised to be at a meeting at three."

As he stood behind her chair to help her rise, Marion noticed the elderly lady at the next table nodding admiringly, approving his gallantry. McGregor signalled the waitress to bring the bill. Marion's eyes, now soft and full of affection, moved him. He took her hand and kissed it in a courtly fashion.

Marion pulled on her gloves protectively. "Take care of yourself, Thaddeus. You're very important to all of us, you know."

After a moment's silence, McGregor whispered: "I'd rather just be important to *you*. Marion," he continued, gathering his courage, "perhaps . . . when I come back from the war, there'll be no need for a stalemate between us?"

Marion didn't trust herself to reply. McGregor tucked her arm safely under his as they walked out of the restaurant.

Even after he bade her good afternoon and hailed a taxi, Marion couldn't sort out what he had said or not said, or why he had insisted on taking her to lunch. It wasn't until almost an hour later, when a motion put before the Coloured Ladies Club, about the need for more members, seemed about to be defeated that she suddenly exploded.

"Look at us, sipping tea as if we're gentry – as if we're well-to-do white ladies at the MAA. Unlike them, however, because our husbands aren't presidents of banks, we desperately have to find ways to raise money to continue doing worthwhile things for our community – like maintaining our two beds at the TB sanatorium, our four plots in the Mount Royal cemetery, and providing dinners for shut-ins. We've always taken care of our own people!"

Marion forced herself to seem calm. "Yet, last spring, we rejected Miss Torrie Delacourt, a close friend of Langston Hughes, who, as we just discussed, would draw a large crowd if he agreed to come to Montreal to give a reading. Well, ladies," she concluded, "I propose to resubmit her name. We need to broaden our membership."

The members were stunned. Miss Delacourt, who worked at Rockhead's – to be accepted as one of them! What about those mysterious years she'd spent in Europe?

Marion sat down, then stood up and awkwardly passed around a plate of Mrs. Brock's asparagus sandwiches.

Unexpectedly, Angela Brock laughed. She was one of the few women present who did not need to work outside her home, and had graduated as a young lady from Spelman College in Georgia, as had her mother. Thanks to her plantocracy grandfather's legacy, the Brocks were one of the few truly upper-class Black families in Montreal. Marion looked at her in surprise.

"I do declare, Miss Delacourt might breathe new life into our group. I think I'll vote with Marion. Who are we to cast the first stone?" she asked the members with her customary candour, as she, too, passed around dainty sandwiches with their crusts carefully cut off.

Amelia Hall harrumphed. "Talk about puttin' the cat among the pigeons! Whatever has come over you, Marion? Hmmph . . . Ah fear you'll live to rue *this* day."

⚓

CHAPTER XIII

The first snows of winter hovered, heavily weighted with moisture. People scurried along quickly, knowing that if the temperature rose, the snow would turn to sleet. Then, if it fell during the night, the sleet would turn to ice, and the steep rise of rue des Seigneurs would turn into a toboggan run for the children, resulting in bruised backs – or even broken hips for the elderly.

Emily sat in the window seat, half reading, half watching the world outside. She hadn't been well for a few days – nothing specific, just a kind of ennui, an exhaustion that worried Marion. Suddenly, as if back to her old zestful self, she squealed, "Mother!" She could hardly contain herself. "Mother! Otis is wearing a zoot suit!"

Marion hurried to the window. "Dear Lord, no! He can't be serious. Emily, run down and catch him. Ask him to come back right away." Emily leaped down the stairs, not hearing her mother add, "Don't forget to say please."

Otis Thompson returned, broad-brimmed hat in his hand, overcoat flung over his shoulders, his wide-lapelled suit jacket hanging smoothly to fingertip length above ballooned trousers, narrow at the ankle. "What's the matter, Missus Willow? Emily

wouldn't tell me. Are you okay?" Both he and Emily followed
Marion's slim figure into the parlour. Marion shooed the reluctant Emily out of the room and closed the door.

"Otis." She sat down at her Regency desk. "Please understand, I don't mean to dictate to you. I know you have a date
tonight with Marushka to hear Oscar Peterson play at Victoria
Hall."

He nodded happily.

"Well, that suit is just not appropriate."

"What?"

"Aren't you wearing what they call a zoot suit?"

"Yes," he said proudly. "They're all the rage in New York.
What's the matter with it? A bit loud, but it's cool." He pirouetted
to show it off. "Cool, that's what they say when something's hot
stuff!"

"Otis, Marushka's from a very conservative family."

"Right on! Her mother's still in Tzarist Russia."

"Be that as it may, wearing a suit that's rather loud and high
fashion might make her doubt you. Oh, Otis! That's not really it at
all. Marushka's too wise to judge you on appearances, but others
aren't. Victoria Hall's where well-to-do white couples go to
dance. If you arrive in a zoot suit, they'll just think you're low
class."

"I don't get you. Why should I care what they think? What
are you trying to say – that I should dress white?"

"No, no. That's not what I'm trying to say." Her voice suddenly sounded weary. "Please, just humour me and wear your
smart grey flannels and blazer. I promise you, I know I'm right –
but I don't know how to explain it."

"Damn! Damn! Damn!" Otis marched out, hazel eyes blazing
with annoyance, and stomped up to his room. He changed in less
than five minutes.

Marion was still at her desk when he came back down. "Now
I'm late," he announced. "I promised to pick Marushka up at

seven." She looked up. She tried to smile, but sadness still lurked in her eyes. "Now you look like your uncle."

Otis walked over. He put an arm gently around her shoulders. "Then I must look all right. I know you care," he added with chagrin.

"Have a nice time."

He began to hum "Stardust," as he fox-trotted Emily to the door. She squirmed happily and squealed, "Otis!" Still humming, he went down the stairs.

⚓

Marushka was waiting in the studio, playing Debussy's *Golliwog's Cakewalk* to relieve the tension. She had had a difficult time. Her mother had started a long tirade on the worthlessness of men in general and West Indians in particular.

"But you loved my father."

"He had other women."

"I don't believe you."

"One even came to his funeral."

"Oh, Mamushka, you were just jealous. You imagine the worst. That sometimes happens, they say, in a mixed marriage. One never feels really secure."

"So, why do you want to marry this boy? You're not of his race."

"Yes, I am. I'm what they call mulatto, and what people see is what they believe you are. One has to accept that. I'm dark-hued, so I'm coloured. Mrs. Willow explained it to me."

"They don't see you as coloured or different at work. They think you're like all the other salesgirls. No?"

"That's the problem. I can't even let Otis meet me after work, for fear they'll suspect I'm not all white." Marushka had unbraided her hair for the second time, letting it fall in a cascade down her back, trying to decide how to wear it. "It's even worse when they believe you're white and going out with a Black man. It's somehow as though you're doing it for sex or cheap thrills." She had shuddered, hoping her mother would sympathize.

"Marushka! Watch your language!"

It had been no use. Her mother's fears were based on overprotective love and her own traumatic experiences. She had hugged Dame Orlova and had slipped away to the studio to wait.

It was nice having an undemanding friend like Otis. She enjoyed being included when he took his little cousins to cricket matches. Daydreaming sometimes, Marushka fantasized that Mrs. Willow was her godmother or aunt. Like Emily, then, she would no longer feel so alone. From the frightened, almost aggressive adolescent who'd arrived just before Pippa's birthday, Emily had grown into a little mother hen, fussing about her sisters' well-being, shaping herself, even in speech patterns, after her beloved new mother.

How naturally they reinforced each other, Marushka thought. Instead of being confined to the house, the girls could now go anywhere, as long as they were together. Mrs. Willow was teaching them to go uptown to pay household bills and the weekly life insurance premiums.

Laughing to herself, Marushka recalled the day she'd seen them walking along beside a crippled man. Pippa, always compassionate, had instructed her sisters to limp as they passed him. "We don't want him to feel he's alone with his affliction," she had whispered.

Dutifully, they had limped past, turning to share a *simpatico* smile with the old man, and had then resumed their natural stride. Surprised and then furious, he had shouted curses at them. "He's simply ungrateful!" Pippa had declared to her sisters, amazed at his anger, and had proudly walked on.

Marushka remembered Otis's story of Pippa visiting funeral parlours with wildflowers for un-wept-for guests. Would she and Otis ever have children as warm and wonderful as the Willow girls? A flush rose-bronzed her cheeks. "How bold I'm becoming!" she scolded herself, but inside was an incandescent glow of happiness.

The door chimes rang. It was Otis.

Otis carefully parked his uncle's Chevy illegally in the crowded Westmount Library lot across the street from the Y. The blowing snow hurried the young couples, some in uniforms, across the park, up the stone stairs, and through the massive Gothic wooden doors of Victoria Hall. Checking their winter coats and boots, they hurried to join friends in the lower hall where the young impresario, Johnny Holmes, led Montreal's most popular band of local white musicians.

Tonight was special. Through his friend Rodney, Otis had obtained two tickets to attend a celebration for the new pianist in Johnny Holmes's band. When the group had lost two pianists in quick succession to the army, saxophonist Art Morrow had asked Johnny to audition young Peterson, who had already won the Ken Sobles Amateur Hour at the Rialto Theatre playing boogie-woogie, and had his own weekly radio spot on Montreal's most popular radio station, CKAC. Here was genuine musical talent. Holmes never hesitated. He hired young Oscar Peterson at once to play with his band at the weekly dances.

Take the A Train, the saxophone crooned. Marushka's escort hummed along softly, moving his shoulders to the rhythm. *That's the way to get to Harlem*. Gently, he led Marushka onto the dance floor. There was a such a feeling of ease holding her in his arms. Instead of dancing on a dime as he liked to do, they swung out. "Easy does it," Otis told himself. He didn't feel compelled to show off his store of fancy footwork. At the Cozy Corner in Plage Laval, or at Chez Maurice Danceland, where most of his friends took their dates, he'd have be-bopped at centre stage. Dancing with Marushka was something else. Cuddly, yes, cool and light on her feet. Her laugh was a low bubble. She held his hand when he offered it, but wasn't mushy. He'd obviously have to teach her how to dip and break, but when he informed her of his good intentions, she responded, "Then I'll teach you how to waltz."

"Deuce. Forty all." The girl had class.

Other couples glanced at them with admiration. All but a handful of the eight hundred young people who attended the Victoria Hall weekly dances were high school seniors or college kids, familiar with musicians like Johnny Holmes, Oscar Peterson, and Maynard Ferguson from their graduation dances and school proms. They envied couples who danced in harmony.

They were mostly of Anglo stock, from middle- and upper-class families who wouldn't allow their daughters to go to night-clubs where alcohol was available, or to the racy dance halls in Verdun, or to the amusement parks on the outskirts of the city. In fact, unless a girl was a Molson, a McTaggart, a member of the E.P. Taylor family – or one of the Upper Westmount debs who graduated from Miss Edgar and Miss Cramp's private school and patronized the tea parties at the Ritz, or had dates who could afford the Normandy Room at the Mount Royal Hotel – this was the weekly social event of the winter season.

Airmen, navy and army officers in uniform were always in the crowd. Ordinary servicemen on a forty-eight-hour leave were warned off; most of the girls were too prim and proper to seduce easily. Still, tickets were usually sold out and lines began to form before the massive doors opened at eight.

Oscar Peterson's fingers moved magically from "Take the A Train" to Cole Porter's "Night and Day." Trumpet in hand, Johnny Holmes brought his orchestra to an intermission break. The eighteen musicians stood, put their instruments down, wiped their damp foreheads with white handkerchiefs, and acknowledged the applause.

The ten-thirty intermission found Marushka and Otis near

the bandstand. Rodney beckoned them to make their way backstage. Marushka and Daisy, Oscar Peterson's sister, embraced. Sheet music that Daisy couldn't find at Layton's, her favourite store, or at Archambault's, was often below the counter at Ogilvy's. Daisy, dark, diminutive, and with deep dimples, was her little brother's mentor and best friend.

Meeting his idol left Otis Thompson almost tongue-tied. The lad wasn't yet eighteen, but his fame as a keyboard wizard, as a prodigy, was commonly acknowledged and a source of great pride in the community.

Like Oscar, he knew Maestro Lou Hooper, so they chatted about him. Maestro Hooper's skill in orchestrating Negro spirituals, classical jazz, and choir arrangements was legendary. From the church choir to Rockhead's, he arranged musical scores that were deeply rooted in the South and in Harlem. In a way, he had been instrumental in steering Daisy and then her brother to the Hungarian-born classical pianist and teacher, Paul de Marky, who was challenging young Peterson to stretch his horizons.

In the Peterson family, music was a way of life. In their devotion to their children's education, the Petersons, like Marion Willow and most parents in their small community, rigidly maintained their high standards and values. They sacrificed for a principle: their children's future was more important than theirs.

Some young people fell by the wayside. Tuberculosis was rampant in the thirties and forties. It took its toll on the immigrant communities, as well as on the mainstream. Little Oscar Peterson, in fact, just as he was starting public school, had had to spend a year in a sanatorium. When he seemed stronger, the doctor advised his father not to let him tax his lungs with his trumpet; the piano became his solace.

That incredible night, when Oscar Peterson was finally acknowledged as an indispensable member of an otherwise all-white dance band – the night that launched his meteoric rise to the number-one spot as the greatest jazz pianist in the world –

that night, for Otis and Marushka, was the turning point in their friendship.

Back in the dance hall, while her escort was away buying Coca-Colas for them, a rather clean-cut, tall, blondish soldier asked Marushka to dance. She felt she ought to honour his uniform by saying yes.

"What's your name? Mine's George," he said.

"Maria," she answered automatically, then realized that she had given the name she used at work, not the name she used with her family and friends. It didn't matter, it was only one dance; then she'd return to Otis. Otis, returning to the hall, watched quietly. She looked so graceful. The orchestra was playing "Dark Eyes"; her head was flung back; her dark, curling hair was escaping from its ribbon. She was so beautiful. He felt proud and possessive.

"Who's the chick George has?" he heard a serviceman with a black beret standing near him ask another. "I could get a hard-on for her."

Otis tensed. One of the glasses he was holding tipped, spilling Coke on his trousers. He wiped it off with a hanky. When he looked back up, the black-bereted soldier was cutting in on his friend George. Marushka seemed to be politely manoeuvering to escape them both.

The music swung into a slow "Body and Soul" two-step rhythm. George reclaimed Marushka. She looked as she felt – trapped – and though she still wore a demure smile, her body was resisting both the music and her partner. "Enough is enough," Otis's heart decided. Placing the drinks on a nearby table, he moved quietly to the couple and, sliding his hands between them, snarled: "Thanks, ole man." He twirled Marushka away.

"Did you see that?" George asked his friend, as he joined his buddies propped against the wall.

"Forget it," his friend advised.

"No darky's going to take a girl from me."

"Forget it. You're not at Plage Laval. This is a classy joint. He's probably the pianist's brother."

"If it's so classy, what are darkies doing here?" George asked, his spleen churning.

"You're not at Roseland – I said, forget it!"

A bouncy redhead in platform shoes tripped against his large army boots, giggled, and said, "Sorry." George forgot the darky, asked the redhead: "Wanna dance?"

Marushka wanted to leave. The evening had been dreamy until the servicemen intervened. She reminded Otis of her promise to be home before twelve. Otis didn't want the evening to be over yet. "It's only eleven. Let's go to Ben's for smoked meat."

"Ben's? I've never been there. What's it like?"

"It's a Montreal landmark. You'll enjoy it."

They went to get their coats. "Button up, now, baby. It's cold outside," Otis advised. They left the hall, retrieved the Chevy, and then drove east along Sherbrooke Street to Metcalfe Avenue behind the Mount Royal Hotel.

⚏

Ben's, a hole-in-the-wall delicatessen in the heart of Montreal's shopping, hotel, and tourist centre, was famous for smoked meat sandwiches at twenty-five cents each. Freshly sliced, with the meat so thickly piled on that the rye bread often had to be held together with a toothpick, the sandwiches were served with cucumber pickles and the city's best French fries. Ben's special fruit punch cost fifteen cents and chocolate milkshakes twenty. A bar stool counter provided room for about twelve people. In the main room, up to thirty could be accommodated at white formica tables seating four each.

The delicatessen was busy from 7:00 AM till 2:00 AM. Even then, if you could stand the smell of the Javex used to wash down the white and black tile floors, Ben's was the place to be, as the very late-night musicians and visiting Broadway stars dropped in for Ben's wonderful breakfast omelettes.

Ben's food was strictly kosher. The roast chicken served at lunch had probably been inspected that very dawn by the Rabbi who supervised the Jewish market on St. Lawrence Main Street. The cherry cheesecake was far moister than that served at Lindy's on Broadway, in New York, and the owners of Ben's were on a first-name basis with the real "movers and shakers" in Montreal. Colour and class meant nothing to them. "Behave, enjoy, and pay your bill" was their creed.

Young people felt sophisticated, taking their dates there. To make waiting customers feel part of the crowd, Tilly the cashier would make the odd, offhand remark: "You should have been here earlier. Tommy Dorsey was in." People dared not scoff, for covering the walls were photographs of visiting celebrities, from Joe Louis and Franchot Tone, to Fay Wray and Peaches. If the owner, Ben Kravitz, noticed you had a nasty cold, he would send a steaming bowl of chicken soup with matzoh balls – free.

Parking nearby was difficult, with the swirling storm clogging the streets; parking lots were full. Otis and Marushka trudged the two blocks through slush before the steamed-up glass windows of Ben's greeted them. All the tables were taken.

The head waiter shrugged. "Maybe a twenty-minute wait, maybe only ten." Someone was trying to signal them. A tall, bearded man with horn-rimmed glasses stood up at his table. "Maria," he called, "there's room here." It was Mark Reitman, the young assistant manager of the furniture department at Ogilvy's.

"Would you rather not?" she asked Otis, noticing his puzzled frown.

Otis shrugged. "Any port in a storm," he replied, then followed her to the table.

"Good to see you," Mark said, pointing to the two empty seats at his table. "Hey, weren't you two at Victoria Hall tonight?

Maria, this is my wife, Sarita. And you are . . . ?" Mark asked, offering his hand to Otis.

"I'm Otis Thompson." They shook hands, rather like gladiators in an arena. Otis settled Marushka in a chair and sat himself down stiffly, slowly looking around.

Mark turned to his wife. "Maria's a godsend in the music department. She's the first one they've ever had there who knows the difference between Wagner and Dvorak, or who can show a customer how to negotiate Chopin." Sarita's smile warmed Marushka. "You're obviously as bright as you are beautiful," she whispered. Marushka blushed, shook her head. Wet snow flipped over onto Otis's jacket. "Oh, Otis. I'm so sorry."

Without a word, he wiped it off. For a few minutes, silence hung heavily. The waiter intervened; huge illustrated menus were shoved between them, one for each. Their choice was unanimous: "Smoked meat on rye." Otis gave the order for all of them. Mugs of hot coffee were plunked on the table. The ice broke.

"What do you think of Peterson's technique at the piano? Wow! He's phenomenal!" Mark imitated his rapid, light fingerwork on the table, humming "Body and Soul."

"No way, man," Otis interrupted. "It's like this." Stretching his long brown fingers, he rotated his supple wrists to emphasize the mobility in his thumbs and little fingers. He staccatoed a basic boogie-woogie beat, using his left hand to show how the fingers split the octaves.

"See, he's influenced by Duke Ellington's mastery of harmonic chords. It's a soul thing."

Mark tugged at his beard. "But that doesn't explain his arpeggios, the technique of rapid movement on the treble notes."

"You mean, like Rubinstein's?" Marushka questioned.

"Yes, but more like the way Liszt would have tickled the keys." Mark's twinkling eyes showed he agreed with her observation.

Otis's green eyes revealed that he did not. He threw up his

hands. "No, Marushka. Who would you give credit to? Liszt, De Marky, Art Tatum . . . Steep Wade . . . or the *community* that created him."

Mark removed his glasses. "That's poppycock. You can't isolate it!"

"Here we go again. Ole Whitey's discovered him, so he must be for real. Damn!" Otis pushed his sandwich away and waited, muttering, "Ai-yai-yai," till his bile subsided. "Man, let me tell it so you white folks can understand. Duke Ellington pioneered a way of playing that is innovative, expressive and in harmony with race spirituality. That's where Oscar Peterson comes from. That's what marks him as someone whose going to be head and shoulders above other jazz pianists of today."

"But you can't deny the European influence. Music doesn't have boundaries," Mark started to protest, but Sarita cut him off tartly. "Yes, it does, and until Europe acknowledges the influence of jazz on its culture, there's no dialogue."

Otis stared at her, incredulous, then smiled. "Right on."

She deliberately changed the subject by asking Marushka, "Why does Otis call you Marushka? Mark calls you Maria. Marushka's Russian, isn't it?"

Should she? Marushka cringed inwardly. Should she explain that Maria was her name so that no one at work would question her background? If she told the truth, would Mark give her away? She felt her shoulders sag and a faint cramp meandered across her lower tummy. She'd lose her job. Department stores didn't hire coloured girls. Yet, why should she deny her heritage? A cool, firm hand closed over hers.

"Marushka's mother is Russian." Otis's deep voice was gentle, taking command. "It's difficult for most people to pronounce, so she calls herself Maria."

The cramp receded. Sarita was saying something about her family coming from Poland. Otis's healing hand was still holding hers, calming her.

"Otis is right. Marushka's a far prettier name," Mark said.

"Sarita is, too," his wife chipped in. "But people don't like Jewish names. I'm blonde, I've cultivated a Westmount accent, and I don't look particularly Jewish to most people. I'm Sara at my job as a teller in the Toronto Dominion Bank, but if management knew! *Oy veyss meer!*"

Her laugh was infectious. She had great charm, Otis realized, as well as good judgement. It would be nice for Marushka to have her as a friend. He hoped he hadn't been too hard on Mark. But, Otis still resented the fact that white people had to approve before outstanding men of colour were acknowledged. It pained him.

Sarita's comment reminded Marushka that even McGill University, through its quota system, discriminated against Jews in the medical faculty. She so wanted to share with Sarita the fact that she was "passing."

Otis's hand tightened on hers. "It's almost twelve," he said. "Your mother will have a candle in the window."

Sarita laughed. "You, too? Before we married – "

"Sarita," Mark lovingly interrupted. "They don't want to hear your *yenta* tales."

"I'll come and visit you on the fifth floor sometime, without Mark," Sarita said, with a twinkle in her eyes, as they parted.

"Please do. I'm near the elevator," Marushka replied, noticing Sarita's state of pregnancy, which had been hidden under her cloak and under the table.

⚜

The jewelled light of the vestibule lamp at the Russian Ballet Academy twinkled against the falling snow as, hand in hand, Otis and Marushka climbed the front steps. Leaning against the academy's brass plaque, Otis pulled Marushka close to him.

"No," she murmured, but his lips, trembling against hers, filled her with such a feeling of his vulnerability that she put her arms around his neck. "Thanks for the nicest evening I've ever had."

The grilled door opened as if by magic. "Dame Orlova's magic," Otis thought, as he floated the forty-nine steps back to the Willows' door and the twenty-three steps up to his bed.

The depths of sleep evaded him. He tossed and turned. He lost a sense of what was real and what was imagined, when a tall, austere doorman at Ogilvy's barred his way to the fifth floor. Taking one look at him, the man announced, "No coloured people work here." Otis woke with a start. Slowly, Marushka came back to him. Her incandescent smile filled him with such peace that he softly fell into a deep sleep.

CHAPTER XIV

Christmas had long come and gone, leaving behind two brand-new navy blue Red River winter coats with red woollen leggings, red sashes and red woollen tuques for the two older girls. Efuah didn't get a new coat. Philippa's old brown one had been cut down, but a lovely fur collar had been added. And Efuah discovered brand-new long leather leggings – just like the ones the girls at the Christian Science Sunday School wore – tucked under the tree for her, along with a one-person wooden sled. And, for her beloved "Winnie-the-Pooh," a warm winter sweater. In Emily's stocking, there had been a recorder, and, naturally, for Philippa, a new book by her favourite author, Lucy Maud Montgomery. The ladies at the Y had sent each child a silver dollar.

The most unexpected gift came from Mademoiselle Laroche, the lawyer for whom their mother enjoyed working and discussing the rights of women. The envelope contained three gift certificates worth five dollars each from Dupuis Frères department store.

Marushka and her mother had invited the entire family, including Otis and Poppa Dad, for Twelfth Night, their Russian Christmas, for a feast of traditional foods. After that, the Willows' Christmas tree was left in the shed to dry for kindling. Its oil-filled needles, when dropped on the kitchen stove, released a rich pungent scent. The smaller branches crackled and popped in the stove itself, helping their home-made "coal," created from old newspapers soaked in water, then kerosene, and rolled into tight balls to dry, catch fire.

After that magic season, life slipped back to normal. Emily was upgraded from Royal Arthur School to Montreal High School, a half-hour walk from home. She had to wear a uniform – a white middy blouse, navy skirt, and black Oxford shoes.

In February, on Valentine's Day, three new school bags came, nestled in a green box marked Marshall Fields, which meant that Edmond Thompson had had a successful meeting in Chicago with J. Phillip Randolph or the Brotherhood of Sleeping Car Porters in Chicago. Marion knew that while the gifts would thrill the children, they were really meant to mollify her. Mollify or woo her – which?

Life would be so much simpler, at least on the surface, as Edmond's wife, she realized. He was tall, he was handsome, he was sealskin dark, with skin that was smooth to the touch. He had seniority in his job, and skill on the cricket field. And their social circle was comfortable. With him, there would be no surprises, no alien places to explore, no incidents where they'd learn they weren't wanted. Above all, he was a true Garveyite. He believed, as she did, in the need for self-sufficiency for Black folks. Yet something – and not just his exotic mistress – kept Marion from committing herself.

They were due to attend the Debating Society's launch of the Spring Program at the United Negro Improvement Association's hall on Fulford Street – an invitation she'd accepted with pleasure. Although Marushka had come to babysit, Marion didn't really feel comfortable. Otis was not due to return from his run to Winnipeg until the weekend – and his gentlemanly behaviour since meeting Marushka had been exemplary – but still she couldn't shake off a certain fear. When she had boasted to Vashti about the reformed Otis, the older woman's retort had chilled her. "Hunh. That's 'cause Mistress Delacourt is wearin' him out. He can afford to be cool 'round young girls."

Was Vashti right? Or was that remark just more of her "narking" against Edmond and his nephew? Was there an underlying cause, or did it lie in Vashti Dobson's over-protective nature?

In the hall mirror, Marion adjusted her cloche hat, nipped the long, bushy tail of her silver fox shoulder stole into the fox's toothless mouth, and checked her lisle stockings to see if her pencilled-on seams were straight. "Not much breast, but not much bum either. Not bad for a thirty-two-year-old mother," she decided, laughing at herself.

Poppa Dad helped her into her camel-hair coat and fox-trotted her to the car, but she became fearful again as he opened the door of the Chevy, helped her in, then walked to his side to start the engine. Seeing the girls pressing their faces against the window and blowing kisses to her, Marion knew she didn't really want to spend time with anyone but them.

⚑

In retrospect, like the stalemated war in Europe and the collapse of Singapore, the winter of 1943 was a dreadful season. Emily's school report card was distressing. Her classroom teacher at Montreal High obviously intended to assembly-line her students through ninth grade, but there were too many gaps in Emily's knowledge not to disrupt the teacher's "make-notes-while-I-lecture" methodology.

Emily, conscious of cause and effect for the first time and now responsible for her own actions, needed time and space in which to expand. Her mother and sisters supported her explorations, but at school, she discovered, they couldn't care less. "'Make sure your uniform is neat and clean, pay your school fees on time, don't flirt with boys, and don't blot your copybook,'" she mimicked, telling Pippa about attitudes there.

Philippa, anxious to be with Emily at Montreal High, achieved excellent graduating grades at Royal Arthur. She earned her weekly allowance on weekends, taking care of two war babies. Efuah limped through fourth grade, superb in mathematics, incorrigible in spelling, communicating freely only with her sisters, and increasingly in street French with Sylvie Vachon.

It was proving to be a difficult spring as well. Otis, determined to become a man of substance and worthy of Marushka, became deeply involved with his uncle, trying to organize a railway porters' union. He spent less and less time with the girls.

Marushka was torn between playing the piano twice a week at the army canteen as part of Ogilvy's volunteer group, attending to her mother, who was enjoying a season of rheumatic aches and pains, and trying to fit music lessons for Emily in between the Saturday ballet classes.

Marion feared that once school was out, the children would end up playing on the sidewalks of rue des Seigneurs that summer. She doubted she could find enough activities to keep them occupied indoors. After the Williams twins' unfortunate experience the previous summer, camp was not high on her agenda. The centretown YWCA had an excellent summer program, but wouldn't allow coloured children to use the swimming pool. Marion, livid, wouldn't enroll them there, even for knitting lessons.

Yet Vashti Dobson's caution – "the Devil finds work for idle hands" – haunted her. If only she could find a sanctuary for the children for the summer, she could double up on her hours at the Y. Or perhaps she should try to find Poppa Dad's elusive farmland somewhere in the northern Laurentian woods, and camp out there for July and August, among the blackflies and the mosquitoes, earning money by taking care of five or six foster children at the same time. Unknown to the family, Emily

slipped into St. Anthony's Church and lit a candle to help her
mother decide. The gods intervened.

⚔

Two hundred miles or so, as the crow flies, due southeast of Poppa
Dad's Laurentian farm, but still in Quebec, the very proper and
prosperous Eastern Township farming communities of
Chatsworth, Huntington, and Stanstead nestle quietly against
New England's northern borders. While most of Quebec had
been populated by seventeenth-century settlers from France, welcomed naïvely by the indigenous Crees and Abenakis who were
then banished to reserves, the lower Eastern Townships, deserted
by the already decimated Mohawks, were peopled by staunch
Anglo Royalists. After the American War of Independence in
1776, the British deliberately enticed sheep and dairy farmers
from Scotland, along with weavers and woollen-mill owners from
northern England, to create a buffer between the rebels in the
United States and the resentful Québecois.

Slowly, however, very slowly, the French were repopulating
the territory. Their bishop warned, "We will reconquer with the
cradle what they conquered with the sword." Only the counties
around Lake Champlain still held their own, remaining British to
the core, though their numbers dwindled through attrition and
the Anglo practice of having only "two and a half" children per
family.

Ninety acres of that particular patch of Eden, north of a ham-
let known as Chatsworth, were owned by Andrew Windsor, a
sturdy, no-nonsense, third-generation farmer who loved the gently rolling countryside of southern Quebec, protected on the
south by the rock-strewn, rugged Green Mountains of Vermont,
sheltered on the north by the fertile apple orchards of the far
Rougemont Hills, and watered by meandering tributaries of the
Richelieu River.

The Windsors' children had grown up and gone away. The eldest, Ernest, who was serving with the Red Coats – the famous Royal Canadian Mounted Police – was stationed in the Northwest Territories, more than two thousand miles away. The younger son was at Guelph Agricultural College in Ontario, while their daughter Phyllis, driving an ambulance in London, dodging bombs, and madly in love with a British RAF bomber captain, had decided to cultivate her garden in England.

The Windsors' big white house, shingle-roofed with dormer windows, was almost empty; only Andrew's spinster sister, Abigail, haunted its upstairs rooms. In the yard, two rather moth-eaten reindeer and a collie dog roamed, wondering what had happened to the three youngsters they'd grown up with. Alice Windsor – who had yearned to be a foster parent to some of the British children sent for sanctuary in Canada during the early years of the war – now gently hinted, almost every holiday, that it would be "an act of kindness" to invite some city child to the farm for a summer of healthy living.

Her husband rarely responded. Andrew always hoped his own children would come home and really didn't enjoy adjusting his routine to accommodate others. Finally, at Easter in the year of her Lord 1943, her husband, deciding that "it would be a way of showing God our gratitude for the hospitality shown to our off-spring by strangers," agreed to have one inner-city child for a summer of fresh air and sunshine.

A friend in Kingston, who had graduated from Queen's University with Alice, suggested she write the Children's Aid Society in Montreal. The Windsors' April letter was unearthed on June first in a tray on Mrs. Brown's desk, a victim of the Society's FILO system – first in, last out. Anxious to get away on her own summer vacation, and knowing how dependable Mrs. Willow was, Mrs. Brown dispatched the original letter with a note scrawled across it: "Emily's health might benefit from this. Please reply directly."

Alice Windsor received a reply to her letter in mid-June. The Windsors decided that it would be acceptable to have three children instead of just Emily since, as Mrs. Willow claimed, they were inseparable. She had also volunteered assurances that the children were tidy, very well behaved, in good health, and that character references from Reverend Lorenzo West of the Union United Congregational Church would be forthcoming.

The Windsors were Methodists, but a United Church minister's word seemed acceptable. What really cleared the decks was when Mrs. Willow, who abhorred charity, insisted on paying twenty dollars a month towards the children's board. "Now," the Windsors agreed, "this is the sign of a woman of judgement." It was all arranged by mail.

CHAPTER XV

The drizzle and then the morning mist that had hidden the young cornstalks, Guernsey cows, and meandering river during the early morning gave way to a pale sun as the old steam engine lurched to a stop at the wooden railway station. Coal dust lay on its windowsills. Peering out the cinder-pocked coach window, Philippa's felt her spirits lift when she saw the antique charm of its old Victorian fretwork and the beautifully lettered station sign that read *Chatsworth, Quebec. Population: 342.* Emily organized their luggage while Efuah searched for her straw hat. Then, together, they alighted.

As Alice Windsor moved quickly down the platform towards them, Philippa noticed that she was rather plump, with brownish hair just turning grey; her complexion was not weathered as a farmer's wife's should be, but fresh, like a young girl's. Her smile was a friendly one.

The girls stood together, waiting to be claimed, as Marion had instructed. But the closer Mrs. Windsor approached, the weaker her smile became. She stopped, searched in her bag for her glasses, then looked carefully, first at Emily, then at Pippa, and at little Efuah. Putting two of her fingers against her mouth, she murmured, "Oh dear, there must be some mistake!" Philippa looked around, but there were no other little girls on the platform. The woman seemed so distressed that, in pure compassion, Pippa volunteered, "Don't cry, don't worry. Maybe your little girl will come on another train."

"Little girl! We'd only asked for one, but agreed to have all three, and I'm sure you're the ones. But no one told me you weren't... Canadian! Dear me, dear me," she fretted, with two fingers still pressed against her mouth. "You're African, aren't you?"

Pippa dwelt on the lady's reaction for a moment. "To tell the truth," she reasoned aloud, almost to herself, "I guess, because of Daddy, we are African, although we don't look the same colour as those in *The National Geographic*." She looked at Emily, who was barely brown, and at her little sister, who was verging on ebony; she herself was what Torrie referred to as café au lait. But then she recalled a conversation she had overheard between her mother and Amelia Hall. Miss Amelia had advised Marion to be quite candid when describing how the girls would be dressed, their ages, and when the train from Montreal would arrive in Chatsworth, but to skip the inconvenient fact of their colour. Pippa remembered that her mother had not agreed. Unable to bring herself to use colour as the outstanding characteristic of her children, Marion had included a snapshot of the girls instead in her detailed letter to Alice Windsor.

Yet Pippa's mind kept tugging at an inner door to which there was no handle. Shrugging, she decided simply to follow the lady, and beckoned to her sisters to come along as they headed towards the truck parked alongside the platform.

Alice Windsor, shaking her head in bewilderment, drawing on all the Christian fortitude she possessed, piled the children into the back of the old Ford pick-up truck and drove through town, past the obviously curious townsfolk, far faster than she was wont. She only allowed herself to turn around and inspect her guests once she was on the dirt road heading towards the farm.

Throughout the trip, the roar of the engine, the hot sun, the flying stones, and the constant jolting left the girls silent, gripping the sides of the truck, each deep in her own thoughts. Suddenly, Pippa's memory jolted open that inner door, bringing back a scene she had conveniently forgotten.

✢

In mid-June, two days after school closed, Pippa was leaving the Westmount Children's Library, her arms loaded with borrowed books, when she saw Torrie Delacourt drive up. Getting out of her car, Torrie raised a critical eyebrow at Pippa's huge pile.

"Oh, they're not just for me," Pippa protested. "They're for Emily and Effie as well. We're allowed to keep them for ten weeks on summer loan." Without her customary humour, Torrie inspected the collection. Not one of them was by a Black author. With unexpected passion, still standing on the library steps, Torrie expounded on the importance of reading about the Harlem Renaissance. "People like you and me made Harlem the literary, if not the jazz capital of America in the twenties and thirties. Your mother should try being as meticulous about your mind as she is about your manners!"

Pippa felt compelled to defend, not her choices, but the quantity of books. "Mother allowed me to borrow as many as I could 'cause we're going to stay on a farm all summer. And if it's dull, we'll probably read a lot." Unloading her books onto the hood of Torrie's car, Pippa dug into her pocket to pull out a letter. "See? We're going to the Eastern Townships – near the American border." As she opened the unsealed envelope, a capricious breeze wafted its contents out of her hand; the pages pirouetted for a moment or so before drifting carelessly into a puddle of water. Pippa stared, close to tears. "The letter's ruined! I promised Mother to mail it. She'll be so cross!"

Torrie tiptoed into the puddle and plucked the letter, its

envelope, and a floating photograph from the water. "I can take them home and dry them out," she assured Pippa.

"Would you?" Pippa asked gratefully. "You promise you'll mail it, too? Cross your heart?"

Torrie crossed her heart, countering, "If you promise to come and choose one of my books to add to your summer reading."

⁂

What Pippa did not know, however, was that, as Torrie was climbing the high, winding stairs to her apartment later that day, she rediscovered the soggy letter in her purse, and realized that it was indeed ruined. "I'll just have to rewrite it," she decided.

In her elegant living room, late that same afternoon, stretched out languorously on her chaise longue, letter in hand, she finally managed to decipher what Marion had written. "I declare! I never met a woman who was so naïve. Why show those farmers the girls are Black? They'll only find some excuse not to have them." Torrie put the photograph of the girls on a blotter on top of a radiator to dry. After placing a Cole Porter record on her gramophone, she selected a sheet of lovely cream-coloured notepaper, consulted the damp envelope, and, sitting at her desk, picked up a gold Parker fountain pen. Guardedly, she began to reconstruct the letter.

When Torrie was finished and had addressed a new envelope, she licked it shut, stuck on a stamp, and, picking up a designer cardigan, left her apartment. The letter in one hand, she slowly and gracefully descended the stairs, her distinctive feline walk so like a fashion model's. She sauntered to the corner of rue des Seigneurs and St. Antoine, and slipped the letter to the Windsors into the red mailbox. As she returned home to await Edmond's evening visit, she smiled like a cat who had swallowed a canary.

⁂

When Alice Windsor and the girls arrived at the farm, her tall husband laughed and joyously threw little Effie into the air, then caught her with gentle hands, grinning broadly. "This will test your missionary zeal for sure," he teased his wife, as he took the girls upstairs to see their room. It was at the top of the house, a big bright room with dormer windows and white-painted metal beds – three beds, carefully made up. Flowers were on the wash-stand, frilly curtains at the windows. "It's such a beautiful, happy room," Pippa thought, as she looked around in awe.

Mr. Windsor explained that he hoped the girls would feel less homesick being all in the same room. "This is the room our daughter Phyllis grew up in."

Uncle Andy, as he instructed the girls to call him, suggested they unpack, wash up, and come down for supper. Once the door was closed, Emily inspected the closets, Efuah bounced from bed to bed, and Pippa opened the windows to lean out. A cherry tree grew just outside the window. "It's just like *Anne of Green Gables*, only it's real," she breathed happily.

⚓

The next day, the telephone rang incessantly. A neighbour called to ask Mrs. Windsor if it was true about her visitors. "Are they actually sleeping under the same roof?"

Gradually, the number of voices joining the party line could be heard clearly, all burning with the same curiosity. Mrs. Windsor answered guardedly and then hung up, but the others stayed on the line gossiping. Ten minutes later, when she picked the phone up to call her son in Guelph, they were still there, clucking like hens.

"Who are they? Where do they come from?"

"Africa," one answered confidently.

"Are they really black?"

"No . . . well, one is, and one is sort of dark brown. The other is . . . well, beige."

"What were they wearing? Do they have shoes? Do they speak English?"

"Who knows? ... Of course, they must. The missionaries must have taught them, eh?"

"Isn't that what Abigail was sent to do in China – or was it Africa?"

"Too bad she was so sick when she came back home. She never talks about it. Never!"

"That was years ago."

"Speaking of missionaries, has anyone told the Vicar? Better ring him up, he'll want to know . . . ."

At the rectory, Reverend Carver listened to the caller in astonishment, barely concealing his irritation at being the last to hear. A trim, well-dressed man in his mid-thirties with curly hair, he burned with ambition and, fancying himself a rather good orator, thanked the caller, implying that he had actually known all along, then hung up.

In the living room, his wife, a pretty blonde woman dressed in black and white, hair fashionably bobbed – "almost a carbon-copy" of Carole Lombard – was mixing a jug of martinis and popping olives into her mouth. Clearing his throat, Reverend Carver announced that Mrs. Windsor had three heathens staying with her: "Three girls from darkest Africa! This is an interesting turn of events, yes indeed. Alice attended the Missionary Society last week and didn't say a word. She's a sly one, isn't she?" Rubbing his long fingers together, he said, "I've been looking for an evangelical theme for a sermon." Satisfied that God works in mysterious ways, his wife offered him a martini.

No one seemed to think for a minute that the Willow children might actually have been born in Canada. Reverend Carver delivered a rousing sermon the following Sunday on the effectiveness of the church's missionary program, taking up an extra collection for the cause. With great gusto, the congregation sang: *Suffer little children to come unto me.*

A few days later, the three girls returned with Aunt Alice to the village of Chatsworth. She parked the pick-up on the main street in front of the general store, suggesting that the girls go across the street to the bandstand while she did her shopping. Her list must have been a long one, for Emily, becoming bored, suggested they look for some postcards to send home.

"Small-town life is charming," Pippa observed.

"No, it ain't," Emily cautioned, as she noticed how people stared at them. It was more than staring – people were gawking! Some stood on the sidewalk in disbelief and, as the news spread, others came out onto their porches to squint across at the girls. One lady tried to take a picture of them. Another tried to feel the texture of Efuah's curly hair. Both times, Emily intervened.

Cars slowed down along the tarmac. The whole village seemed to have ground to a halt to stare, muttering and scratching their heads as they inspected the curious new arrivals. Only Emily seemed to understand what was going on.

Chatting with the store owner as he filled out her order, Mrs. Windsor heard someone rush in and shout: "You'll never guess what I saw!"

"What's going on?" the clerk in the storeroom called out. "Is it a fire?"

When Alice Windsor saw the object of the townsfolks' focus, she steeled herself, opened the door, and headed across the street. Relieved, the girls ran to meet her. Aunt Alice took Efuah by the hand and, slightly flushed but dignified, led her girls back to the store to complete the shopping.

⚓

Uncle Andy was furious. Sitting around the kitchen table, the family discussed how best to help the community learn to accept people who looked so different. Miss Abigail, his older sister, explained to Emily that the townsfolk weren't evil people and

were far from ignorant, but they were guided by the only information they had ever been given – that is, that people who were
Chinese or African, or from lands on the other side of the world,
were heathens.

"Our people are taught that it's the duty of a good Christian
to rescue heathens and save their souls," Aunt Alice told them.
Emily stated that they were already Christians. In fact, she boasted that she was both Catholic and Protestant, and that her sisters
went to both the Christian Science and the Union United
Congregational Church sunday schools.

Miss Abigail protested: "Going to church is not a social pas-
time!"

"Since when?" Uncle Andy retorted.

Pippa and Emily mulled the situation over in their bedroom.
"Wouldn't it be much wiser to ignore these people, if they mean
no harm? And if we stick to our good manners," Pippa added,
"God will stay in His heaven and all will be right with the
world."

Emily's resolve didn't last twenty-four hours. Two boys, who
came with their parents to visit, asked the girls if they knew
Tarzan and scratched their own armpits as though they were
apes.

Cautioned by Pippa, Emily ignored them. But she felt the sisters ought to work out some kind of code to deal with such children, who were not actually rude and never called them "nig-
gerblack," as the French kids in Montreal did.

"We need to know a secret language of our own. Otherwise,
we become victims of other people's ignorance," Pippa said,
echoing Torrie's caution.

Emily had the answer – pig Latin, a language common on the
streets of Little Burgundy, but quite unknown on the farms of the
Eastern Townships. Using it could keep people bewildered and at
bay. "Instead of saying 'give it to me,' you say, 'ivgay itay ootay
eemay.' See, it's a twist-around! You put the first part of the word

at the end, adding 'ay.' A cow is 'owcay' . . . a cat is 'atcay' . . . and if it's sick, it's 'icksay'! Understand?"

Patiently, Emily schooled Pippa to speak pig latin, but Pippa insisted on adding a few touches and twists of her own to mystify the language. Crucial phrases, such as "don't do that" or "we'll be found out," became simply "Ixnay!" When they decided to throw the sound "ob" between each syllable in a verb or name, even Uncle Andy didn't recognize himself as "Anobdy." Practising as they washed dishes or ran alongside Uncle Andy's wagon down the hayfield, helping to rake in the first crop, they developed speed and created tonal nuances in their secret "African" language.

Effie couldn't handle pig Latin at all. Her lisp got in the way. She couldn't spell anyway, and as she preferred animals to most people, except for Uncle Andy, she didn't need to talk. Her sisters were so competent, in fact, that all she had to do was nod her assent.

That summer, the Windsor household became, in a sense, an extended family. Aunt Alice grew quite accustomed to the girls. Miss Abigail was delighted to discover that they knew how to use a toothbrush and say prayers at night, that they stood up when elders entered the room, and, like the Windsor children when they were young, that they objected to having their hair brushed.

Efuah, the old collie dog, and Uncle Andy were inseparable. Her little hand tucked safely in his, she explored a beaver lodge, found a robin's nest, bathed a new-born calf, and learned how to drive the hay wagon.

One afternoon, to escape a visit from Reverend Carver, Pippa and Emily went exploring. At the western edge of the hay-field, beyond a gully, was a small forest. Deep inside, they discovered a sugarbush of magnificent maples, sweeping up to shadowy heights, and on the ground delicate ferns growing in the shade. "It's like a magic kingdom." They hugged each other in delight.

In the middle of this secret world nestled a high, tin-roofed sugaring-off shack made from square-cut logs. Puzzling over the separator and other sugar-making equipment, they crawled into the side lean-to where the wood was kept. At that time of year, it was empty except for a lantern hanging on a nail, an enormous steel pot – a relic of an older time – and a couple of stools. It was snug and private, a perfect little hideaway. Then, in the distance, the girls heard the bell ring for supper.

Racing back, they found to their dismay that Reverend Carver was staying for the evening meal. When Abigail came in all dressed in black, the three girls politely got to their feet and stood until she was seated. Reverend Carver, impressed by their manners, murmured, "Proper little Africans from the upper class – a chief's family, no doubt."

Mrs. Windsor asked the minister to say grace. He delivered a long and florid one, all about the Lord moving in mysterious ways to reward the faithful who struggle without recognition, and adding references to the heathens brought out of darkness into the light. A chorus of "Amens" followed, and the roast chicken was finally served. When Reverend Carver had departed after supper, and the girls had helped with the washing-up, they kissed Aunt Alice and started to climb the stairs to their room. As they passed the door to Miss Abigail's room, it opened. She invited them in. They hesitated, then timidly entered, pushed from behind by Emily.

This was obviously the room that Abigail had grown up in as a child and returned to as an adult – an odd mixture of oak furniture, Victoriana, dolls, and lots of embroidered mottos. Abigail laid aside the sampler she'd been embroidering and condescendingly opened an old tin locker-trunk, slowly and carefully. From it, she took out several photographs and wooden African artifacts, including a mask wrapped in some old printed fabric. The artifacts had a peculiar, acidy-mouldy smell that caused Pippa to wrinkle her nose.

Miss Abigail tensed. "Why, that's the natural smell of the earth where you come from. And this is the kind of bowl you ate out of."

Guardedly, Efuah asked, "What did we eat?"

Having gained their attention, Abigail handed them other

things, hoping against hope for a cultural response. She showed them a picture of herself teaching four native women how to wash themselves in the river without removing their clothing. "Don't you remember anything?"

Pippa, thoroughly bewildered, shook her head, avoiding the anxious watery eyes that, she realized, mirrored the burnt-out zeal of the frustrated aging former missionary. "Azycray," Emily explained quietly, hoping to comfort Effie, who seemed on the verge of tears.

Pippa picked out an ornately carved, long-toothed wooden Ghanaian comb, observing, in pig latin that it was do doubt designed to get through their woolly hair. But the sticky, spidery-mouldy feeling of the beautiful little moon-faced ebony-wood doll with a beaded necklace, but no legs, repelled her.

"Most of these things are really so strange – and so old. You should send them to a museum so people will know what 'once upon a time' used to be like," Pippa suggested. "The Royal Museum in Toronto would probably be glad to have them."

Miss Abigail's composure snapped. Pushing the artifacts out of sight, she hissed at the girls, "They're heathen idols, that's why you don't recognize them! Our Saviour, in His mercy, has allowed you to forget and deny your past."

Emily was about to protest, but found herself and her sisters being shooed out of the room. "Mercifully saving herself more anguish," Pippa commented, safe in their own room.

"She don't seem like Uncle Andy's sister at all," Effie observed. "She gets so cross!"

"She's probably had a thwarted love affair," Pippa said wisely. "That's why she's so crabby. Let's forgive her."

People of the township continued to be curious, but in rather charming ways. The Missionary Society organized separate fund-raising strawberry socials in Franklin Corners, Covey Hill, and Huntington, at which, after much urging, the children sang some half-remembered Negro spirituals. Emily had a naturally beautiful voice. Pippa's voice was neither as melodious as Emily's nor as raucous as Efuah's, but, blinded by their colour, no one seemed aware of the dissonance and the applause was enthusiastic.

July slipped happily away. They helped Uncle Andy and the farmhand, Maurice, with tasks around the farm, read books in their secret hideaway, and learned to embroider samplers with Miss Abigail.

Mid-August was the Eastern Townships' important annual country fair, with livestock auctions, produce contests, animal judging, baseball games, and potato-sack races, as well as family picnic baskets full of fried chicken, potato salad, baked ham, and fruit pies. Proceeds from the bake and jam sale would go to the missionary fund.

Bored at being the subject of both over-solicitous concern and supercilious smiles, Pippa and Emily wandered off to look for the United States border just before lunch. They had been told that one could see Vermont, with its soaring ski peaks, across the pasture. To prove to themselves that Canada was not really bounded by a three-thousand-mile fence – and, even more, to boast that they'd actually been in the United States – they decided to have a look at it, at least.

By the time they returned to the picnic site, the Windsors' lunch was over. Miss Abigail, having no intention of unpacking the basket again, ordered them to do without food as punishment for having wandered off. Exhausted as well as hungry, Pippa and Emily threw themselves down on a grassy hill and watched other children stuffing themselves.

Jody, the little freckled fat boy who lived on the next farm, ventured up, munching a sandwich, a chicken leg in his other hand. Pippa and Emily looked yearningly at him and he suspiciously at them. Finally finishing the chicken, he smacked his lips, then ambled off without a word. Two minutes later, he was back. "Want some?" he offered, holding out two juicy chicken legs.

Pippa seriously considered the gift for a few seconds, but remembering Miss Abigail's admonishing words, shook her head. Emily didn't waver – she grabbed the chicken legs and handed one to Pippa. "I'm so hungry I could even eat you!" she told the plump little boy. When she reached the bone, she ordered: "Don't stand there! Go get some more!"

Jody scampered off. He looked back at the two girls grinning at him, their jaws munching in slow motion. He ran straight over the hill to his mother who, rather than interrupt her stream of gossip, pushed another piece of fried chicken into his hand and shooed him away. It couldn't have been easy for him to give up a juicy, golden chicken thigh, but weighing the girls' strange behaviour against the loneliness of always being ignored or called Fatty by the other children, he decided in their favour. He came trotting back up the hill, holding his "tithe" in front of him as he puffed along.

Recognizing a good thing when she saw one, Emily took Jody's offering and sent him back again for more, suggesting that he include some of his mother's famous chocolate cake. "And don't you dare tell on us or something dreadful will happen to you!" she said ominously.

The third trip yielded the fat courier nothing, for by that time his mother had exhausted her neighbour's store of gossip and was changing the baby's diapers. Tired, a tiny bit frightened, and beginning to weary of the new game, he sauntered back to inform the girls, "There ain't no more."

Efuah had joined her sisters. Not wanting to share the last morsel of chicken, Emily threatened Jody anew. His legs behaved like limp spaghetti as he struggled over the hill, anxious to put ground between himself and those Africans. At Sunday School, the teacher had told him that the girls' ancestors used to eat people, and Emily *had* murmured something about his being so nice and fat. Sweat broke out all over his body.

His mother, engaged with a new gossiper, was completely indifferent to his terror and refused to give him more food. Jody decided to tackle his Sunday School teacher, but she, knowing him to be generally overfed, sent him off, ignoring his stuttering pleas. He walked slowly towards the hollow, rehearsing his speech, but when he saw Emily eyeing him, grinning wickedly, he flew back to his mother, blubbering that the African girls were going to eat him if he didn't give them more food.

Absent-mindedly, Jody's mother patted his bottom. "Yeah, yeah, and if you don't stop annoying me, I'll lend them my pot to boil you in!" With that, she fell into a lively discussion with her friend as to whether Africans really did eat people. This was too much for poor Jody, who fainted dead away.

The next morning, the telephone party line was buzzing with his incredible tale. By noon, stories were being exchanged, punctuated with case histories of missing missionaries; as the townsfolk reminded each other, leopards did not change their spots, and cannibals never became vegetarians.

Back at the Windsor farm, Aunt Alice and Miss Abigail anxiously pressed extra helpings onto the girls' plates, to Uncle Andy's amusement and amazement. "Cool it," he advised his wife, and left for the annual Farm Marketing Board's week-long seminar at Guelph University. Aunt Alice didn't really believe her guests would revert to being cannibals, but dared not take a chance.

Pippa and Emily were triumphant, and began to speak in "African" whenever they were in public, even at the dinner table. Soon the entire neighbourhood was in a welter of confusion and speculation about the half-savages at the Windsor farm, and Emily delighted in playing to their suspicions. Whenever she wanted an apple that another girl had, she'd smack her lips and eye the girl appraisingly. If these hints were insufficient, Emily would saunter up and poke the girl's arms thoughtfully, while asking the quivering child's weight. No one would run anywhere near Efuah at races, so she walked off with all the prizes at the Athelston Athletic Day, the week after the picnic.

⚡

One morning, Jody's parents were arguing loudly – as usual – because Jody refused to go outside. He claimed he was terrified of being eaten by the girls. His mother was sympathetic: "What if it's true?" But his father, a thin, defeated-looking man with a mean streak, thought it was ridiculous. "I won't have him skulking about the house all day," he said roughly, and dragged Jody outside, closing the door behind. Then he went into the barn, foraged for his bottle, and started drinking home-brewed moonshine.

Jody, keeping a wary eye out for the girls, sat down by the boundary fence, took out an apple, and started looking for worms in it. He didn't see Efuah come to her side of the fence until she spoke. "Hello." Jody jumped in terror.

Efuah apologized. "It's just a joke, Jody. We're not really cannibals. We just find it fun to fool everybody."

He calmed down, and the two shy children, about the same age, decided to be friends. Efuah invited Jody to come and play in the secret hideaway. When she appeared with him at the sugaring shack, the other two girls apologized as well, although Emily couldn't resist adding, "We won't eat you – unless we get *really* hungry."

"What are we going to do with him?" Pippa asked. "Could we initiate him as an African? Some North Africans look like him."

"Well, as long as he's not going to be a missionary!" Emily insisted. Crestfallen, Jody asked, "Couldn't we pretend I was a Mohawk? I mean, a redskin? I've always wanted to be an Indian."

Pippa took charge. "Let's make this a spirit or long house. I saw a picture of one once in a *National Geographic*. We need to plan a secret ceremony place."

Four little minds took wing. No one could get through chores fast enough to return to the shack. Jody saw their hideaway as an Iroquois long house. Emily considered it a spirit house. Pippa saw it as a magic medieval castle, with the woodshed as a dungeon. Efuah, who preferred the wide-open fields, rarely visited, unless she had a bird with a broken wing to nurse, or kittens to save from drowning.

Increasingly, Pippa included Jody in her activities. He made a wonderful audience, held spellbound by her recollections of their royal African childhood. He was also a good handyman, willing to dig a moat around the shack.

The girls gave Jody importance in the eyes of the other children, since he, in turn, could keep them spellbound, boasting of his escapades with "those African princesses." Jody was no longer just the "fat boy."

One Friday evening, about a week after the three-county picnic, Miss Abigail, accusing Pippa of breaking a crock in the pantry, sent her to bed without supper. Normally, that was standard punishment for a fib or for disobedience, but these were not normal times.

Pippa hadn't broken the crock, Emily was furious and insisted on joining her sister in protest. Efuah, in tears over the affair, nobly abandoned her supper to support Pippa's cause, but she was soon starving. To pacify her, Emily gathered some chokecherries from the tree just outside the bedroom window.

Sleep came soon. In the morning, Pippa insisted that they maintain their fast until Miss Abigail apologized. At noon, while Pippa was half-asleep with a migraine headache, Emily sneaked down to get some milk. Finding none in the pantry, she poured some of the apple cider from the old wooden keg into a clean flower vase.

Tiptoeing back up to the bedroom, she shared her drink,

giving the largest portion to little Effie. Delighted with this refreshing liquid, Emily refilled the vase and filled up their porcelain water pitcher for good measure. When the supper bell rang, all three girls were fast asleep. Neither Uncle Andy nor Aunt Alice could wake them up.

The next morning, Sunday, Emily woke at dawn. Hearing the cows ambling in from the pasture, she woke the others and they hurriedly dressed so they could eat with Uncle Andy and the farmhand, and then help with the milking. As the womenfolk didn't get up until six, it was a treat for the girls to have breakfast with the men, for both Uncle Andy and Maurice told them great tall tales. Morning was usually their favourite time. Even though it was early, Jody was on his side of the fence, waiting for them to appear.

On the way to the barn, Pippa found a tiny dead sparrow that had fallen from a nest. Deserting Uncle Andy and the cows, the children knelt beside it in sympathy. Deciding it deserved a decent funeral, Pippa raced back to the house for the Windsor family Bible. She ordered Effie to search the barn for a trowel to dig a tiny grave, and sent Emily to borrow a sharp carving knife from the kitchen to whittle a cross.

Effie called across the field to Jody to invite him to join the funeral ceremony. Accordingly, he went to search his barn for a shoebox. Miss Abigail, who had seen Emily saunter out with the carving knife, heard Effie announce cheerfully, "Jody's here!" Suspecting that the girls hadn't eaten a morsel of food for thirty-six hours, and petrified at the prospect of fat little Jody with her unfed, heathen house-guests, she simply froze, like Lot's wife.

The girls gleefully sang all four verses of the funeral dirge, "Shall We Gather at the River," and taught Jody to recite part of Tennyson's mournful "Crossing the Bar." After the bird's funeral, all four picked fresh flowers to place on the mound, wiped away their tears, and, forgetting that Uncle Andy was haying in the north pasture, trekked off to their spirit house to read *Hiawatha*.

At eleven, Jody's mother telephoned to ask if the Windsors had seen her son. He'd not been home since before breakfast. "Those girls are always trying to lure him over for strange heathen ceremonies involving Indian feathers and such," she whined.

⚊

Efuah, not up to playing Minnie-Ha-Ha because her tummy was aching, was allowed to go back to the house. On the way to the bedroom, she leaned over the stairwell to tell Miss Abigail that she had a tummy-ache and that her bowels were threatening to run like water. Instead of enlisting sympathy, this announcement seemed to add an element of frenzy to her immediate demand on the telephone: "Clear the line." Efuah continued to struggle up the stairs and, after three visits to the toilet, felt well enough to lie down.

The strange fears, the half-suspicions, the coincidences were more than Aunt Alice could bear. The Willows had no phone, but she remembered the girls saying that their mother worked at the Westmount Y. The manager there put her through to a "Mistress Amelia Hall," who, after inquiring what the problem was, muttering, "Enough is enough," guaranteed that someone from the family would be at the Windsor farm before the day was done.

When Efuah awoke in the attic room, its dormer windows reflecting the low-lying western sun, she saw Pippa and Emily, trying bravely not to cry as their mother practised her preferred method of dealing with children who misbehaved – a spanking on a bare bottom bent over her lap.

"Putting people on is one thing, but scaring them half to death is another! Have you any idea what it costs in gas to come down here? A month of Emily's high school fees – that's what!" Marion continued to fume. "Now, all three of you must apologize to Mrs. Windsor. But *only* to Mrs. Windsor. I'll listen to your explanations on the way home. Now, go on downstairs," she

instructed Pippa and Emily. "And while you're there, collect anything that's in the wash. Effie, you stay here and help me pack."

Bottoms stinging, noses sniffing, Pippa and Emily dried their
tears and left the room. Marion took the suitcases out of the clos-
et. While emptying out the drawers of the dresser, she came across
an envelope, so creamy in texture that she stopped to look at it
curiously. It was addressed to Pippa. "What elegant handwriting!"
she acknowledged. "I wonder who . . . ?" But her sense of deco-
rum would not allow her to pry. She finished packing, then went
down to check on the other two girls, instructing Efuah to bring
her own bag down.

As Marion strode onto the side porch outside the farmhouse
kitchen, carrying the luggage, she heard Mrs. Windsor reading
aloud to Pippa and Emily from a letter she held in one hand. It
was written on the same, creamy notepaper as the envelope.
Marion listened, feeling increasingly uneasy.

"'You'll find them full of spirit and rather inventive,'" Aunt
Alice read. Then, speaking directly to the girls, she chided, "Well,
your mother *did* warn me. But not about everything!"

Marion, her senses on full alert, moved forward. "That sounds
like my letter, but it doesn't *look* like it. It's not even my handwriting!" she said, not realizing she was speaking aloud.

"Oh, yes!" Aunt Alice hastened to assure her. "This is the letter you mailed from Montreal in June, describing the girls. I must
say, you do have beautiful penmanship, Mrs. Willow."

Marion reached for the letter. Aunt Alice, a bit perplexed,
reluctantly gave it up. Pippa, realizing that something was terribly
wrong, elbowed Emily. Quickly, they took the suitcases across the
yard to Otis, waiting in his uncle's green Chevrolet parked in the
drive.

Aunt Alice's puzzlement turned to consternation as Marion
concentrated on the letter. When Pippa came back onto the
porch to get another suitcase, her mother turned to her. "Pippa,
what has happened? This isn't . . . ?"

"Mother, it no longer matters," Pippa reassured her. "Aunt Alice has forgiven us. Let's go before it gets dark," she urged.

Marion looked at Pippa for a moment with fire in her eyes, then, hoisting the last suitcase, headed down the stairs and into the yard, her face flushed with embarrassment and chagrin, the sparks in her eyes dissolving into mistiness.

"You bested them," Otis said to Emily with a conspiratorial wink as he packed the suitcases into the trunk. "I'm mighty proud of you!"

Otis's remark provoked Marion into a rare indiscretion. "Otis Thompson! If you say things like that to my girls, how will I ever be able to teach them the fine line between not being a victim and yet not trampling on other people's sensibilities? When you take that attitude, you're as bad as Miss Delacourt!" She stopped abruptly, wiped her eyes, and slipped into the front seat of the car. Otis tried to look contrite while fitting the last suitcase into the trunk.

The girls ran over to kiss Aunt Alice good-bye. She hugged them back tightly en masse, saying: "Good-bye, my dears. It's been wonderful having you here! And not to worry. We've all learned a lesson."

The girls walked slowly back towards the car where Marion and Otis were sitting in the front seat, silent but tense. Just then, Uncle Andy came out of the barn and, seeing them ready to leave, hurried down the lane towards the car, carrying three jars of maple syrup in a shallow basket. The girls rushed to him. Putting the basket down, he hugged each one tightly, lifting little Effie up off the ground when it was her turn.

"Uncle Andy!" Effie asked. "Promise you'll tend the little bird's grave for us?"

"I promise, Cleopatra, if you promise to come again. Come back next spring for the 'thugaring off,'" Uncle Andy said, mimicking her lisp fondly.

The girls scrambled into the back seat of the car. Picking the basket up again, Uncle Andy crossed to the car and passed it into the back seat. He put one ruddy hand on the car door and gently placed the other on Marion's shoulder for a moment. "Good-bye to all of you," he said. "Come back soon, you hear?"

Just as the old green Chevrolet revved up to pull out onto the drive, Jody came running across the field, carrying an old wire birdcage. Proudly, Jody climbed over the fence and approached, wordlessly offering the cage to the girls. Inside was a little broken-winged bird, cheeping faintly. A tiny dish, stuck between two wires, was filled with chokecherries for it to eat. The girls smiled happily, while Marion shook her head in mock exasperation.

At last, the car pulled away from the Windsor barnyard, leaving Aunt Alice and Uncle Andy watching and waving. The car moved slowly off down the driveway, past Jody, who was running as fast as he could through the field until the car began to pick up speed. Puffing, he waved a final disconsolate good-bye. Efuah squirmed around in the back seat so she could wave back vigorously.

Fretting in the front seat beside Otis, Marion murmured, "Do you know what your *friend* did to my letter? Well, just wait till I finally come face-to-face with that . . . that interfering woman!"

CHAPTER XVII

Torrie Delacourt, feeling rather exotic in dragon-patterned silk pajamas, relaxed full-length on her chaise longue facing the mirror-panelling in the front room. The music of Duke Ellington's "Mood Indigo" spinning on her gramophone filtered the late summer air with arabesque sounds.

She was entertaining Edmond Thompson and they were both in good spirits. Edmond was drinking a glass of lager beer, but a bottle of aquavit stood temptingly on the table near him. Torrie drank her aquavit from a small glass, chasing it with sips of Edmond's beer.

"Still think you in Europe, don't you?" teased Edmond, picking up the bottle. "Ak-wa-vite," he pronounced slowly as he read the label.

"It's Danish, and it's called aquavit," Torrie commented. "It's far better with Tuborg lager. Ah! Lunch at a *krol* in Copenhagen! Someday, Edmond, we must go there."

"What if your Norwegian lover is still about?" Edmond trusted he sounded sarcastic rather than jealous.

"No chance. He disappeared one day in early spring, the day the Nazis invaded Norway... March the tenth, 1940. He and that Quisling." Torrie's dark, almost purple eyes moistened. Her voice seemed to come from faraway. "I still don't understand it. Lars was such a quiet man . . . such a gentleman."

"Gentleman? He picked you out of the chorus line of the Cotton Club in Harlem, then took you to Europe!"

"Edmond, you don't understand," Torrie protested. "He fell in love with me. We had ten wonderful years together," she added wistfully.

"He bought you! He kept you!"

"Yes, he did – and I was worth it!" Torrie's temper began to rise. "Oh, Edmond! Why get so uptight about my years in Europe? How else could I have met people like Paul Robeson, or Bricktop and Josephine Baker in Paris? Being someone's mistress in Europe is a vocation, not a shame."

Torrie's voice started to take on a more nostalgic tone. "Lars was a travelling sales representative for a Swedish firm of 'widget' makers. His wife stayed in Oslo, directing Ibsen plays. Apparently, she hated to travel. But because of it, Lars and I were able to stay in lovely old medieval towns near the European capitals where he did business."

Laughing, Torrie got up and turned the record over. The soothing music of "Body and Soul" began to reclaim the romantic mood. Selecting a photograph album, she sashayed over to Edmond's chair and, leaning over, began to explain the photographs.

"That's Paul Robeson and Essie, and that's me going into the Hermitage Museum in Leningrad." Torrie slowly turned the pages over, reliving those cherished moments. "Paul must have had an intuition about the hardware that Lars sold. He warned me to keep my own bank account. That was in thirty-six – years ago. Look, here's Bricktop."

Edmond laughed. "Heard about that red hair of hers! They say she wouldn't allow Negroes into her nightclub in Paris."

"True. I mean . . . with exceptions." Torrie felt she should defend the indefensible, arrogant blues singer who was a close friend of Josephine Baker. "She catered to the Prince of Wales crowd. Then, after he and Wallis Simpson married, Bricktop threw a fabulous party for them. When Paris fell, I think she went to Mexico."

Torrie's elegantly manicured finger paused on another photograph. "That's Langston Hughes, with the poet Claude McKay in Paris."

The doorbell rang, disturbing their concentration.

"Who can that be?"

Edmond went to the window and looked out, careful not to disturb the sheer curtains. "Good God!" he cried. "It's Marion Willow!"

Torrie immediately hid the glass of beer and the bottle of aquavit. "Mrs. Willow? Why?"

The doorbell rang again. Torrie took a deep breath and started to move towards the front door. "Maybe my application to join the Coloured Ladies Club has been accepted," she gloated.

Edmond was aghast. "I've got to get away!"

Torrie turned, hissing in sudden fury, "Then hide!"

"No!" Edmond retorted. "I'm a gentleman – I'll leave." He disappeared down the hall towards the rear of the apartment just as Torrie opened the front door.

Marion Willow, modest in her tweed skirt and freshly ironed white blouse, was standing on the landing, a pencil and sheet of paper in one hand. "I thought you weren't in. I was just about to leave you a note," she stammered, as though sorry the door had opened.

"Oh no, I . . . Do come in, Mrs. Willow."

The sound of the back door shutting could be heard faintly. Marion momentarily reacted, then, noticing the photograph album open on the chaise longue, asked, "Oh, do you have company?"

Torrie, smiling, quipped what she hoped was a joke. "Just the milkman."

Believing her, and relieved, Marion complained, "Oh, I can't

get mine to use the back door and come through the shed. Even
the iceman comes up the front stairs and drips icewater all down
my hall!"

Realizing that Marion had missed the joke, Torrie smiled
smugly. The woman was far too earnest. Torrie wound up the victrola and discreetly hid the photograph album. "Perhaps you'd like
to hear this new recording?" she asked. "It's a new classic by the
baritone Rolland Hays."

"No, thank you. I didn't come to be entertained."

Torrie indicated the Queen Anne chair for Marion, then sat
down in a straight-backed chair. For a moment, there was only
silence in the room.

"Can I offer you some tea?" Torrie asked.

"No, thank you."

"You might be interested to know that since I've applied to
become a member of the club, I've unpacked some of the delicate
Dresden china teacups I managed to collect in Europe."

Marion was suddenly able to focus. Looking very uncomfortable, she admitted, "I came about something else."

Torrie didn't intend to be helpful. "Pray tell."

"Miss Delacourt . . . did you rewrite a letter of mine last June
addressed to the Windsor family in the Eastern Townships?"

"Yes, I did. Why?"

"You admit it! But why?"

"You mean, why do I admit it? Or why did I do it?" Marion
did not respond. "Well," Torrie continued, "first, you'll find that I
never lie."

"You rewrote my letter, taking out the photograph and omit-
ting to tell the Windsors that the children were coloured."

"You didn't know how to tell them either," Torrie flung back.
"I knew how much you wanted them to have a happy, safe summer away from the street urchins in Montreal. Forewarning the
Windsors didn't seem wise. Children should be judged on who
they are, not on what they look like – don't you think?"

Marion glared at Torrie for a moment, trembling with suppressed emotion. To give herself time, or perhaps to regain control over her feelings, she moved over to the bookcase, looking aimlessly at the books on the shelves. When she began to speak, it was almost as if she were thinking out loud.

"You're from the States where there are lots of Negroes, but when you're a minority here in Canada, it's easy to develop a sense of inferiority. I don't want my girls to become victims of other people's stupidity or outright bigotry. How can I help them to grow up with self-confidence and pride, when to be coloured is to be at the bottom of the ladder?"

To cover her emotion, Marion pulled out a book of poems and thumbed through it, stopping as she reached one she recognized. "Langston Hughes," she murmured, then read aloud, "*Life for me ain't been no crystal stair. It's had tacks in it, and splinters, and boards torn up. And places with no carpet on the floor – bare.*"

As Marion read, Torrie joined her by the bookcase and recited from memory. "*But all the time I'se been a-climbin' on. And reachin' landin's, and turnin' corners, and sometimes goin' in the dark where there ain't been no light. So don't you turn back. Don't you set down on the steps 'cause you finds it's kinder hard. Don't you fall now – for I'se still goin', honey, I'se still climbin', and life for me ain't been no crystal stair.*"

Torrie took the book from Marion's unresisting hand and put it back on the shelf. Marion stared at her in wonderment.

"You came here to give me hell, didn't you?" Torrie asked. "I shouldn't have interfered, but... but I admire your kids! And while you're busily providing them with the breeding that's sorely needed in our working-class families, I can give them the street smarts they need to survive."

Marion remembered Alice Windsor's anguish. "Street smarts! The children terrorized Mrs. Windsor – and God knows who else!"

"So what?" Torrie shrugged dismissively. "Missionary zeal terrorized Africans for centuries."

"That's no excuse."

"It's a reality. It's what makes white folks so schizophrenic. They're told they're superior – and they're afraid to discover they're not!"

"I can't cope with you." Marion threw up her hands. "Just leave my girls alone!"

"But I could give them – Philippa, in particular – a sense of identity. She needs to know more about her own people, her own culture. She gobbles up British literature as fast as she can get it, and she's a wonderfully imaginative child. But if you don't know who you are, where you're from, you have to take other people's word for it. Please, even if it's just Philippa. Let me share these books." Torrie made a broad, all-encompassing gesture.

Marion looked past the bookshelves at the African sculptures and exotic textiles in the apartment. Slowly, she began to relent. Her shoulders relaxed, her hands unclenched. "Not Emily, nor Efuah.

"Mind you," she hedged her ambivalence a bit, "I think it's . . . I mean, I realize that letting Pippa read philosophers, like Dubois and Frederick Douglass, and learn what our poets have written would expose her to more of her father Kofi's world, his belief in the power of the ancestors. Maybe she'll even want to go to Ghana someday to meet his family!

"But only Pippa, and only to share your knowledge of Negro culture. Not your, excuse the word, 'tactics'! I intend my girls to use their education, not their bodies, to escape the trap of poverty and consignment."

Torrie stood, hurt. "You don't approve of me?"

Marion backed to the front door, opened it, then turned back. "I can't pass judgement. I don't really know you . . . but I don't think I want to." She walked out, closing the door gently behind her.

A few days later, Edmond Thompson, in a well-cut, glen-plaid suit, standing at the coat-check counter at Rockhead's Paradise, nervously turned a grey fedora in his slim fingers and waited for Torrie. Beyond him was the main room of the nightclub, with its small tables, dance floor, dimly lit bar, and jazz orchestra, playing Ellington's "Take the A Train." The coat-check girl took hats from a couple of navy officers in spotless white uniforms, who were then greeted by the hostess, Torrie Delacourt.

Dressed in elegant maroon velvet with a lace collar, Torrie ignored Edmond and addressed the officers in immaculate Parisian French. "*Bonsoir. Est-ce que je peux vous aider? C'est votre première visite, n'est-ce pas?*" They bristled with pleasure. She escorted them to a ringside table.

The club's clientele was mostly white, but not exclusively. There were businessmen, a number of soldiers and sailors on leave, two not-so-subtle gangster types, and a gaggle of American tourists searching for the Montreal of Prohibition times. Men watched as Torrie passed, but never breached club etiquette. She exuded an aura of sophistication that made the patrons admire her, without daring to take liberties.

At a table by the dance floor, Otis Thompson and his friend, Rodney Brown, were being served by an alluring Black wait-ress. Rodney, feeling cocky in his zoot suit, snaked one arm around her waist. "Sister, you sure sportin' one fine brown frame!"

The waitress deftly brushed him off. "Don't touch the mer-chandise!"

Otis, in his more conservative hand-me-down flannel trousers and tweed jacket, missed both Rodney's comment and the waitress's snappy putdown. He was preoccupied, watching Torrie as she walked smoothly back to the entrance where his Uncle Edmond stood, waiting for her.

Edmond quickly reached out and, holding Torrie by the wrist, moved to one side. "I'm not staying," he explained.

"Then why come?" Torrie asked coolly.

Edmond mustered up his courage. "Torrie. I . . . we've talked about this before." Taking a clean hanky out of his breast pocket, he wiped his forehead. Torrie stiffened, waited for him to continue.

"Don't toy with Mrs. Willow," Edmond said. "She's a lady."

Torrie winced. Then she squared her shoulders and raised her chin. "Meaning I'm not?"

Flustered, Edmond sputtered, "That's not what I meant."

With great dignity, but coldly, Torrie retorted, "Edmond. Piss or get off the pot."

Edmond held up his hand to calm her down. "Torrie," he said admonishingly.

"Edmond, why do you hanker after that wishy-washy widow? She's afraid of men, and thinks that because she's bringing up her girls as well-bred young ladies, no one will ever call them nigger."

Torrie's moist eyes and suddenly gentle smile reflected her true concern for the Willow girls. "If that's all she's afraid of . . ."

Then she stiffened again and her eyes hardened a little. "Well, she's wrong! Someone's got to teach them about reality or they'll never survive to be the 'emancipated women' she intends them to be." Her hand went up to cover her face. "And now she's adopted that half-breed! She needs help!"

"Not yours, Torrie. And she's too proud to ask for help. Look, let's talk about it when you get home."

Torrie momentarily recaptured her mischievous mood, saying coquettishly, "My place . . . or yours?"

"You know I no longer have a key to yours."

"*Tant pis*," Torrie said dismissively.

Edmond was angry again. "I'm warning you, Torrie. Desist! They're her children!"

"Not Emily." Torrie looked at him speculatively. "Tell me, Edmond. Where were you, that night in 1929, when she was conceived?"

Edmond was taken aback for a moment, then his face closed down. Without another word, he jammed on his grey fedora and started down the stairs. Torrie watched him go, her pain visible. But, as new customers came up the stairs towards her, she resumed her elegant mask.

CHAPTER XVIII

E mily's "bad blood" began to show itself within weeks of their holiday in the Eastern Townships – their "African summer," as Pippa renamed it. It wasn't measles, wasn't mumps, wasn't the flu – and no matter what herbal remedies Amelia Hall sent home for the child, Emily just couldn't seem to summon up the energy to do more than amble listlessly to school and then home to bed. By mid-October, Marion decided that forcing her to attend her classes was unjustified punishment. Pippa collected the lessons from Emily's teachers and patiently fed her the information, along with food from her supper tray.

Dr. Marcus Cohen at the Children's Outdoor Clinic prescribed iron injections. "How can a child of fourteen have tired blood?" Marion asked.

Old Dr. Valliers, after ordering X-rays of Emily's chest, ruled out tuberculosis, but seemed to agree with Vashti Dobson's suspicion about sickle cell. "Anemia," he said, calling for more blood tests. "Leukemia?" he questioned on Emily's medical chart.

"Isn't that cancer of the blood? Is there any cure?"

"We'll just have to wait and see."

Marion was absolutely shattered. Poppa Dad waited with her in the out-patient corridor for the results of Emily's third set of blood tests. "What about blood transfusions?" he asked. "We could easily round up any number of donors. What about a private doctor?" he suggested to assuage Marion's grief and depression. "I've some money put aside."

Marion insisted on taking Emily back home. The social worker read the official Children's Aid Society guidelines and threatened to wash her hands of the matter if Mrs. Willow didn't leave Emily in the old, greystone Children's Hospital at the corner of St. Antoine and Guy. "It's not far from your home and there are visiting hours every evening." But Marion was unwilling to leave Emily all alone in an atmosphere where the staff felt it was "just a matter of time."

Poppa Dad signed off his normal and usually lucrative Chicago run in order to have time to help Marion, who, in the past year, had still not been able to contact Dominic. Maybe, she felt, he could provide the clue to her illness. Evening after evening, the old green Chevy prowled from respite centres to old folks homes, from Brewery Missions to alms hostels, looking for Dominic.

Marushka, fluent in French and near a telephone during the day, dogged the municipal bureaucracy. "Surely, a Dominic Capriccio is somewhere in your files? Yes? Well, what forwarding address do you have?"

Otis questioned friends, fellow railroad workers, and bartenders at Rockhead's who had access to the minor Mafia circle, but no one seemed to know what had happened to the old Italian fruit vendor.

⚓

Torrie was the one who finally found him. Pragmatic, no-nonsense Torrie traced his name through a list of paupers' graves. Edmond hadn't the courage to tell Marion, whose grief at his apparent loss was so deep she could barely hide it when she was with Emily or the girls. Dominic had died soon after Emily had found a home with the Willows. Torrie suggested to Edmond that they have Dominic reburied and a tombstone carved before they inform Marion. In their eagerness to deny that Emily might not make it, her friends had all joined in a conspiracy to protect Marion, leaving her free to concentrate on Emily. Marion continued to go to work, both at Mademoiselle Laroche's apartment on Côte des Neiges and at the Y. Even Dame Orlova took turns looking in on Emily, bringing her hot, iron-rich beet borscht.

But, by mid-November, Emily had to be hospitalized. Her weight had dropped, her freckles faded. Beside herself with worry, Marion focused on the West African prayer that she remembered Kofi invoking when Efuah was born. "If you have come," he had chanted, holding the baby out to the sun, "then you must stay with us."

"Since you have come," Marion whispered to Emily, lying lethargically in the sterile hospital bed, "then you must stay with us."

The last week in November, Emily seemed to rally and was allowed to rest in the sunroom. Full of excitement, Pippa and Effie, who were not allowed into the hospital, dragged wooden boxes to the flat space under the sunroom's west window to peer in at Emily. She saw them and walked slowly to the casement window.

In sign language, the girls told her everything that was happening. Pippa hugged Effie to demonstrate that Otis and Marushka were still in love. Effie stole Pippa's hat and hid it behind her back to indicate that Maurice Vachon was still up to his old tricks. But when Pippa tried to imitate Torrie Delacourt's walk down the long, winding stairway of her home, they fell off their boxes laughing, and the nurse, hearing Emily hiccuping with laughter, and thinking that she had gone into convulsions, ordered her back to bed.

There is no life, truth, intelligence or substance in matter.
All is infinite mind and its infinite manifestations,
For God is All-in-all.
Spirit is real and eternal. Matter is mortal error.

Marion recited this creed over and over again.

Denise Laroche wheeled herself into her tiny kitchen. "Marion, have you become a Christian Scientist?"

"I'm trying to be. I need to be. How else can I save Emily's life?"

"Mind over matter," Mademoiselle Laroche murmured. "It can be dangerous, you know that," she warned, her French-accented English trembling with concern. "Isn't Emily a provincial ward?"

"The child's technically a total orphan. I'm responsible for her." Marion had to hold onto the counter to keep from trembling. "The doctors have given up. They say it's just a matter of time." Marion's fist hit the countertop defiantly. "She has to live! She *will* live!"

Her employer wheeled herself closer and took Marion's hand. "My aunt is one of those Christian Science practitioners." Suddenly, she giggled a low throaty musical scale. "Her husband's a Christian Science dentist. I drew the line at him – there IS pain!" Again, she began to laugh softly, sharing with Marion her memory of his pulling her tooth when she was twelve, denying that pain was real. The gentle laughter cemented their empathy. "Don't let them talk you out of your belief. She'll live – you'll see," Denise said. "And to help, I'll ask my priest to say a mass for her."

All the way along Westmount Boulevard on her way to the Y, Marion murmured,

There is no life, truth, intelligence or substance in matter.
All is infinite mind and its infinite manifestations,
For God is All-in-all.

Across St. Stephen's Park she marched, declaring under her breath,

Spirit is immortal Truth; Matter is mortal error . . . .

"Did they call from the hospital?" she asked Vashti as she changed into working clothes in the linen room at the Y.

"No news is good news, honey. Jes' relax. Silent ribbas run deep," she added to console Marion.

"*Matter is unreal and temporal,*" Marion chanted loudly. "Oh dear God, give me strength. Give me back Emily," she pleaded as she vacuumed the long corridor rug, certain that no one could hear her.

Vashti waddled over, turned off the machine, and hugged her. "Go home, child. Ah kin finish dis."

Marion found no news at home, just two little children making newspaper flowers for her to take to the hospital. How could Emily have wormed her way into our hearts so completely, she wondered, unless God, in His infinite wisdom, had meant her to be there? Her mind repeated Kofi's African invocation: "If you have come, then you must stay with us."

Her friend, the unflappable Mrs. Brock, was herself a Christian Science practitioner. "Perhaps," Marion thought, "if Otis is willing to stay home this evening, I'll go and visit. I'll bake her some gingerbread."

⊞

To ease into their session, Angela Brock suggested that Marion describe Otis. Marion explained that he had a mercurial personality, and carried around a load of pent-up rage and frustration. "Otis is capable of spending an afternoon with the girls, being gentle, sweet, and funny, and then going directly to Rockhead's where, I suspect, he vents his spleen.

"He usually just rants against the uncivilized passengers he's forced to bow and scrape to, the 'Uncle Tom' attitude of the older porters like his uncle, and the unbearable restrictions of his life." She paused. "His anger is justified, of course, but I fear Otis is the proverbial 'accident looking for a place to happen.'"

When Mrs. Brock didn't indicate agreement or disapproval, Marion felt the urge to explain. "An acquaintance of mine – you know, the lady I insisted that the club reconsider for membership – suspects he has a high IQ. He's devoured most of my second-hand books, as well as the writers on Black history that he borrows from Miss Delacourt. He and Pippa both read voraciously." Marion paused. "What else can I say?"

Angela Brock smiled and nodded, indicating that Marion should explore further her reactions to Otis.

"True, he's taught himself auto mechanics and keeps his uncle's ancient Chevy in perfect repair," Marion continued. "He amazes me, really. I think part of his enormous frustration stems from knowing that as a young man who doesn't come from a well-to-do family, he's denied any opportunity to study formally, or to pursue a respectable trade or career without being beholden in perpetuity.

"I used to think we women had it hard, but now I think Black men suffer a 'double whammy.' White men, fearing Negroes' sexual prowess, deny them competitive jobs, while we women turn inward from them, through sisterhood and children, yet judge them as the adults they've never been allowed to be. Inside, I feel an infinite sorrow for Otis, yet sorrow is a precious treasure shown only to friends . . . and I fear to show him my sadness lest it undermine him." Marion sighed into silence.

"It's just as well, my dear," Mrs. Brock said, and began to lead Marion to think more positive thoughts about both Otis and Emily. Closing her Science and Health, she advised Marion of her prerogatives: "Try to replace mortality with immortality when thinking of Emily, and silence discord with harmony when dealing with Otis's emotions."

"Easier said than done," Marion's weary spirit thought, yet she needed a lifeline. *If you speak,* she remembered reading in one of the books of Senegalese proverbs that her mother's father had left, *speak to her who understands you.* For a brief moment, she thought of Torrie Delacourt, but just as quickly rejected the thought. Her life was complicated enough!

CHAPTER XIX

E mily could hear the night nurse singing snatches of rollicking shanty songs half-under her breath as she trudged through the quiet wards, tucking in blankets, feeling foreheads, willing the children to sleep. Suddenly, stomach cramps made Emily groan. She'd been to the bathroom twice, but couldn't force a bowel movement. Now the pain was searing. Nurse Jeannie hurried over. Just as suddenly, Emily's pain ebbed away, but in its place a warm, thick liquid oozed from between her legs. "I'm so sorry," Emily said, her lackluster eyes apologizing to the nurse. "I couldn't help it. I'm afraid I've wet the bed."

"Not to worry." As the nurse propped her up, she saw the trail of red on Emily's nightgown.

"I'm bleeding!" Emily panicked. "Am I going to die?"

"It's just your menses, child. You know, the curse. Have you never had it before?"

Emily shook her head. Then another spasm struck.

Nurse Jeannie eased her down, consulted the chart at the foot of the bed, and frowned. "Almost fifteen, and the child's never had her menses!" With sardonic humour, she chuckled. "This could well be part of the problem. Men doctors!" Until she went off duty at four in the morning, Nurse Jeannie paid special attention to Emily, instructing her how to wear protective absorbent pads and how to relax her muscles to minimize the pain, speculating on why so many females seemed to suffer the same debilitating syndrome Emily exhibited. Was it purely physical, or did it stem from an inability to cope with the pressure of change?

The nurse thought about the symptoms of fatigue, muscle weakness, and swollen lymph nodes that were registered on Emily's chart. Tests for the sickle cell trait were suggested in the notes of one of the interns, but leukemia was being investigated. "Silence is the door of consent," she thought to herself. "She'll need someone to fight for her."

⁂

Next morning, something made Marion decide to look in on Emily before going to work – some strange urge to share the sense of "it's going to be all right" that Angela Brock had imparted the evening before. Tucking the embossed card with Mary Baker Eddy's Christian Science poem in her tapestry carry-all, she hustled the girls off to their respective schools, then walked the four blocks to the Children's Hospital. Parents weren't welcome during the busy morning routine, but the head nurse indulged Mrs. Willow – "who is," she confided to the intern, "a cut above other parents in the district, even though she is a darky."

Emily was sleeping soundly, but her freckles were showing. Marion kissed the pale forehead, tucked the card under her pillow and, purposely taking deep breaths, left the hospital humming a half-remembered Negro spiritual, "One Day at a Time, Sweet Jesus," to comfort herself. But fear haunted her still. Trying to evoke a sense of calm, she parroted the Christian Science creed on the denial of mortality: *There is no life, truth, intelligence or substance in matter.*

Up the steep incline of Guy Street hill she trudged. Crossing Dorchester Street, she subconsciously substituted lines from the Langston Hughes poem:

And sometimes goin' in the dark
Where there ain't been no light.

"What's the matter, lady?" A young man in uniform stopped her, touching her shoulder solicitously as though he knew her. "You okay?"

"Was I talking out loud?" Marion felt her face redden.

He smiled crookedly, trying to hide his prematurely decaying teeth. "Naw, you was jus' mutterin'." Suddenly, he seemed embarrassed, too, and started to walk on.

Marion recognized his crooked smile. "Wait. You're Maurice Vachon, aren't you?"

"Yeah. Me, I enlisted in the army."

"My! You do look handsome in uniform. Please tell your mother when you get home that Emily's taking a turn for the better."

"*C'est bon, n'est-ce pas?*" he asked, and, walking on, began to whistle.

"Pull yourself together," Marion scolded herself. "Making a spectacle of yourself on a public street! A true Christian Scientist would have been more calm. Better take a streetcar up Côte des Neiges or you'll be late! Denise Laroche may waste your time arguing about the rights of women, but you still have to give her three hours worth of work."

Yet, the feeling of elation, the budding of hope, the awareness that disease and matter could be dispelled propelled her through the day, letting her be civil, even cheerful, as she greeted the new manager, Alfred Jones, when she sprinted through the Y lobby at noon.

Early in December, Emily was pronounced well enough to be released, with reservations. Cosseted and fed lots of fresh vegetables, cod liver oil, chicken broth, and endless cups of Ovaltine, she was almost back to normal by Christmas. Dr. Valliers called it a reprieve. Marion didn't argue – she knew it was a miracle!

Now she could focus on Pippa's needs – and Efuah's apparent lack of them. Effie was now speaking French, with no lisp at all. "I must invite Madame Vachon in for tea," Marion decided. "I know she's been -mothering Effie, just as Miss Delacourt has been playing *Pygmalion*'s Professor Higgins for Pippa's mind." Overwhelmed, Marion allowed herself a moment of self-pity, wondering if her world was falling apart. One image repeated itself over and over in her mind. It was the snapshot Miss Delacourt had kept, the one intended for the Windsors last summer. She had noticed it, elegantly framed, hanging in Torrie's parlour – the three girls standing in a lane, grinning from ear to ear, Pippa dressed in her new Red River coat. "Perhaps, as Kofi warned, it takes an entire village to rear a child. On the other hand," Marion's mind countered, "too many cooks spoil the broth." She was too exhausted to decide which was the truth.

⚜

After Christmas, at Efuah's insistence, Sylvie Vachon was included in Marushka's invitation to Dame Orlova's second annual Twelfth Night feast, January the sixth, 1944. At midnight, when Otis and Marushka announced their engagement, the four sleepy girls suddenly came to life and began to plan their part in the wedding.

Marion quietly hid her concern behind a glass of plum cordial. She saw Otis abandoning his dreams of serving as an apprentice auto mechanic – a future as an independent man, an entrepreneur, no longer dependent on the railroad. She foresaw problems with Marushka's easy ability to "pass" and earn her living in a world that Otis could never enter. But when Otis's uncle opposed the marriage on the same grounds, Marion took the couple's side and convinced Edmond to give them his blessing.

Otis thought of nothing but Marushka, and during the long war-weary winter of 1944, they were absolutely happy. Otis steeled himself to settle down and work hard, but even love couldn't negate the subservient status of a sleeping car porter. The work was still gruelling and mindless. There was no hope of advancement and his tips depended on his ability to keep "smiling and scraping" through endless days of humiliation and racist slurs.

Yet, before the snows of winter had vanished – on the very day of the Coloured Ladies Club's successful fund-raising recital by the American poet, Langston Hughes, organized by the club's newest member, Torrie Delacourt – Marion was forced to banish Otis from her home.

CHAPTER XX

We need to talk. The note brought up to the linen room on the Y's third floor was unsigned. "Who sent this?" Marion asked Mr. Jones.

"A lady . . . a coloured lady. She's in the lobby still," Thaddeus McGregor's replacement replied, a pained expression on his face.

"Thank you. Please tell her I'll be right down."

Alfred Jones did as he was requested, then faded back into the front office woodwork. "Those women upstairs have far too much freedom," he muttered. "I'll have to work out an organizational chart. Imagine! I've just delivered a note, as though I were a lackey!" Peeking out from behind his half-closed door at the woman who had made him do such an uncharacteristic thing, he marvelled inwardly at the vitality of her beauty, not admitting to himself that his deeply subliminated libido had impelled him.

Torrie continued to tiger-pace the Y lobby, her sable coat rippling behind her. Finally, she flung the coat off, nestled into one of the leather club chairs, lit a cigarette, and watched the snow beat tattoo patterns on the window. Marion, fighting a sense of impending doom, stood silently behind Torrie's chair, watching the same late-winter snowflakes, wondering if little Effie had worn her woollen leggings to school. Suddenly, a throat-clearing sound from the manager's office forced Marion into action. She touched Torrie on the shoulder. Startled, Torrie stood up.

"How dare you ask my boss to deliver a note, as if he were a messenger or something!" Marion quietly hissed.

Torrie stubbed her cigarette out in a heavy glass ashtray. "It was urgent. It's Otis."

"If Otis has had another brawl at your nightclub, that's no concern of mine!"

"Goddamn your haughtiness! This is serious," Torrie insisted. Another throat-clearing warning from the office made Marion realize they shouldn't stay in the lobby. She signalled Torrie to follow and went up to one of the second-floor conference rooms.

Subtle William Morris patterned drapes cossetted the room with a dusky, quiet elegance that Torrie described as "Madly male!" They settled into the matching chintz easy chairs grouped around the large fireplace. Impulsively, Marion lit the log fire, laid for an evening meeting. She needed its warmth to counteract the tension that had been destroying her composure for the past three days.

Speaking as much to herself as to Torrie, Marion muttered peevishly, "If you only knew how, ever since you've come to Montreal, you've disrupted our lives. Why can't you just leave us alone? And now this!" She got as far as the words, "My boss will – " when Torrie scornfully interrupted.

"Screw your boss! The ole letch actually ogled me when I came in. Are you afraid of him because he's white? Hell, child, we're in Canada, not the Deep South. You gotta stand up for your rights!"

Her vehemence startled Marion. "Miss Delacourt, there is nothing to discuss. Otis behaved unspeakably, and I ordered him out of my house. That's all!"

With a curious intonation, Torrie asked, "Don't you consider Otis family?"

"Not really," Marion replied, without the slightest hint of remorse. "Not since I realized he was probably one of your lovers – at least until he met Marushka. Anyway, I don't want to discuss it. He was a brute, violent – and in front of my daughters! Hit the girl he's supposed to love and expected to marry. He was drunk."

"He was more than drunk. He was hurting," Torrie explained.

"Are you condoning what he did?"

Torrie tried to reply, but Marion wouldn't give her a chance. She suddenly needed to make Torrie understand the world she lived in and the standards she had to erect to protect her family. "Men get away with violence too often in this world. Just tell me why, if Otis Thompson is mad at the world, he should be allowed to take it out on the people who love him."

"Black men don't usually have many alternatives."

"Black men. White men. It doesn't matter . . . it's wrong! You live with violence. I don't have to – and I won't!" Marion's voice broke. Anguish misted her eyes.

Without pity, Torrie informed Marion that if she didn't pull herself together, she would soon be embroiled in more than household violence. The entire Black community would be involved in a "whole shitload of trouble" if they didn't find out where Otis was – and soon. "I know you don't want to know and don't want to be involved. But Otis's little blue recruiting book has been found."

Marion blinked. "Found? But Otis is always so careful. How could he lose it?" Her withdrawn body betrayed her fear of knowing.

"The railway dicks found it – and they're bloody triumphant!"

"Dear God! What if it actually gives the names and details about unionizing the porters?"

Like a bulldog, Torrie wouldn't let her be. "Listen. I don't think they're certain, but they'll try to make Otis confess – if they find him. And we've gotta prevent that. Girl, listen to me. All hell's about to break loose! We've got to do something."

Almost in a monotone, sagging under the weight of what she began to fear was guilt, Marion repeated twice, "I don't know where he is."

Changing tactics, carefully taking off her fur hat, Torrie offered, "Maybe I should tell you what started it. You may not be aware of the incident that lit Otis's powder keg." She inhaled from her cork-tipped cigarette. "It began on Friday. I was waiting for Langston Hughes due on the Delaware–Hudson train from New York for our club's fund-raising recital Saturday – remember? *Comme d'habitude*, the train was late, so I went through to the arrival platform. As the attendants lowered the steps of the first-class car, I saw Otis, looking awfully fed up, lean out to hail a Red Cap with a luggage dolly." Marion listened silently, her body poised in a defensive posture.

Torrie continued. "Moments later, he emerged supporting an elephant of a man, gross and sweaty. Otis was trying to calm him down. Too drunk to manoeuvre by himself, he was not too drunk to bellow out orders – and insults. He said Otis was – and these were his very words – 'the world's best shoeshine boy! Sambo, you sure deserve a fifty-cent tip.'"

Torrie's dark eyes brimmed with hate. "Can you imagine Otis's humiliation? Damn those Okies!" She swallowed hard and continued. "Just then, I spotted Langston stepping out of the tourist-class car. I hid behind a post so Otis wouldn't know I'd been there." To cover the silence created by Marion's lack of response, Torrie felt compelled to explain. "I caught up with Langston later. Don't want him to know how unpredictable life can be for coloured folks here in Canada. Prepared dinner for us at my place – wish Pippa had been able to be with us. He was in such good form. His book, *The Big Sea*, is selling well." Sighing, she added, "I sure miss the tempo of Harlem." With a shrug, she tucked away the memory and returned to the present.

"The next day, Saturday, Otis came into Rockhead's early in the afternoon, raging drunk. Wasn't even four o'clock. Hadn't seen this side of him in months. Not since he met Marushka. Believe me, I was worried! Put a waitress in charge of the table set-ups, ignored the normal kibitzing of the band during their sound check. Shooed everyone away, sat Otis at my corner table, and tried . . . tried to get the whole story.

"It was obvious that Otis was angry – crazed, even. I asked him what had happened and he told me – he was fired! A month before his wedding day and he's unemployed. Bet it burns their butt that 'Sambo, the world's best shoeshine boy' is also a union organizer. As you know, Otis has been in the vanguard of civil rights, helping to strengthen the Canadian Brotherhood of Sleeping Car Porters, although he hasn't been nearly as militant as some of the Toronto porters like Harry Gairey. Well, when Otis stepped off the train on Friday, he walked straight into a round-up. Anyone suspected of union activities was fired. Someone had ratted. And that blue book is the proof they need!"

Closing her eyes, Torrie forced herself to revisit the scene she'd witnessed so briefly, but which was etched indelibly on her soul.

"The station platform had been almost deserted – except for two men in overcoats waiting near the train. Rodney Brown came running from the station's main concourse, pushing a lug-gage cart and grimacing sympathetically at Otis. But the fat man had shrugged off Rodney's offer of help. 'No, no . . . I wan' my own boy,' the fat man said drunkenly. 'He's got savvy, speaks French. I kin give 'im a job cleanin' up my place . . . gotta bar in th' East End . . . need a bouncer like Sambo here. He's the world's best shoeshine boy.'

"Otis, suppressing his fury, put the fat man's bags onto Rodney's trolley. The two men waiting nearby entered the train just as the fat man flipped Otis two quarters. They fell, clinking, onto the ground. Otis refused to pick up the coins. The fat man

laughed and threw down two more. 'Hinkty nigga!' he said scornfully. 'Dollah's a lotta money for you folks.'

"Rage forced Otis's fists to stay down by his side. He turned
away to re-enter the coach, muttering, 'Gotta finish my work.' To
calm himself, using body language, he began to hum, with
increasing bravado, *Steppin' out . . . with my baby.* The two men in
overcoats – railway detectives, as it turned out – barred Otis's
entrance back into the coach. One held up Otis's little blue notebook. 'Gettin' careless, ain't you, boy,' he snarled. 'Found this on
the floor in there. Now we know you're a Union organizer, as
well as a *hinkty nigga*, eh? Get your things, boy. You're fired!'"

Full of pent-up fury, Torrie continued. "True, at Rockhead's
Otis called it like it was – overt racism and exploitation. But he'd
been drinking for twenty-four hours and couldn't even pronounce the words anymore. He was simply a tight package of
misdirected violence, smashing his glass into the table because he
couldn't smash the bosses – smash white society.

"I tried to get him upstairs into one of Rockhead's offices to
sleep it off, but for the first time I had no influence over him. He
actually shoved me aside, staggered down the stairs and out onto
St. Antoine. Said he was going home . . ." Torrie turned away. Her
voice broke. "I'm sorry. I'm so sorry, Mrs. Willow. I tried, but I
couldn't stop him."

Marion's head went back, then swivelled to ease her neck
muscles. She suddenly reached out for Torrie's hand. "Please, call
me Marion. You mustn't blame yourself. You obviously did what
you could." Despite her reluctance to take up the story, Marion
found the words spilling out, as if she were a doll wound up to
perform. "We were expecting Otis for dinner that night. I'd been
teaching Marushka how to prepare cassava pie." Marion paused as
her mind reconstructed the scene.

"We planned to eat early since I'd promised to take the girls
to the Langston Hughes recital. Pippa, perched on a stool in the
kitchen, was reading parts of his novel out loud. As I recall,

Marushka then said something about realizing she'd found a safe haven, that marriage to Otis would complete her search for identity." Marion's voice faded to cover a threatening sob.

A log fell forwards in the fireplace, sending sparks flying. Skillfully, Torrie rolled it back with the fire tongs. The action gave Marion time to recover herself, but as she continued, her voice became as tense as her body. "Suddenly, there was a banging on the front door. Pippa was the first to respond. Again – banging and scuffling! Pippa raced out of the kitchen and down the stairwell in time to see Otis slam the front door and fall back against it, cradling a bottle of whiskey. 'I wanna see my fiancée,' he yelled.

"'No, you don't, Otis. You want to get out of here before anyone sees you,' Pippa pleaded. But it was too late to avert the scene. Otis was in a mood for confrontation and, in his drunken muddle, he identified Marushka as the enemy – his enemy. He pushed Pippa out of the way, lumbered up to the kitchen, and grabbed Marushka by the shoulder. He shook her for emphasis during a rambling, irrational diatribe on the subject of passing. 'Black is Black. White is evil. You only play at being Black. You've denied your people. You've denied me!' Then he slapped her. Oh, Torrie! If you'd been there, you'd have known why I had to act quickly. I couldn't let violence happen in our home, with the children as witnesses."

Torrie leaned forward to comfort Marion. "You were probably the only person on earth who could have stopped Otis at that moment."

"I picked up a bowl full of soapy water from the sink and threw it in his face," Marion explained. "I actually threw that bowl of filthy dishwater in his face!" She shook her head, still amazed and dismayed at her own daring. "He released Marushka. Taking his arm, I walked him to the door. He'd disgraced himself, behaved in a bestial manner, trotted out racist filth in front of my daughters. 'You're no longer engaged to Marushka, and you'll never again be welcome in my home!' I think I said. I remember reaching into his pocket to retrieve his key and locking the door behind him. I had to do something. Dear God, was I right? Did I react too harshly? Did I even stop to think that he didn't know what he was doing, or that he needed us?"

Torrie's fingertips massaged Marion's cold hands. "You did what you had to do. Poor bugger," she added. "Now he's lost both his job and his family. I know he's tried to talk to Marushka, but it only confirmed that he's lost her too."

Moments passed in silence. Torrie felt compelled to mediate. "Even though I'm disgusted with him, I feel I have to do something. I could get him a job as Rockhead's chauffeur and errand boy – at least he would dress well! But Rufus has warned me in the past that Otis dabbles in the numbers racket and drinks compulsively under pressure. I've tried to reach him all weekend, but I can't track him down. I'm afraid Otis's lost!"

"Or else enlisted." Marion's tears were real.

Darkness had fallen. The logs had burned to ashes. Still, Torrie and Marion sat there in silence, every once in a while shaking their heads, individually and sadly. "Poor Otis," Marion said. "He dared to dream."

"What about Marushka?" Torrie, ever the pragmatist, asked. "Were the gods jealous of her, too? Will she always be an outsider looking in?"

A fumbling sound at the door warned them that someone was turning the handle. Involuntarily, Torrie flung her hand against Marion's mouth to prevent a sob escaping. "Ole Whitey's snooping around out there." Footsteps could soon be heard moving softly away. "I declare, Mrs. Willow. You the weepingest woman I know. But crying's not gonna change anything. We've got to get the book back!"

Facing Marion to get her full attention, Torrie asked whether she couldn't pretend the book was hers, but Marion shrugged it off. "Why would I have a book like that? Can't we just telephone and ask for it back?"

"If you say you're his aunt, they might give it to you," Torrie agreed, picking up the telephone from the table near the wall.

Marion reacted quickly. "Better not. It goes through Mr. Jones."

Torrie, shrugging, informed her that she was quite willing to go down and seduce Mr. Jones while Marion made the phone call. Her dare broke the tension. Realizing that Torrie was serious, Marion relented. Suddenly, Torrie took on another persona. She perched on the table and preened, like a cat with a canary in her sights.

"Dial W-E-7-4-2-0," she ordered. Submissively, Marion did as she was told, asking who they were calling. Torrie took the phone from her and waited for an answer. "Sergeant Tom? It's Torrie Delacourt... Torrie, from Rockhead's." She paused. "Tonight? Well, since Dizzy Gillespie's due for a jam session – of course I'll save you a seat." Laughing, she quickly added, "No, not *that* kind! As a matter of fact, I'm in the hot seat myself right now, and you can help me...Yeah, well, I'll owe you one.

"Look, somewhere in your office is a small blue notebook. One of your boys picked it up off the train on Saturday." The moments ticked by. "Sergeant Tom" must have been looking for the book. And he must have found it, for, breathing a sigh of relief, Torrie murmured into the telephone, "Yes, that's it. Honey, that book's my bread and butter! Time's money... and so are those names!"

Marion was horror-stricken. "No, don't!" she mouthed, but Torrie simply shook her head and grinned wickedly. Continuing with a warm laugh, Torrie assured the sergeant, "No, honey, your name's not there! Those are my *community* customers. Porters, mainly – lunch-hour stuff. Check it out if you want." She paused for a moment. "Your name's in a little RED book – red hot!" Torrie hunched the phone between her left ear and her shoulder, fished another cigarette out of her purse, and lit it. Blowing smoke upwards, she scolded, "Oh, stop being such a prig, Tom!

You haven't a leg to stand on. One of your inspectors made a silly mistake – took it from one of the young porters who's got the hots for me."

Marion realized that she didn't want to know what Sergeant Tom was saying. She wished she could block out even Torrie's side of the conversation. Still, Torrie's voice went suggestively on. "'Course not! Not as good as yours! Look, I just want the book back." Torrie made a 'moue.' "You're wicked, Tom! . . . You mean tonight AND tomorrow night? For one frigging book? Stuff it! You can KEEP the book. AND you get no more wholesale-price crates of Jack Daniels through ME!" She stubbed out her cigarette.

"I know you were just joking, Tom . . . Okay, we have a done deal then?" Standing up, Torrie brought the conversation to a close. "See you at eleven, Tom – WITH my little blue book. Bye for now," she added flirtatiously, and turned to Marion in triumph. "*Inshallah*. Now, we've got to get Otis safely home to you and Marushka."

But Marion protested. It was no use. She didn't want Otis back. She couldn't take any more problems and repeated her suspicion that he'd already enlisted in the army. Torrie did not intend to be put off. She argued, then appealed to Marion: "You can't just let him go off like that, thinking no one cares." Torrie even confessed that that's what had happened to her and she'd had to take to the streets. She didn't want that happening to Otis.

Defensive again, Marion spat out, "If he's that weak – " But Torrie interrupted, saying with mock humility, "To err is human, to forgive divine."

"Forgive?" Marion asked. "Until the next time?"

For a moment, Torrie simply glared at Marion, and then, exasperated, hiding her sense of defeat and rejection, she put on her fur hat and long leather gloves. Throwing her beautiful sable coat around her shoulders, she hissed angrily, "You fool! You stubborn fool!" She could hear Marion plaintively defending herself, saying something about Otis's abusiveness, but by then Torrie was in high dudgeon.

Rounding on Marion, she hissed, "Who's being weak now? Damn it, you don't deserve the love Otis feels for you and your girls!" She strode to the door, opened it, and went through, only to pause at the threshold, saying hotly, "Just wait and see how long your precious respectability keeps you warm at night. Even Edmond won't forgive you!" Controlling her temper, she closed the door very carefully behind her.

Left alone, Marion shuddered as she fought for control of her own mind and body. "No one has the right," she said to herself, "no one has the right to resort to violence." Haltingly, she walked towards the fireplace and poured herself a glass of water from a jug on the mantel. Suddenly, instead of drinking the water, she threw it on the dying embers of the fire. As they sputtered angrily, she crumpled onto the sofa, fighting an urge to weep.

Nothing, all that long and drea-ry winter, managed to erase the scene of Torrie's confrontation from Marion's mind. Even the bitter report that she had to table to the January Club Meeting – which Torrie attended, gray-wrapped in understated respectabili-ty – that yet another family from the Black community, all but the youngest child, had died from tuberculosis, seemed as cruel as los-ing Otis.

At school, Pippa was forced to endure a teacher who harassed her, hoping to break the uninhibited spirit that produced poems as homework, instead of traditional compositions for the teacher to grade. Emily's mid-winter bout of her recurring illness was far briefer than the previous one. Doctor Valliers congratulated her on Emily's progress, but somehow Marion still felt inadequate and her spirit troubled.

Though she understood the urgency that had provoked Torrie, Marion found herself unable to condone Torrie's seduc-tive tactics to retrieve Otis's book. She was certain that it wasn't her own moral judgement that bothered her, but rather, the ethi-cal challenge that Torrie's success presented. "I am haunted," she realized," by things I do not understand, and cannot control."

Torrie's unselfishness brought to mind a short story by O. Henry about a devoted couple intent on pleasing each other.

The wife had cut off and sold her hair to buy a chain for her husband's pocket watch as a Christmas gift, not knowing that he had sold his precious watch to buy a tortoiseshell comb for her beautiful hair.

Restlessly, Marion twisted the radio dial, searching for the weather forecast. More snow was predicted. Pippa was in the country, at Ste. Anne de Bellevue's military hospital, spending her Sunday afternoon reading to Trevor, who, wounded in a training camp accident, was undergoing medical treatment to restore his sight. Her train was not due back until six, yet, scraping snow from the crusted window, Marion was astonished to see Pippa climbing out of the yellow Buick convertible. The top was down. She couldn't tell who else was in the car, but prayed that it wasn't Edmond. Pippa had once mentioned that Torrie, concerned about Trevor's blindness, visited him occasionally. Obviously, Torrie had given her a lift home from the hospital.

Taking her apron off and slipping on a shawl, Marion hurried down the stairs and out the door, calling in a clear, inviting tone, "Miss Delacourt? Miss Delacourt! It's time for tea. Won't you come up with Pippa?"

Pippa stood looking up at her mother, smirking happily as Torrie stepped out of the car. "Delighted! Just have to park the car in the Vachons' backyard. Be there in a minute."

Marion set the kitchen table with her good Madeira lace tablecloth, while Pippa fetched the Aynsley tea service from the china cabinet. "Thank goodness I've got freshly baked gingerbread."

When Torrie came in, Marion listened to the joint report on Trevor's progress, and then suggested that Pippa, taking her hot cocoa and gingerbread man, join her sisters in the front room to do her homework. Pippa agreed readily, realizing that, although a whole year had passed since her mother had promised, the two of them were finally having tea alone together.

Cutting the warm gingerbread loaf into slices, Marion

offered Torrie a choice of sour cream or lemon curd topping.

Their conversation was desultory until Marion admitted, "I need to confess that, although I once resented your playing Svengali to my daughter, now I appreciate what you've tried to do. I want to thank you for being there for Pippa. You've strengthened her sense of self-worth immeasurably through your introduction to, as she calls it, 'the souls of Black folks.' She now talks about 'entitlement.'"

The bittersweet smile that Marion remembered seeing on Torrie's face at the picnic was there again. "Entitlement? You owe me nothing. I need to thank you for being there for Emily."

"Emily! Why Emily?"

"Hadn't you guessed? She's so like me when I was young. No mother, no father, buffeted by social rejection, not knowing who I was. All I owned was the determination to survive against all odds."

A withering feeling of chagrin filled Marion. "How blind prejudice makes one."

"As a youngster on the streets of Kansas City," Torrie continued, "I had an unfathomable curiosity about the world outside, and, admittedly, a fine brown frame; that was all. But Emily – she'll more than just survive, because you've claimed her. She has such an exquisite voice, she could become another Marian Anderson. You've groomed another asset to the race."

Suddenly, Torrie found herself being hugged by the last person in the world she would have claimed was impulsive. Now, she found that it was her turn to fight back tears.

"Nonsense," Marion was protesting, "You have more than a beautiful body. You have grace, undeniable grace. Race and sex are not problems for you. I hope you'll be able to impart that to my girls."

Whether to check her tears, or simply to regain her brittle composure, Torrie's throaty voice enquired, "Would that be needed, my dear, to balance your Puritan *politesse*?"

"Puritan or not, I know I'll soon be in trouble if you don't clear out of here," Marion said, suppressing the amusement she felt at being called Puritan. "Edmond Thompson usually has dinner with us on Sunday – and he's not ready for the two of us to be friends."

"They never are," Torrie answered with a mischievous smile.

"Promise me something, Miss Delacourt – I mean, Torrie?"

"Don't worry, I shan't repeat our discussion."

"That's not what I was going to ask."

"Pray tell."

"Be there for Otis, too. Promise you'll be."

"I promise."

***

Marion was grateful when Torrie came "a-visiting" on Shrove Tuesday – with her rare edition of a well-thumbed book entitled *Caroling Dusk*, an anthology of poems compiled by Countee Cullen, another Harlem Renaissance poet and a friend of hers. They shared the evening with a lacklustre Marushka and an ebullient Amelia Hall, reading aloud over a tray of Torrie's open-faced smörgasbord sandwiches, the girls learning how Mardi Gras was celebrated in New Orleans.

***

The joyless Lenten season of that frigid winter limped along. Otis caught the odd glimpse of Marushka through frosted windows. He even dared to browse through the music racks at Ogilvy's, but she would not look at him. Once, he spotted her at the movies holding hands with a boy who was definitely not a Negro. The next morning found Otis trying to walk off a deadly combination of anger, grief, frustration – and a bad hangover.

The Union Jack and the Red Ensign, fluttering outside an

army recruitment office, caught his eye. The winter offensive of the Nazi *Luftwaffe* against England was still taking its toll on both human lives and spirit. Land mines hindered the Allies, slogging up the "boot" of Italy. The Canadian army, in dire need of more men, was actively recruiting. Otis enlisted and left for army camp without exchanging a word with either Marushka or the Willow family.

In their hearts, Pippa and Emily never abandoned Otis, but they would never betray their mother to the point of actually speaking with him. Pippa, who got news through Torrie, was not above lobbying Marushka on his behalf. Marushka seemed unmoved, however, even by the news of his enlistment – and, of course, there was now the matter of her new boyfriend.

Devastated by her glimpse of Otis's other side, Marushka felt utterly betrayed. Encouraged by her mother, determined that her life was not over, she agreed to "keep company" with Jean-Pierre Saumier. Their relationship wasn't deep. He certainly didn't have Otis's charisma. He was a pleasant enough person, probably capable of only one minor act of courage in his life. This had occurred when he'd turned his back on family tradition, went to L'École des Beaux Arts instead of Brébeuf College, rented a backyard shed as a studio, and proceeded to imitate Jean-Paul Riopelle as an *automatiste* painter.

Marushka enjoyed the parties and Québecois concerts that Jean-Pierre took her to, and the glamorous, self-consciously Bohemian lifestyle he led. But the truth was, she hardly thought about him from one meeting to the next. Jean-Pierre considered Marushka the most exotic woman he'd ever met. He was dying to bed her, but didn't dare try. What if she refused him? To his Beaux Arts friends, her dark, White Russian heritage was highly romantic. They had no idea that, to him, she was an "ice maiden." His Roman Catholic parents were another matter, though, and young Saumier didn't intend to risk having his allowance cut off by keeping unsuitable company.

Marushka was surprised when he invited her, on the first day of Spring, to Sunday dinner at the Saumier residence, perched high on the exclusive Outremont slope of Mount Royal. Her impression had been that Jean-Pierre had very little to do with his family. She was still more surprised when, on the way to dinner, they stopped at the Café Prague on Park Avenue for an espresso coffee – and a coaching session. To his credit, he was embarrassed about it. However, the burden of his message was that it was not necessary for Marushka to mention her origins, nor the fact that she lived in Little Burgundy and was close friends with people of colour. He suggested a plausible alternate biography, then declared his undying love.

Humiliated, Marushka realized that this was actually her first direct encounter with personal bigotry. Fighting her pain with gentle compassion, she opted out of the dinner. Trudging the long, cold walk home from the coffee shop alone, only one thought repeatedly hammered itself into her head: "This is what Otis constantly went through. This devaluing of one because of colour. This is what he was trying to talk about that night. One drop of blood from an African ancestor shapes who he is and who I am – that's the bottom line."

The Willow girls were dressed for church and waiting for Poppa Dad as Marushka came down rue des Seigneurs. It seemed that Reverend Lorenzo West had arranged a special evening service to honour the neighbourhood boys who would be leaving to join the Third Canadian Division in England. Marion urged Marushka to come along. On the steps of the church, Pippa took Marushka aside to warn her that Otis would probably be inside, since he was on a week's leave between finishing boot camp and his posting overseas.

The Union United Congregational Church was adorned with fragrant Bermudian lilies. The gospel choir was in full attendance, and over a dozen young Black men in uniform were sitting with their families or their girls. Otis sat alone in a pew towards the front, next to the aisle, wearing the black beret of a private in the Tank Corps of the Canadian army.

When Marion, with her three girls, slipped in beside Amelia Hall, Marushka kept on walking. Heads turned. Pippa's face lit up with an enormous smile as it became apparent that Marushka was headed straight for Otis. She slid into the pew and took his hand as the choir began the opening hymn, "Onward Christian Soldiers."

Marion tried to concentrate on the hymn, but other words from a Christian Science melody took over unbidden. Stretching her arms to encircle her three "jewels," two of whom were now as tall as she, she sang silently, gratefully,

> *Oh gentle presence, Peace and Joy and Power.*
> *Oh Life Divine, that owns each waking hour.*
> *His habitation high is here and now.*
> *His arms encircle me and mine and all.*

CHAPTER XXII

They had just five days in which to plan Marushka's wedding. Dame Orlova insisted it be Russian Orthodox. Visions of wafting incense, tinkling bells, and bridal crowns danced in her head. No time to lose. As soon as Marushka left for work Monday morning, Dame Orlova dressed, telephoned for a taxi, and directed the driver to the Russian Orthodox Church of St. Nicholas, perched imperiously at the corner of Sherbrooke and rue St. Urbain, planning her strategy *en route*. The reassuring sight of the five gold onion-domed cupolas on the church's roof allowed her to pay the taxi fare without vexation.

She shouldered her way through the dusty green double doors, then peered into the various musty, candle-lit recesses, hoping to see the familiar long shaggy grey beard of a priest. In desperation, at the chancel steps, she called, as softly as she could, "Father, Father." Women, she knew, were hardly expected to be seen, much less heard, in the Russian Orthodox Church.

A scruffy, non-frocked, burly man appeared from the vestry. "No, the archimandrite is away for one week. No, no one else can perform the ceremony. No, there can be no deviations from the traditional service. There must be three weeks notice. Yes, I know there's a war on. Hasn't Mother Russia lost more men, women and children than all the other Allies put together?"

Dame Orlova was getting nowhere. She tried another tack, but obviously the old codger had never been a St. Petersburg resident (he called it Leningrad) and didn't approve of the atmosphere she intended to create. He not only referred to her as "Comrade," but above all, immune to her charm, he wouldn't let her borrow the church's jewelled bridal crowns. "Peasant!" she snarled as she left.

Miss Delacourt had more luck. "Yes, Reverend Lorenzo West will be pleased to perform the ceremony, if we can provide him with a printed copy of the Russian Orthodox *Order of Holy Matrimony Service* within a few days. Yes, he allowed that it would be a charming gesture for little Effie and Sylvie Vachon, as bridesmaids, to carry censers of burning incense."

Marushka and Otis, consulting by telephone, drew up the invitation list: from Ogilvy's, Grace and Monique, Sarita and Mark Reitman, and Francis, the artistic young window decorator who'd been such an uninhibited friend. Rodney Brown and Rufus Rockhead, of course, but could Marushka stand two of the girls from the Rockhead chorus line who were particularly nice? At Amelia Hall's insistence, Staff Sergeant Thaddeus McGregor – who, for his obvious management skills and his age, was still assigned as recruitment officer by his Black Watch Regiment – was also invited. When the guest list grew to forty, Mrs. Willow had to arbitrate.

Emily and Pippa volunteered to deliver invitations to neighbourhood guests. "Better telephone them," Marion advised. "There's no time for RSVPs."

Monday morning, at work, Marushka went down to the furniture department to let Mark in on the good news. Mark informed his wife Sarita, who responded with delight. Arriving at Ogilvy's that afternoon – her new baby, David strapped like a papoose on her back – she bombarded Marushka with suggestions.

"Would you like to borrow my bridal veil? It's been blessed

by the Rabbi. I think the orange blossoms could be steamed back into some kind of recognizable shape. You're wearing a wedding gown, aren't you? No? Don't be silly! War or no war – you must wear white! I'll ask Flo Gibson if there isn't a window display dress you can have at a cut rate. She's Montreal's best fashion buyer, so surely she can arrange it for us! Now, for something new. New white shoes from Ogilvy's – you get ten percent off as an employee. Something borrowed . . . a dozen things come to mind, but my veil's your best bet. And something blue . . . surely, Emily, Pippa, and Effie could be allowed to buy a sexy pair of blue garters!"

⚜

Monday evening, Dame Orlova ordered the overseas operator to put through a call to the Braithwaite residence in Christchurch, Barbados. The connection was so full of the sound of waves breaking on the shore that she could neither hear properly nor speak clearly, so Mrs. Willow had to come over to the Russian Ballet Academy to explain the emergency to the Braithwaites. "No problem," Cyril Braithwaite Senior declared. "Our youngest son, Randolph, is at Trenton Air Base in Ontario, training with the RCAF. Yes, yes! He'd be proud to give his little niece Marushka away. I'll call him at once and arrange everything. Congratulations!"

Tuesday, during the staff tea break at the Y, when Marion floated the idea of Amelia Hall perhaps preparing a dish for the wedding luncheon, the occasion turned into a strategy session.

"Sweet Jesus, child. Can you imagine coloured folks eating Russian beet borsch' and potato pancakes?" Amelia asked. "War effort or no, that weddin' feast has to be prepared by us'ns if it's bein' served in the basement of our church. I'll be supervisin' the cooking. Gertrude," she ordered as the waitress entered the kitchen. "See that you'all are free, available, and in a Christian

mood on Saturday. Contact Rosie the Riveter – I mean, Clara.
See if she'll help out. No way I'll be here at the Y the Saturday of
the wedding!"

Vashti Dobson was not to be upstaged. She insisted that
Marion should ask those "fine-feathered biddies" at the Coloured
Ladies Club to ensure the quality of the cutlery – "sterling silver,
of course!" – and provide the finest glasses, teacups, and dishes.
"Cain' have Marushka's uptown visitors feelin' grass don' grow on
rock stone," she tsewpsed.

That evening, Amelia ran afoul of Dame Orlova's Tartar
blood. A tug of war ensued. Finally, the menu was adjusted
to include *kulebiaka*, a spiced salmon loaf baked like beef
Wellington, and *pirozhki* or potato dumplings. Tea was to be
served, but only with lemon and *only* from the Orlova family's
copper samovar. Dame Orlova did concede, however, that after
she baked the wedding cake, Amelia would be allowed to provide
it with instant mellowing and aging, using her famous Demerara
rum icing.

The thorniest part emerged on day three, Wednesday. Dame
Orlova, encouraged by Pippa to consider Miss Delacourt a "kindred spirit" – after all, she had actually visited Russia ("twice!"
Pippa stressed) – decided to seek Torrie's assistance with the order
of the wedding service. Dame Orlova felt that Torrie would
instinctively understand the need to have the marriage service
reflect Marushka's Russian heritage. Selecting two sheets of her
precious, though slightly aged, watermarked writing paper, she
wrote:

My dear Miss Delacourt,
May I express our appreciation for all you have contributed,
as a member of the groom's family, to the upcoming nuptials.
However, as you have a special relationship with the officiating
minister, would you explain to him and give him these guide-
lines on the meaning of the Russian Orthodox ceremony?

He doesn't seem to understand when I try to explain, and insists on reducing the service from the customary two hours to less than forty minutes. The following notes outline the accepted order of procedure in our faith.

May the Holy Theotokos and all the Saints guide your actions.

Tatiana Orlova Braithwaite (Mme.)

THE EASTERN ORTHODOX WEDDING SERVICE

The Orthodox wedding service is divided into two parts. The first is the betrothal (or engagement), and the second is the crowning (the actual wedding).

I.   The Betrothal

The betrothal takes place in the narthex (the back of the church) and the crowning takes place in the church. The couple are betrothed by blessed wedding bands which are placed on their right hands, then exchanged three times.

II.   The Wedding Service

The wedding begins immediately after the betrothal. The bride and groom hold candles to show their willingness to accept the true light of God into their marriage. The bridal pair stand on a white cloth, symbolic of their first steps together into their wedded life, sharing good and bad, joy and sorrow, whichever is their fate together.

III.   The Three Prayers

Three prayers are offered for the couple (approximately ten minutes per prayer). In the first, the priest asks God to bless the marriage and grant to the bridal pair all the blessings necessary for the happiness of their wedded life. In the second, the priest prays to God to preserve them, to remember them and the parents who nurtured them, "for the prayers of the parents make firm the foundation of the home." In the third prayer, God is beseeched to "unite the bridal pair in harmony and marry them in one flesh."

IV.   The Crowning

The bridal pair are crowned as a sign of their office as King and Queen of the family. Crowns are a sign of Christian purity, undefiled and victorious over adversities. The Orthodox Church crowns her people, expressing her love and hope that each will earn the Eternal Crown granted to the faithful servants of Christ, the Eternal King.

V.   The Epistle

The reading from the Epistle describes the relationship between husband and wife, and their duties to each other and the family. (Marushka has asked to replace this with a reading from The Prophet by the Persian poet, Kahlil Gibran.)

VI.   The Bible Reading

There must be a reading from the Bible, describing God's approval of marriage through a description of the wedding in Cana, where Jesus performed the first miracle by turning water into wine.

VII.   The Common Cup

As a symbol of the "common cup" of life, wine is given to the couple to share three times.

VIII.   The Ceremonial Walk:

The priest now binds the right hands of the bridal pair together and leads them in a circle around the altar, while the choir sings three hymns proclaiming joy on behalf of the newlyweds. (Please note: No musical instruments may be used.) The priest holds a cross as he leads them in their first steps of marriage. After the service, people are invited to proceed to the wedding feast.

"Dear Lord," Torrie commented when she received Dame Orlova's letter. "No one will sit through all that." Twirling her hair into a low bun, she fitted a brown velvet cloche over her head, slipped into her brown sable coat and, with toe rubbers covering her high-heeled shoes, descended, leather-gloved hands carefully holding the winding banister, down the forty-three snow-packed steps to the street. Within minutes, her yellow Buick was purring its way towards Reverend Lorenzo West's study.

That week, slushy rue des Seigneurs became even slushier as the Willow girls raced back and forth from Torrie's apartment, where her "critical-path" chart was posted on a wall mirror, to Madame Vachon's sewing room, to the Willows' busy kitchen, and to Dame Orlova's drawing room, where copper and silver were being polished at a furious rate.

Thursday evening, Reverend Lorenzo West invited Otis to the rectory, both for a talk over a glass of sherry, and for a discussion as to how the ceremony could be simplified without hurting the bride's feelings. The minister admitted to finding the pageantry quite irresistible, but feared the logistics were unmanageable. "What a brouhaha!" Otis observed. But weddings were for women and all he wanted was Marushka.

On Friday morning, Marushka's handsome window-decorator friend, Francis, arrived at the church with armfuls of white silk calla lilies and evergreen boughs. Painstakingly, he arranged Dame Orlova's precious triptychs and her supply of religious icons, urns, and silver candelabra with such elegance that the chancel of the Union United Congregational Church became a medieval sanctuary, albeit eclectic.

Hearing her sad tale of the missing Russian bridal crowns, Francis persuaded Marushka's mother not to worry. At lunch hour, he burrowed through the artifacts of the rental department at Malabar's Theatrical Suppliers and emerged with two exquisite crowns that had been created for the recent Montreal Repertory Theatre production of Shakespeare's *Richard III*.

"Truly something borrowed," Marushka admitted triumphantly when he produced them at Friday evening's wedding rehearsal.

The wedding morning dawned gently, with both a light brushing of snow and the promise of spring. The entire Rockhead chorus line, in fur hats and fashionable foxfur "bum freezer" jackets, arranged themselves demurely in the fourth pew on the groom's side of the church. Twelve of the sixteen members of the Coloured Ladies Club sat near the door, intending to slip out quietly and head downstairs to assist with the serving of lunch before the traditional ending of the ceremony.

Two young men in uniform, whom even Torrie had never seen before, served as ushers. Their melodious West Indian voices and courteous manners, coupled with the Old World grace with which they extended their arms clad in blue RAF-officers' uniforms to guide guests to their seats, "provided proof" – Vashti Dobson observed, using the old Jamaican saying, "An orange never bears a lime" – "that Marushka comes from good stock." The ushers were fellow Barbadians, friends of Randolph Braithwaite.

Edmond Thompson, waiting in the lobby with Efuah Willow and Sylvie Vachon, impatient for the bride to arrive, seemed disturbed. "How come Torrie and Marion seem in cahoots?" he asked himself. In fact, neither seemed to be competing for his services. He wasn't happy about it.

The little girls were dressed in Madame Vachon's interpretation of Dame Orlova's description of Russian flower girls. Long red ribbons flowed gracefully from flowered crowns, embroidered white satin blouses were tucked into wide, gaily striped skirts, gathered tightly at the waistband. Red patent-leather Mary Jane shoes replaced the suggested high red Cossack boots. Each child clutched the chain of an incense-filled brass ball. Edmond stood ready to light the wicks, which would release exotic fumes for the betrothal ceremony, to be held in the vestibule.

The church was more than half full and filling fast. Suddenly, a strange, droning sound, as though a thousand queen bees were swarming outside the church, seeped through the closed outside doors. Heads turned discreetly towards the vestibule. A second, almost wailing sound slowly assaulted the old stone church as Thaddeus McGregor began to march up the outside steps – his bagpipes pressed against his Black Watch-blanketed shoulder, his cheeks puffed out, his diaphragm raised.

"Oh, dear God, no!" Marion gasped, rushing to the back of the church, leaving Emily and Pippa alone in the second row. Carefully, she closed the vestibule and then the church doors behind her to block McGregor's entry. "Thaddeus! At the reception, not the church!" she said.

"I came prepared to pipe the bride in," he announced. "I even found a song with roots in Africa!"

"You can't. We're not permitted to play instruments, not even an organ, at the ceremony. It's against Russian Orthodox tenets."

"But this is the church for coloured folks, is it not?" He glowered, lowering his bagpipes.

"Nevertheless, we respect all traditions. Please, just come sit with us."

Thaddeus, crestfallen, considered his options. Deep inside, he felt an atavistic urge to be part of the event. External pride made him fear he was intruding. Reluctantly, he turned to go.

"Please, Thaddeus! We need you."

"Right-ee-o, lass!", and into the church and down the aisle he marched, one large freckled hand clutching his winded bagpipes, the other proudly holding Marion by the elbow.

Heads turned as they passed, and tongues wagged. Marion heard someone murmur, "Well! I never would have believed it if I hadn't seen it with my own eyes!" At first, she cringed, but then she threw her shoulders back, knowing that, like Torrie, she was now a marked woman. She slid into the second pew and made room for McGregor.

Across the aisle, Dame Orlova crossed herself. The groom's guests were an odd lot. Little did she know that, right behind her,

Sarita and Mark Reitman were plotting to break glasses at the reception, in the Jewish tradition – or that Madame Vachon's husband had made the wedding wine in his own cellar.

⊕

In his embroidered surplice of creamy white, Reverend West, noting that it was twelve noon exactly, bade the congregation to kneel in prayer as he made his way into the vestibule of the church for the betrothal ceremony. At the door, he signalled the congregation to rise as he made the sign of the cross, and then to sit as the four members of the choir began to hum, "Oh, Perfect Love" in four-part *a cappella* harmony.

Modestly encased in a flowing choir gown of maroon and beige, her graceful long hands pacing out the tempo, Torrie indicated to Emily that she should now move to the front of the quartet. Emily's wide hazel eyes caught the trusting twinkle of Torrie's smile and began to sing. The bell-like clarity, the incredible purity of tone, and, something rarely heard in a contralto, an almost modest sweetness, reminded Torrie of the great Marian Anderson's celebrated voice. Marion Willow, sitting in the second row, breathed deeply, tears of pride in her eyes.

"Now, now! Steady on, old girl," Thaddeus McGregor murmured, patting her hand. "It's an uncanny voice she has! Reminds one of Jenny Lind," he added with admiration.

The church was hushed. The light that filtered through the high stained-glass windows – prismed by the bright, flickering candles and reflected in the Golden Crown of the Russian Virgin on the central triptych – filled the chancel with divinity.

> *O Perfect Love, all human thought transcending,*
> *Lowly we kneel in prayer before thy throne.*
> *That theirs may be the love which knows no ending,*
> *Whom thou for evermore dost join in one.*

Outside in the narthex, the betrothal ceremony was almost complete. Emily finished her solo. "Now, follow me," the minister instructed Otis and his best man, Rodney Brown. "Be careful not to step on the white mat at the altar, and stay to the right. Lieutenant Braithwaite, wait three minutes, then bring Marushka." Turning to Efuah and Sylvie, the reverend said, "Now, girls, walk slowly and look straight ahead. Mr. Thompson, I'm counting on you to keep things moving! Good. Are we all set? Remember, the crowning comes almost last – and you, Randolph, as the one giving your neice away, must hold her crown over her head. Rodney, you hold Otis's. Are we ready?" He flexed his shoulders and flipped his gown so that it would flow behind him.

"Everything's copacetic! Let's get the show on the road," Rodney urged.

Edmond Thompson opened the vestibule doors. The heady scent of myrrh wafted behind little Effie as she walked slowly down the aisle, concentrating on pointing her new red shoes straight ahead. Sylvie, her bright Shirley Temple curls mixed up with her red hair ribbons, swung her censer in a high arc, looking from side to side for her mother's approval.

A hush, an intaking of breath, and the soft whispered echoes of "Isn't she beautiful!" followed Marushka down the aisle. At the altar, Otis didn't dare to turn. It couldn't be true! He sensed, with a deep feeling of calm, that all his life he would remember this moment – the moment when he realized he would never again be all alone.

"*Dearly beloved*," Lorenzo West began, ignoring his Russian text. "*We are gathered together here, in the sight of God and in the face of this congregation, to join together this man and this woman in Holy Matrimony.*"

Deacon Stevens, looking more and more inscrutable – he was distressed that the minister wasn't following the agreed-upon text – pushed the two tall white candles towards him.

Lorenzo West blithely ignored him until he had finished his standard solemnization litany. Then, switching to the suggested Russian Orthodox text, he handed Marushka and Otis each a candle to hold. *"For the servant of God, Otis Lee Thompson, and the handmaid of God, Marushka Natasha Braithwaite, who now pledge fidelity to each other, and for their salvation, let us pray to the Lord . . . that there may be granted unto them children for the continuation of their race. Let us pray."*

For the next half hour, he faithfully followed the Orthodox exhortation, telling the pair what the sacrament of marriage consisted of and how they ought to love God, pleasingly and honourably, in the wedded state. Before the conclusion of his long, yet lyrical, supplication, the neighbourhood Catholic church bells pealed one o'clock. An hour had passed and he wasn't even halfway through the Orthodox text.

Downstairs in the church kitchen, Amelia Hall fretted. It had been forty minutes since she'd put the blasted Russian salmon pie in the oven. She reread the recipe aloud: "'Bake the . . . *koolybakky* one hour in a 400-degree oven. Serve at once with a pitcher of sour cream.' How can a body be expected to time the servin' of this here foreign food when that foolish woman won't agree to a proper ceremony? How kin Ah serve it crisp and hot," Amelia asked the stove, "when in twenty minutes that pie will begin to overbake?" The final wedding march hadn't even been played yet. People hadn't yet drunk toasts or even sat down at the decorated tables in the community room!

"All this foolishness! What's wrong with good ole-fashion' Baptist vows." Amelia lifted the lid on her shrimp gumbo. "Sweet Jesus, these shrimps will be cremated if the ceremony goes on any longer!" The golden brown buttermilk biscuits were already beginning to shrink and the rice to sweat. "How long, dear Lord? How long?" Moving the sweet-and-sour lamb ribs to the back of the oven, Amelia added a cup of whiskey to the gravy for the fried chicken. The church superintendent, who had refused to participate in the foolishness, was complaining that the ice for the fruit punch was melting.

Upstairs, the service droned on. The turning of water into wine at Cana in Galilee was being read word for word from the Russian text.

"Enough is enough!" Resolutely, Amelia removed the lids from her bubbling pots, carried the powerful spiced gumbo casserole to the air vent that wafted warm air up into the chancel. "Sweet Jesus, forgive me!" she intoned. On the stairs leading up, she placed three pans of simmering cinnamon-spiced, brown-sugared sweet potatoes. Under the choir's air vent, she lit a match to the rum sauce, initially intended to be poured over the deep-dish bread pudding dessert.

Hidden behind the altar, Deacon Stevens thought it was his obligatory drinking to the last drop of the "common cup", after the couple had drunk three sips, that was creating euphoria in his soul.

Rodney Brown, holding the jewelled crown over Otis's head, began to salivate as the fumes of Bacardi rum drifted past his sensitized nose. Lieutenant Randolph Braithwaite, holding Marushka's crown, recognized the spicy Barbadian scent of baked sweet potatoes, and breathed happily, but resisted the urge to smile.

The twitching noses of the twelve members of the Coloured Ladies Club informed them that their presence was required downstairs. In single file, they rustled, on tiptoe, into the vestibule and down the stairs. Edmond Thompson, amused by Amelia Hall's subtle strategy, tried to keep from adding to the restlessness beginning to pervade the congregation. As the children's Poppa Dad, he had to set a good example for the two little bridesmaids wiggling beside him in the front pew. With amused sympathy, he watched the choir suppress their impatience by looking heavenwards.

Suddenly, Torrie's composure caught his eye. Calmly, as though nothing calamitous were happening, she was managing to restrain the singers by passing along sheets of music, and urging Reverend West to speed things up by handing him, with due submission and grace, as though it was part of the ceremony, an almost burnt-out candle.

"She's got class," Edmond admitted to himself. "Class and grandeur. She'd make it in the community if she had the stability of a good husband," he thought judgmentally, subconsciously releasing an erotic bubble that began to swish around in his bloodstream with increasing abandon. He felt proud that Torrie's actions, cool and collected, seemed to restrain the congregation as well, helping them to ignore the succulent smells that threatened to disrupt the solemnity of the ceremony.

Valiantly, Reverend Lorenzo West plodded on: "*And thou, O Bride: Be thou exalted like unto Sara: and exalted through, like unto Rebecca: and as thou multiply, like unto Rachel. Rejoice thou in thy husband, fulfilling the conditions of the law: for so is it well-pleasing unto God.*"

Watching for the reverend to reach out to receive Marushka's crown, Marion whispered to Thaddeus McGregor: "I think, right after he takes Otis's crown, if you were to move towards the door, and then start playing "Amazing Grace," it would seem like part of the ceremony."

Thaddeus nodded conspiratorially. "Right-ee-o! Capital idea! That will do it!" Slowly, he slid along the aisle towards the wall.

The moment Reverend West reached for Otis's crown, he noticed, out of the corner of his eye, a stout white man with a slightly mottled face standing in the wall alcove at the end of the second pew, in the far right corner of the church, hoisting a set of bagpipes to his lips.

Instinctively, Reverend Lorenzo West raised his arms heavenwards. Desperately, he tried to recall the final prayer of the Russian Orthodox service, but all that came to his drying lips was a tried-and-true phrase: "*What God has joined together, let no man put asunder. Amen!*"

"Amen!" the audience echoed spontaneously.

To the dramatically piped melody of "Amazing Grace" coming from near the doors, the couple kissed. Deacon Stevens urgently beckoned them towards the vestry door. The music of the bagpipes swelled, bidding the congregation to stand.

Dame Orlova, holding onto Randolph's arm, indicated to Efuah and Sylvie that they should rescue the small white carpet. They did, putting the borrowed crowns safely in the centre of the mat for good measure. Smiling like Cheshire cats, they followed the official party into the vestry.

Marching down the centre aisle, Thaddeus McGregor gave full vent to his deep windpipes. He was a happy man. He sensed that he'd won his personal war – now he could go overseas to deal with the Jerries!

> *Amazing grace, how sweet the sound, that saved a wretch like me.*
> *I once was lost, but now I'm found. Was blind, but now I see.*
> */ / /*

Like the Pied Piper of Hamelin, he proudly led the guests down to the wedding feast.

The few stragglers left behind in the church, including young Corporal Trevor Wilson, moving restlessly from side to side, his damaged eyes covered by bandages and dark glasses, were joined by the wedding party as they emerged from the signing ceremony in the vestry. Spellbound, they stayed to listen as Torrie's *a cappella* choir, with Emily singing the lead, wrapped up McGregor's anthem, proclaiming:

> *Through many dangers, toils and snares, I have already come;*
> *'Tis grace has brought me safe thus far, and grace will lead me home.*

CHAPTER XXIII

The penultimate year that Efuah was forced to race across the slippery railway tracks to Royal Arthur School, in the snow and sleet of the winter following Otis's wedding, her sixth-grade teacher worked hard to correct her lisp by helping her to enunciate her S's, L's and R's. An enlightened woman, she encouraged Efuah to stay after school to do her homework so that she might enter Montreal High, if not on a scholarship, at least eligible for the science stream – rather than general studies, which could only lead to a job as a clerk. Efuah's dream was to become an animal doctor. The previous Christmas, Uncle Andy (who signed himself "Anobdy") had sent her *My Friend Flicka*, and for her birthday, his old copy of *Smoky, the Cow Horse*.

But staying after school isolated Efuah, who knew she would never have Pippa's intellect or Emily's talent, and didn't enjoy being competitive. Her teacher, however, wouldn't allow her to retreat within her self-protecting shell.

Neither would Ti-Jacques, who always hid in the lane to pelt her with snowballs on her way home from school. "Nigger-black," he'd yell, his little muscular arms heaving the circular balls of snow at her red woollen tuque.

"French pea soup!" she'd call back, shaping a ball from the high banks of snow that separated the sidewalk from the slushy street.

"Nigger-black, nigger-black," he'd tease.

"French pea soup, French pea soup," she'd reply happily, since her aim was usually better than his. But on the day the schedule for the midterm exams was announced, she was depressed. History and spelling were going to be oral exams – she'd fail them for sure.

"Nigger-black." The quizzical voice of Ti-Jacques pursued her as she turned east along St. Jacques towards rue des Seigneurs, hunched against the increasingly cold world.

"Nigger-black?" Again, his snowball missed its silent target. Crestfallen, Ti-Jacques's short little legs struggled through the narrow snow-filled lane that ran parallel to St. Jacques. He clutched three snowballs against his chest, intending to intercept Efuah at the next corner.

"Nigger-black, nigger-black!" The imperative call followed her.

She walked on.

"Hey! You, nigger-black. Me, French pea soup. You no wanna play today?" he asked plaintively.

Efuah simply trudged on. No yells, no indignation.

"What's de matter?" he asked, catching up with her.

"Nothing." But he heard a sob catch in her voice that worried him.

"Hey! Someone bodder you?"

"No," Efuah sniffed. "I just don't want to play."

Ti-Jacques spurted past her and turned around. Walking backwards, he jabbed his index finger through the cold air and said, "Listen. Me, I your friend. You tell me. Who hurt you, eh? I go beat 'em up!"

Efuah stopped walking. Looking at his funny, kind face, his patched too-large lumber jacket, and his already rotting teeth, she suddenly saw him differently. He was no longer the 'French pea soup' kid who had taunted her all winter – he was, she realized, a lonely boy-child whose only contact with others was combative.

"I'm too old to play snowball games," she explained, reaching for his hand in an offer of friendship.

Crestfallen, Ti-Jacques jammed his hands in his pockets. Suddenly, a wicked smile lit his face. "Hey! Den, you wanna play house?"

"No, that's dirty! I have to go home now." She darted past him and he didn't follow. The rest of the way home, she thought of Ti-Jacques and being called "nigger-black," but it didn't bother her any longer. She knew she had grown beyond him.

⚓

On June sixth, 1944, the day Efuah's exams were to begin, she felt confident, lisp or no lisp. She now knew how to spell, and her teacher had arranged for her to write the test in a notebook.

In war-weary England, the sixth of June was "D-Day," the day the largest amphibious invasion in history was thrown against the Germans entrenched in northern France. The Canadian troops were confident of victory. Juno Beach in Normandy was assigned to the Third Canadian Division to avenge their Dieppe disaster. *The Montreal Star* reported each detail, personalizing the war for local consumption. In August, it printed photos of Winston Churchill and Roosevelt, president of the United States, meeting in Quebec City's Citadel to plan their "Metternich" strategy for Europe.

Once little Effie was safely headed for high school, the family could enjoy Indian summer picnics in the evening, watching the boats go through the locks at the Lachine Canal. Marion used these outings as geography lessons, each child imagining what the countries were like that the freighters delivered their cargoes of grain to – forgetting that, with German submarines still on the prowl, few of the boats would make it.

The reality of war didn't inhibit Marion. Driven by the belief that knowledge was the key to opportunity and that deportment was its conveyer belt, she pushed for excellence. Others might lament, "You have to be as good as white folks," but she knew you had to be better to be considered equal – in reality, as well as in expectations. No matter how grown-up the girls were becoming, all three still had to read aloud each evening. Poetry was Pippa's weapon of choice to counter Marion's unassailable technique of control. Emily, learning *lieder* music, welcomed the discipline to read and recite Goethe. Effie ploughed through *Smoky, the Cow Horse*, then *National Velvet*.

The bitter war-centred winter sped by – not always easily, but never without some moments of laughter and achievement. Pippa won an award for elocution at the Dominion Drama Festival, while Emily won a music prize for singing *Ave Maria* in German. Effie, when asked what she did, replied earnestly, "I applaud."

Yet another high school teacher suggested that perhaps Pippa would be more comfortable in domestic science classes. "She is too intellectually emotional to pursue a major in English literature."

"Never!" Marion protested in a stern note to the principal. Torrie simply advised Pippa to pamper the teacher, explaining that she suffered from "constipated thinking."

Emily felt harrassed when Black soldiers, on weekend leave from the U.S. military base at Plattsburg, flirted outrageously with her at church until, at Torrie's suggestion, she let them teach her how to do the "huckle-buck" at the afternoon socials.

The war's terrible progress was charted in blue GPO letters from Otis and occasionally from McGregor, whose kinsman, Lord Lovat, was again invading France, this time on the Canadians' eastern flank. Thaddeus felt fearless, knowing that Shimmie Lovat was invincible. Eventually, after nearly a year of rough slogging across the northern reaches of Western Europe, Otis and Thaddeus, along with a thousand and one other Canadians, assisted by the combined Allied Forces, liberated

France, Belgium, and the Netherlands. Victory in Europe – VE Day – was celebrated on the eighth of May, 1945. Outside Buckingham Palace in London... jam-packed into the broad expanse of Red Square in Moscow... along the Champs Elysées in Paris... in ticker-tape parades in New York City... and, rather more raucously, in Nova Scotia's port of Halifax... people waved flags, hugged each other, and danced in the streets.

Peace in Europe meant the soldiers would be coming home. Marushka would no longer be a "grass widow." Her son, wee Oskar, would finally meet his father. The girls were exuberant.

"But what about those Canadians who were forced to march to Japanese prisoner-of-war camps after the fall of Hong Kong, the Christmas of '41?" Marion asked herself, as she sat hunched over, polishing silver, to avoid arguing with Denise Laroche about the politics of peace.

Mademoiselle Laroche wasn't affected by the horror of the Holocaust being unravelled as concentration camps were liberated. "Catholic priests and gypsies were interned as well" was her dismissive comment. She wouldn't discuss with Marion the strange wisdom of dividing up Berlin, nor did she seem to think it was a tragedy when brown babies began to be born in the American-occupied sector of Germany.

Children skipping rope on rue de Seigneurs now had a new song from England which Effie was forced to endure.

There was a girl named Starky,
Who went and married a darky,
And for all her sins,
She had three sets of twins,
One white, one black,
And one khaki.

"Should I tell her it's a racist slur, or teach her to laugh at it?" Marion wondered.

Finally, in August, when the war in the Pacific ended at last in a flash "brighter than a thousand suns" over the Japanese towns of Hiroshima and Nagasaki, Marion and her employer exchanged bitter words. "'Peace purchased through an atomic bomb is not peace,'" Marion said, quoting Dr. Robert Oppenheimer, one of the bomb's designers, who had cringingly admitted that the invention was "the shatterer of worlds."

Denise, though crippled since childhood with polio and wonderfully involved in fighting for the rights of women, still felt that the European and Pacific wars had little to do with her cultural survival as a French Canadian. Nothing would change the English attitude of superiority and paternalism in Quebec unless women fought to change it. "Don't be naive, Marion. There's nothing to celebrate, nothing to mourn. Our jubilation will come when half the members of the Supreme Court of Canada are women!"

Little did Mademoiselle Laroche realize that there could be no jubilation in Marion's heart. The ophthalmology specialist at the Ste. Anne de Bellevue military hospital had informed Trevor Wilson that his full sight would never return. They were discharging him, obviously to make room for the war-wounded soldiers being returned by safe sea passage from Europe. Trevor had never seen overseas action. He'd been blinded by "friendly fire" while training at Camp Petawawa in northern Ontario, so his disability pay would be limited. Trevor, who loved to read so intensely, was having to learn braille.

"Why don't they reproduce the books of some of our Black authors in braille?" Pippa protested to the librarian at Westmount Library. "Very few books are available in braille except the Bible, and perhaps one or two classics" was the reply. "Although," the young man added, "with so many blinded war veterans coming home, there should be some demand. I'll try to find out if Helen Keller has written anything in braille. Unfortunately I doubt that the government will provide allotments for cultural pastimes like books."

There and then, not yet fifteen, Pippa decided to become a
braille translator. There was no arguing with her. She applied herself so she'd get brilliant grades and a scholarship to college. Her
only concession was to promise Torrie that she'd keep up her elocution lessons so that she might someday record a series of "talking books" on the Harlem Renaissance authors.

Torrie, indignant at Pippa's selflessness, sent for prospectuses
from the leading Black universities in the United States, favouring
Washington's world-famous Howard University, where the elegant, erudite Rhodes scholar, Alain Locke, presided as the doyen
of Black literature.

Angela Brock insisted that Pippa also apply to her alma
mater, Spelman College in Atlanta, Georgia. Marion herself was
partial to Spelman, it being an all-girls school where deportment
and academic achievement were given equal validity. The
'Achilles heel' of both noble schools proved to be the literature
available from their sororities and residences, which revealed a
decided stratification code for applicants, based on colour and
class.

Class, Marion could swallow, but she was repelled by their
Afro-Saxon belief that the darker shades were a disadvantage,
instead of welcoming the rich range of colours that make up
"being Black." Marion had experienced the subjective intensity
involved in judging by the actual colour of one's skin. Being light
enough to "pass" brought an agony of choices. Thank God, her
children were brown.

"It's not the cost, though how we'd manage, I can't imagine,"
Torrie commented. "It's hiding behind that pigmentation hege-
mony that is destroying the educated in our race."

The offers of scholarships were of no use. Poppa Dad's
promise of a monthly allowance was refused. Pippa decided she
could not leave Trevor without someone to read to him and help
him regain his confidence. Some day, they would both enroll at
Sir George Williams College – the new community-based liberal

arts institution, housed at the YMCA on Drummond Street in the increasingly cosmopolitan heart of Montreal.

Marion admitted to being both furious and a tad proud of her lovely, stubborn daughter. "But what future will you have, translating books into braille? Who will publish them? How will you earn a living?" she asked. It was proving a useless argument, for someone was feeding Pippa answers from *The Communist Manifesto*, and Marion was sure it wasn't Trevor. One more year, mercifully, and she'd graduate from Montreal High.

Emily had already graduated and, at McGill's Conservatory of Music, was considered a star pupil, earning her tuition as a guest soloist, winning the prestigious National Music Festival a second time, while gaining pocket money by playing piano for Dame Orlova's ballet classes. Her health was iffy, but her spirits were high.

Could Marion expect little Effie to fulfill her dream of having a daughter graduate from McGill University? Though she never dared voice it, Marion was aware that McGill was where the best — well, almost the best — Black students from the West Indies and West Africa came to study. McGill was where social contacts were made, where she'd hoped her girls would meet their future husbands — and develop skills in professional careers that would make them "no man's slave."

"*Malheureusement*," she lamented, during her long walks to and from work, "Effie's skills are proving to be more physical than intellectual." Efuah's summer job at the SPCA taking care of abandoned animals was the highlight of her year. Perhaps that was because she was in touch with Uncle Andy, who was encouraging her to attend Guelph and study animal husbandry.

"Where is the potential of race leadership that I've worked so hard to foster?" Marion asked herself. The cards seemed stacked against her. No doctor to research sickle cell and other illnesses claimed endemic to Black folks, no teacher to tell youngsters of their own proud history, no social worker to hold open doors for the ever-growing breed of mixed-blood children who weren't told they were the way the world was going. No, it seemed that no one from her loins would break through the glass ceiling, even if the jobs weren't yet opening up for them.

⚓

It was already twelve thirty. Marion realized she wasn't going to make it to the Westmount Y on time, even if she trotted quickly the two miles along Westmount Boulevard, cutting through St. Stephen's Park, then down Lansdowne Avenue to Sherbrooke Street. "Damn that Mr. Jones and his new punch-in clock!" So what if she was late? She'd just work harder or later, until the residents' rooms were perfectly clean.

Vashti Dobson put her finger on it. "What we spose' to do when we'se finish'? Twiddle our thumbs 'til time to clock out? That Mister Jones ain't got no class, so he's developed clout! Now, Thaddeus McGregor, he used 'suasion.'"

Denise Laroche had been using "'suasion," too – that's why Marion was late. There was a provincial election coming up and Denise wanted every able-bodied woman to vote. She was after Marion to ensure that all the members of the Coloured Ladies Club cast a ballot. "How can I ensure that?" Marion had protested. "It's okay when your Madame Thérèse Casgrain campaigns. No one is going to harass her. She's related to the richest lumber barons in the province. But people of colour – who's going to rescue us when they throw us in jail for daring to vote?"

"You helped fight for the vote, now you've got to exercise your right!" Denise had retorted. "Women in Quebec are chattel, Marion – you know that! What if you have to move this May? Now that your Edmond Thompson's married, who are you going to get to sign your new lease?"

That was a low blow. Marion walked out of the room before the lawyer could say another word. "Damn! Damn! And damn again!" she thought angrily. "Of course, Denise is right, but I wish I'd never told her that Edmond and Torrie had married." Marion turned onto Lansdowne Avenue like a dervish pursued by the furies.

"Vote!" she thought to herself. "I'll never vote again. The first and last time I went, when women first got the vote four years ago, they threw me in jail, saying I'd already voted so it was fraudulent. Threw me in jail – with all those common 'ladies of the evening'!" she ranted inwardly. "As though I was a street-walker or something, instead of throwing the men in. Claimed I couldn't be Mrs. Willow, since the enumerator had described her as a black lady." Normally, Marion would have laughed at white folks' inability to discern colour, but this experience had been too traumatic.

Anxiety had rendered her irrational. If she wasn't home by six o'clock, who would take care of Pippa and little Effie? When offered one telephone call, instead of calling a lawyer, she'd called the only people close by who had a phone, the ladies at the Aberdeen Bakery, and had asked them to ask Mrs. Wilson or Trevor to stay with the girls. She cringed at the memory. She'd been too ashamed to say where she was. Not having someone to vouch for her, she'd had to stay in jail all night.

Kofi's old Ashanti proverb was apt: "When a woman is hungry, she asks that the children be fed." What use would a lawyer have been when she couldn't have afforded one. And Edmond had been out of town, as she remembered. "Politics are so crooked. Mademoiselle Laroche is right – men don't want women to have equal rights."

Determinedly, Marion banished the subject of voting from her mind, as she took the broad front steps of the Westmount Y two at a time. The clock over the information desk read one-fifteen. She sprinted towards the second-floor stairs. The clearing of a throat was audible from somewhere behind the reception desk.

⚜

"Good Lord, Marion!Yo'all musta run all the way from Côte des Neiges," a voice accused her as she entered Amelia Hall's kitchen. "Ketch yo' breath, chile.There's a dish o' gumbo been waitin' for the past half hour. I jes' hasta heat it again."Amelia tried to square her shoulders as she limped lamely towards the large stove, muttering, "You killin' yo'self, child. Oughta let them girls of yourn get a job. Pippa will be fifteen this autumn.They'se been in school long 'nuff. Child, you always punchin' beyon' yo' reach!"

"Well, I already punched in for Marion at one o'clock," Gertrude Martin laughed as she ran into the kitchen, grabbed a tray of key lime pies, then raced back out to the Rotary Club meeting in the second dining room. "Can't stay.They're discussing how to invest War Bond money, now that the war is over."

Amelia held Marion down with one hand as she replaced the quickly drunk cup of tea with a soupbowl brimming with shrimps, red snapper, garlic croutons, and green peppers, bubbling in a golden-red broth. "Eat, child," she advised. "Sweet Jesus knows, you needs nourishment. Vashti Dobson ain't too spry nowadays. Bes' eat, 'fore you try doin' both yo' work and hern."

Marion knew it was no use arguing. Amelia would only take the weight off her feet if Marion sat for a while beside her. Food was her way of showing love.

"What news of 'Rushka? The young un must be growin' some."

"She'll never forget her wedding day, with you turning the service topsy-turvy with the irresistible aromas of your cooking."

"Jus' about two years ago, ain't it? And Otis's unit still overseas.What they doin' over there?" Amelia asked.

"The wedding was only eighteen months ago, Aunt Amelia," Marion said quietly, feeling more relaxed, almost on the verge of mellowness, as she bit into the firm, yet almost chamois-soft body of a large Cuban shrimp. Delicious food did wonderful things to people. Though her own inclination was to be a vegetarian, maybe she should introduce more fish into Denise Laroche's diet. Her employer could well afford shrimp.

Thoughts of the crippled lawyer reactivated Marion's conflict. The ending of the war was not all good news. Marion was still finishing her gumbo when Gertrude returned, announcing that she wished she had surplus money to put in real estate. "With that Mr. Jones, we don't know how long we'll have these jobs."

No wonder the Black community thought Gertrude Martin was psychic. Her hovering about at meetings of the Rotary Club, the Chamber of Commerce, and other businessmen's groups was not so much to provide submissive service as to glean information. She was the one who warned Edmond Thompson that the railways were seriously considering introducing returning servicemen, who were white, into the ranks of the Pullman porters – breaking the Blacks' monopoly (and their union) on those lucrative jobs – calling it integration.

Life as a Pullman porter, a luggage-toting Red Cap, or a dining car steward had never been "no crystal stair," but even those jobs were now being pulled out from underneath them. In factories, as in the First World War, with war plants being downsized and retooled, "last hired, first fired'" was the rule of thumb. The community's thin toehold on mainstream jobs was evaporating. Without jobs, how could they educate their children? More people were migrating to Canada. More West Indian ex-servicemen were opting to settle in Montreal, Winnipeg, and Toronto – more Black visibility to defuse the myth of Canadian tolerance.

⚜

U pstairs, Vashti Dobson was tsewpsing Caribbean sounds of disapproval without uttering a word. Marion, despite her constantly elusive fear of Vashti's predictions, decided to hug the old thing.

"No use you tryin' to get 'round me," Vashti grumbled. "I don' 'prove the way you carryin' on with Thaddeus McGregor and tha's that!"

"Okay, Aunt Vashti. Give me his letter. I've told you before, he's on mop-up patrol in Germany and he writes describing what life's like looking for Nazis. He finds my description of Mr. Jones assembly-lining all of us amusing. That's all."

"I don' finds it funny!" Vashti retorted, stuffing soiled sheets down the laundry chute.

"Then try to remember how decent McGregor was when he was the Y manager." Marion felt compelled to remind Vashti, for increasingly the staff was becoming isolated, separate, detached from the life of the Westmount Y. The residents were different now. They tended to treat Vashti like a day-maid – and an ancient one, at that! Not as a confidante or a resident housekeeper, who took their socks home to mend, replaced shirt buttons, and chided them if, due to late nights, they slept in of a morning. The short-term tenants, soldiers soon to be mustered out of the

"Charlie" regiments, were the worst. One had even asked Marion why she hadn't cleaned the boots he'd left outside his door. Not having jobs to go to, returning servicemen lolled around in their rooms all morning.

"Poor Aunt Vashti," Marion thought. "She's afraid to complain, lest Mr. Jones use it as an excuse to suggest that she's getting too old to cope, and replace her with one of those British war brides. Scrubbing-up's just their speed – most of them were probably barmaids anyway." Laughing inside, she chastised herself for such a spiteful thought.

They worked quickly together to complete changing the beds and cleaning the Y's twenty-one single and five double rooms before teatime. At three-thirty, Gertrude brought their tea tray up to the linen room. "Here's something for your birthday," she grinned, presenting Marion with a bouquet of flowers rescued from the Rotary luncheon. "Take 'em home with you."

Marion had forgotten – or was it being on the far side of that hill, which too soon leads to forty, that had wiped her memory clean? Vashti had a gift for her, as well – a lovely Victorian cameo brooch.

While searching for a vase for the flowers, Marion noticed, tucked U-shaped beside the pillow cases in the linen room, the blue overseas aerogram she had been expecting from Thaddeus. Vashti had obviously intercepted it. As she reached for it, the envelope strangely seemed familiar. Wasn't that her own writing? Why was it marked with a bold RETURN TO SENDER stamp? She cringed, as the meaning slowly sank in. Absurd palliatives to soften the blow flitted through her mind, but she forced herself to face the truth. Some soldiers died on the battlefield; others lost their lives enforcing peace. That's the way Thaddeus would prefer to have gone. She understood why Vashti, with psychic sixth sense, had hidden the letter.

The years had not added an extra ounce nor a fold to Marion's classical Renaissance Madonna face, nor a wrinkle to her long Nefertiti neck. They had taught her, instead, to control her tears, to use a mantra to relieve her pain and to comfort her grief. She tore the letter quietly into small pieces and let them flutter, like autumn leaves, into the wastebasket.

Going down at five o'clock to say good night to Amelia, she found her standing by the kitchen door, a huge box balanced against her bosom. She presented it with the warning: "Yo' not 'lowed to open it 'til seven!"

Although disarmed by her awareness of McGregor's death and overwhelmed by her co-workers' kindness, Marion managed a smile for Mr. Jones, because it was the proper thing to do, when he met her halfway up the stairs and announced, "Your friend the tiger lady is waiting for you outside."

"He's never forgotten Torrie Delacourt!" Marion whispered to Gertrude, who held her flowers as they punched out together. Gertrude, helping her to open the wide front doors, stared in disbelief. It was indeed the glamorous Torrie Delacourt, and smiling beside her, seated in the yellow Buick convertible, was her handsome husband, Edmond Thompson, Marion's former beau.

"Happy Birthday!" Opening the car door, Edmond took the packages. "Can we give you a lift?" he asked Gertrude. "We're taking Marion to Chinatown."

Miss Martin shook her head. "You three sure are some liberated folk!" was her only comment. She turned and walked to the streetcar stop.

Despite Marion's protest and mounting anger, for it was more important than ever for her to spend this special occasion with her girls, rather than listening to reports of the Thompsons' honeymoon, she wasn't able to convince them not to take her to the Blue Dragon Café.

Sensing that Marion was being torn apart by some inner sorrow, Torrie tucked her arm into Marion's. "Stop worrying! You still have us – no matter what!" she whispered. "I will never mean as much to Edmond as you and the girls do. Our job, yours and mine, is to be there for them, always."

Marion still tried to resist. She had already decided to take a taxi home at the first opportunity, pleading a headache. But Torrie held her close as they walked up the restaurant stairs. Slowly, Marion's mind acknowledged that she was feeling more relaxed, tucked inside Torrie's comforting arm. She felt that women and only women understood ephemeral fears without having to discuss them.

She had long been fully aware that Torrie's marriage to Edmond had let her off the hook, and for that she was actually grateful. She could now afford to be a friend to Edmond with the sexual bit out of the way. Still aching, but circled securely within Torrie's perfumed embrace, she knew she had found a true friend. She recalled the old Senegalese proverb: "If you speak, speak to her who understands you." Torrie would understand why she would never publicly mourn Thaddeus, but would always be glad he had once existed. They entered the restaurant.

"Surprise!" three voices yelled. And from the small private dining room appeared the grinning faces of Effie, Pippa, and Emily. "Poppa Dad, you forgot to bring Amelia's cake," Emily whispered, seeing only the flowers in Torrie's arms. "Come, help me retrieve it from the car," Edmond whispered in turn to Torrie, "so Marion can hug her children to her heart's content."

Outside, he found Marushka carrying little Oskar and a festively dressed Dame Orlova looking for the correct restaurant. He ushered them into the Blue Dragon to join the party.

Mr. Woo's brother-in-law, Mr. Lam, the restaurant's chief cook, had outdone himself – preparing an Oriental birthday feast. Torrie tried to pay for dinner, but was turned down – it was Mr. Woo's treat. What he knew, that she did not, was that his wife, born in Trinidad, albeit into a mostly Chinese family, intended to apply for membership in the Coloured Ladies Club, now that Mrs. Willow was its president.

Edmond and Torrie kept the party in stitches describing their hilarious five-day Indian Summer honeymoon, mostly spent trying to find Edmond's acreage, hidden no one knew where in the brilliant autumn foliage of the Laurentian highlands, north of that vast old millionaires' hunting lodge called the Seigneury Club. They finally discovered the farm, four miles from a little village called Notre-Dame-de-la-Paix. The son of a local farmer was occupying the farmhouse, but when the village priest – awed, urged and, no doubt, seduced by Torrie's impeccable French, to say nothing of her fluttering eyelashes – informed the squatter of Quebec's legally binding property rights, he quickly signed a tenant farmer lease. It gave him permission to farm twenty-five acres of Thompson's land for himself, but it also made it mandatory for him to care for the entire farm.

Torrie noticed an eighteenth-century log cabin, built of square-cut cedar beams, nestled into the hillside above the narrow but energetically flowing river that swept southwards through the farm. The cabin was so superbly crafted that only the cedar-shingled roof leaked. The farmer was keeping his new ewes in it. Edmond and Torrie agreed to have it repaired and earmarked as a gift to Marion and her girls – a piece of land in Marion's name, a home of her very own that she would always have as a refuge. The twenty-five acres beyond, Edmond decided, would be deeded to Otis and Marushka for their family. As well, the tenant farmer was instructed to plant twenty-five acres as Torrie's market garden.

"Poor farmer," Marion observed. "It couldn't have been easy to give up his assumed rights to strangers."

Torrie shrugged. "Proves not all the world's victims are Black."

Ceremoniously, Poppa Dad presented Marion with the cabin's door key, with a caution to the girls: "It's your mother's. She must always have priority."

"We'll name it Innisfree," Pippa declared, and proceeded to

recite: "*I will arise and go now, and go to Innisfree, And a small cabin build there, of clay and wattles made.*"

"See? We haven't lost our Poppa Dad, we've just extended our family." Extended – she'd pronounced it without a lisp! Efuah squeezed her sisters' hands in triumph. They both kissed her.

"We may not get to Garvey's Africa, but now we'll always own a part of Canada," Edmond added, his inner soul basking in the unspoken approval inherent in Torrie's gentle smile.

As they lingered, talking in gentle animation, Marion, half listening to Pippa explaining her ambitions to her Poppa Dad, thought to herself, "Perhaps my children are pioneering in fields where there will be no glass ceiling."

Unbidden, and softly, Emily began to sing, as a birthday gift, an old Welsh melody she'd remembered being hummed wistfully on many occasions when her mother felt no-one could hear her pouring her yearnings into the silent night sky:

All through the night, there's a little Brown Bird singing,
Singing songs of love in the darkness and the dew . . . .

Torrie's throaty contralto and Marushka's gentle mezzo-soprano joined Emily's in *a cappella* harmony, as they serenaded the last verse:

All through the night, my lonely heart is singing,
Sweeter songs of love than the Brown Bird ever knew,
Would that his song, through the stillness would go winging,
Would go a-winging to you, to you.

Pippa, noticing that her mother's eyes had begun to mist as though overwhelmed at the richness of her family's creative spirit, to prevent her emotion from flooding over, leaned across the table to hold her hand, then quoted, with almost mock sardonic humour, the last lines of a poem by Countee Cullen:

Yet do I marvel at this curious thing:
To make a poet black, and bid him sing.

Marion breathed deeply, squeezing Pippa's hand in gratitude. A surge of personal power took over. "Life isn't so awful, after all." Raising her Chinese teacup full of green tea, she toasted her family: Marushka and the absent Otis, whom she often thought of as a son; Dame Orlova, who preferred to be called Babushka now, with her cherished, golden-brown, nappy-headed grandson; Torrie and Edmond; and her three precious jewels, Efuah, Pippa and Emily, who, no matter how hard the climb, would always be there, at the top of the stairs.

In the manuscript's text and dialogue, the words "coloured," "Negro," and "Black" can all be found as they were the common self-identifying terms used during that period. The description "West Indian," "American," "Scotian" or "old-timer" (the old-timers were those who came before or during the 'Underground Railway' era) were culturally-specific connotations. Because of the popularity of Marcus Garvey's philosophy, it was generally acknowledged that the heritage of "Black" people was African, and the term "Black" described their shared negritude.

In this regard, the following excerpt from the American book, *Quotations by Black Women: Gumbo Ya Ya*, edited by Rosalyn Terborg-Penn, might be of interest:

> "… it is important to look at the term black, because not all women of African descent identify with this term. In the United States, for example, by law, people with any measurable degree of African ancestry are considered black … In this sense, black symbolizes a cultural milieu, more than it does a color. On the other hand, in many Caribbean and South American societies, women of African descent vary in colors that determine legal status as well as cultural identification."